CHRISTIANE HEGGAN

NOW YOU DIE

MIRA®

MIRA®

ISBN 0-7394-5958-9

NOW YOU DIE

Copyright © 2005 by Christiane Heggan.

Printed in U.S.A.

To Tom and MaryLou Blair
with all my love.

Prologue

New York City
December 10—11.00 p.m.

Lola Malone was only a block from Tompkins Square Park when she stopped abruptly. She had dismissed the thought earlier, but the sound she heard behind her now, although slightly muffled by the thin coating of snow, was unmistakably that of footsteps.

Nervous, she glanced over her shoulder. The dark street was a stark reminder that she had never felt comfortable walking through this area of Manhattan at night. Vibrant with a mix of artists, students and tourists during the day, the East Village turned downright threatening in the late hours. Fortunately, tonight the snow had kept the derelicts away. Most of them, anyway.

Lola peered into the darkness. Except for a homeless person curled up in a doorway and a couple of distant headlights, the street was empty. Maybe she had imagined the whole thing. Fond of old movies, she had rented two nail-biters this week—*Wait Until Dark* and *Whatever Happened to Baby Jane?* Both had kept her on the edge of her seat. No wonder she was spooked. She should have insisted that her cabdriver go down another block, but he had been on his way home when he'd picked her up, and Second Avenue was as far as he'd go.

Sinking her hands into her coat pockets, she started walking again, quickening her step and scolding herself for venturing out at this time of night. What was she thinking?

Then she heard it again. Footsteps. Keeping time with her, moving when she did, and stopping when she stopped.

She cast a quick look around. Just ahead was a passageway she knew connected Seventh Street to First Avenue, where she had to go. The thought of dashing into a rat-infested alley didn't particularly thrill her, but neither did the possibility of being held up. Or worse, raped.

In order not to tip off whoever was following her, she didn't turn into the alley until the very last second. Then, praying she wouldn't slip, she started running, ignoring the quick scattering of nocturnal pests whose foray into a pile of garbage she had interrupted.

She ran as fast as the conditions allowed, keeping her eyes on the First Avenue streetlight a few feet away. A wave of panic hit her when she realized that the stalker was running, too. And gaining on her.

She wasn't going to make it.

As if to confirm her fears, a steely hand clamped on to her shoulder, squeezing so hard her knees started to buckle. "Please, don't hurt me," she pleaded. "You can have anything—"

He whipped her around. A gasp escaped her mouth as recognition hit her. She starred at him in horror, for the look in his eyes was one she had never seen before.

"I warned you not to mess with me, Lola," he said in a gruff voice. "But you did anyway. That was stupid."

"I'm sorry." She swallowed. "I was upset, not thinking clearly." She searched his eyes for a sign of compassion or pity. She saw nothing but contempt. "Let me go and I swear, I'll leave. Coming here was a mistake. I know that now."

"Like I'm going to believe you." He brought his face close to hers. "No one threatens me. Remember that when you're dying."

His hands wrapped around her throat, and she almost fainted from the fear. He was going to strangle her. In a panic, she tried to wedge her fingers between her neck and his hands. It was no use. He was too strong.

Through half-closed lids, she saw the streetlight up ahead, but its glow was beginning to blur. As all her hopes began to fade, she heard something—a faint rustling. The sound had come from the Dumpster nearby. Someone was there.

Her eyes rolled in that direction. Her lips moved to form words she could no longer speak. Help...me. Please...help...me....

One

"Give it back, you worthless, miserable piece of junk!"

Muttering under her breath, Zoe Foster tried in vain to dislodge the heel of her very expensive, black ankle-strap pump from one of Manhattan's infamous sidewalk vents. Exasperated that her efforts were getting her nowhere, she gave a vicious yank and let out a cry of dismay as the shoe came loose, but not the heel.

"Those things ought to be banned from all city sidewalks." Grumbling, she went down on all fours and jiggled the broken heel. After about a minute, it finally came loose, but it wasn't looking very pretty. The black velvet hung in shreds, and there was a deep gouge in the wood beneath.

Zoe slid the battered heel into her coat pocket, then, with one leg now shorter than the other by three inches, she limped to the curb and raised her arm at an approaching cab. "Taxi!"

Although empty, the car sped by, sending a spray of slush on her new shoes. Could tonight get any worse?

"Hey," she shouted at the disappearing vehicle. "Ever heard of road etiquette?"

She looked up and down First Avenue in the hope of spotting another cab, and let out a sigh. Who was she kidding? In this weather and time of night, her chances of getting a taxi were practically nil. She should have accepted E.J.'s offer to take her home in his limo. Her boss had made the vehicle available to anyone who didn't mind waiting until the Christmas party was over. A few had agreed to wait, but Zoe, who had been up since dawn working on her new comic strip, had chosen to leave.

Lifting the collar of her white coat around her neck, she started walking, a little awkwardly because of the broken shoe, and headed for Houston Street, where her chances of finding transportation would be better. As she passed the alley next to the *Herald* building, something, a glimmer, caught her eye.

She turned her head and let out a gasp.

A woman in a long black coat and black boots lay on the ground. She appeared to be sleeping. Zoe hurried to her and squatted by her side. She was beautiful, with long blond hair that cascaded over her shoulders, a fair, unblemished complexion and a sexy red mouth. Her left arm rested on her midriff. Around her wrist was the object that had caught Zoe's eye—a shiny gold cuff bracelet.

"Miss?" Zoe touched the woman's shoulder. "You shouldn't be sleeping here." When there was no response, she shook her gently. "Miss, are you hurt? Can you hear me?"

The woman remained still. Filled with a sudden sense

of foreboding, Zoe slid two fingers inside the blonde's coat collar and pressed them to her throat. There was no pulse.

She started to reach for her cell phone, then remembered that she hadn't been able to fit it into her tiny evening clutch and had left it at home.

Her heart racing, she sprung to her feet, ran back the way she had come and burst into the *Herald*'s lobby. "Aaron, quick," she said to the night guard as he looked up. "Call 911. There's a dead woman in the alley."

Aaron's thick white eyebrows lifted in shock, but he didn't waste time in unnecessary questions. He picked up the phone and dialed. While he talked to the police, Zoe picked up his cell phone, which he always kept on the counter, and dialed the *Herald,* not sure anyone would bother to answer. At the seventh ring, Eddy, the mail-room clerk picked up. He had to shout over the loud party noise.

"The *Herald.* Happy holidays."

"Eddy, it's Zoe Foster," she spoke rapidly. "Get me Mr. Greenfield, please. It's an emergency."

Seconds later, E.J. was on the line, sounding worried. "Zoe, what is it? Are you all right?"

"I'm fine, but you need to come down right away. I found a dead woman in the alley next to our building."

"Dear God. Is it anyone we know?"

"I've never seen her before."

"Have you called the police?"

"Aaron is doing that now."

"I'll be right down."

A few minutes later, the owner and editor in chief of

the *New York Herald* stepped out of the elevator. A worried crease between his brows had replaced his earlier happy expression. Elijah James Greenfield, fondly known to his staff as E.J., was a short, rotund man with a moon-shaped face, twinkling blue eyes and sparse gray hair. Zoe adored him and so did everyone who had ever been fortunate enough to work for him.

"Where is she?" he asked. Then, as Zoe limped toward him, he looked down. "What's wrong with your foot?"

"Nothing. I broke my heel." As she started to lead the way toward the alley, a patrol car pulled up in front of the building and two uniformed officers jumped out. Zoe and E.J. walked out to meet them.

"Good evening," the older cop said. "I'm Officer Curtis. This is Officer Barnes." He looked at E.J. "You're the one who called about a body?" He spoke calmly, as though answering a call about a dead body was a daily occurrence. Considering this was New York City, it probably was.

Zoe stepped forward. "*I* did. She's in there." She pointed toward the alley, but when she started to lead them to the scene of the crime, the officer stopped her. "We'll check it out, ma'am. You wait here."

E.J. turned to Zoe. "Are you sure you never saw her before? Gene just hired two new secretaries. I didn't see either one at the party."

"She didn't look familiar." Zoe looked up the tall building.

He followed her gaze. "I know what you're thinking. Forget it. People don't fall from windows in New York City anymore."

"They do if they're pushed."

E.J. was about to reply when the two policemen returned. Officer Curtis, who seemed to be in charge, spoke first. This time his tone was sharper as he addressed Zoe. "Is this some kind of joke, ma'am?"

Zoe and E.J. exchanged glances. "I beg your pardon?" Zoe asked.

"There's no dead body—in the alley or anywhere in the vicinity."

Two

"But that's impossible." Zoe looked from one officer to the other. "I saw her with my own eyes. I shook her. I felt for her pulse. She was totally unresponsive."

The officer took out a small notebook from his jacket pocket. "When was that, ma'am?"

"Less than ten minutes ago."

He started writing. "Your name, ma'am?"

"Zoe Foster." Because she knew the drill, thanks to the many hours she spent doing research for her comic strip, she added, "I live at 1232 Wooster Street."

"What were you doing in the alley?"

"I had just left a Christmas party at the *New York Herald* and I was heading for Houston Street to catch a cab. As I passed the alley, something shiny—a gold cuff bracelet—caught my eye. That's when I saw the woman. I tried to wake her up, but she didn't respond."

"What did you do then?"

"I ran back into the *Herald* building and asked the night guard to call you."

"Can you describe the woman you *claim* you saw?"

She caught the skepticism in his voice but didn't let it bother her. If she hadn't seen the woman with her own eyes, she would have doubts, too. "She was attractive, well dressed and well groomed, with long blond hair and a fair complexion. The bracelet I mentioned was about two-and-a-half-inches wide and was on her left wrist." She almost added that robbery could not have been the motive or the killer would have taken the gold cuff, but she didn't think the officer would appreciate her input.

The younger policeman, who had been observing her while his partner wrote the information down, pointed a finger at her. "Wait a minute. Are you *the* Zoe Foster? The creator of *Kitty Floyd, P.I.?*"

Grateful for the friendly tone and the recognition, Zoe returned the smile. "Yes, I am."

"You look like Kitty. Maybe it's your red hair—"

His partner shot him a quick warning glance and Officer Barnes snapped his mouth shut.

When the senior officer returned his attention to Zoe, however, his tone had mellowed. "Look, Miss Foster. I'm sure you meant well, but the truth is, there are a lot of parties taking place throughout Manhattan at this time of year. Maybe the woman you saw had a little too much to drink, and she was sleeping it off."

"In a filthy alley? With snow coming down?"

"We don't know the condition she was in."

Officer Barnes nodded in agreement. "And when you touched her, you frightened her and she ran."

Zoe gave a stubborn shake of her head. "She couldn't have run anywhere. The woman was dead."

As if to strengthen her convictions, Zoe walked the few steps that separated her from the alley. Once she reached the entrance, her gaze stopped on the spot where, a moment ago, a dead woman had been lying. A light coating of snow now covered that area. Except for a Dumpster directly across from it, the alley was empty.

The skeptical officer watched her limp back. "Something wrong with your shoe, ma'am?"

She motioned behind her. "I caught my heel in the air vent over there. It broke when I tried to pull it off."

The glance he gave his younger partner spoke volumes.

"Look, I haven't been drinking, if that's what you're thinking. And I'm not in the habit of fabricating stories. Or seeing things. I found a dead woman and, like a good citizen, I called the police."

"I believe her," E.J. said, speaking for the first time.

"Who are you, sir?" the patrolman asked.

"Elijah James Greenfield." He pointed a thumb at the building behind him. "I'm the owner of the *Herald*. Zoe called me as soon as she found the body and I came down."

"Well, Mr. Greenfield, the fact remains that without a body, evidence of foul play or a witness to any crime, there is nothing we can do except talk to neighbors and file an incident report. As for the two of you, I suggest you go home and get a good night's sleep."

The comment almost brought a sharp retort from Zoe, but she, too, snapped her mouth shut. Losing her cool in front of two NYPD officers would not bode well for her credibility.

"How do you like that?" Zoe put both fists on her hips as she watched the two officers head back toward the alley. "They didn't believe one word I said."

"They're a little skeptical, that's all. That's understandable."

"You don't sound so convinced yourself, in spite of what you told the officers."

"Don't mind me. I'm just worried that the woman you saw may be one of our employees. That kind of publicity wouldn't be good for business."

"Or for the dead woman."

"Yes, of course. I didn't mean to sound insensitive." He was watching the alley, looking uncommonly nervous. "Look, why don't you come back upstairs for a minute? I need to talk to my secretary and find out if those two secretaries were here tonight. Then I'll take you home and come back for the others."

At that moment, a cab miraculously appeared. Zoe raised her arm. "I think I'll grab that cab if you don't mind, E.J., but please call me after you talk to Maureen. Something tells me I won't be able to sleep, anyway."

As the cab coasted to a stop in front of Zoe, E.J. kissed her on the cheek. "I'll call you as soon as I know something." He opened the taxi's back door. Once Zoe was inside, he handed the driver a twenty-dollar bill and gave him the address.

"E.J., you don't have to—"

But he had already shut the door.

Three

Zoe's nerves didn't completely settle down until she stepped into her loft ten minutes later and closed the door. Her home had always had a soothing effect on her. No matter what mood she was in or what small disaster had crash-landed on her head, she could always count on the loft's welcoming comfort to erase the day's problems.

Finding an apartment she could afford in Manhattan hadn't been easy. The cost of city living had skyrocketed over the last ten years, especially in SoHo, which had become one of New York City's most sought-after neighborhoods. But when her best friend, Lizzy Min, had told her about a candy factory whose owner was relocating to Brooklyn, Zoe had made the leap from renter to homeowner without giving it a second thought.

She and Lizzy had worked on the place for weeks, scraping, scrubbing and painting until the nineteen-hundred-square-foot, brick-walled loft had become a beautiful, cozy oasis that was a perfect expression of Zoe's personality. The raw space had been cleverly partitioned to form several areas. Just off the small entryway, a galley kitchen had been set up, with compact appliances and a dividing island. The living/dining area was larger, and bursting with colors—easy chairs in sunny yellow, a red lacquered table over a Turkish rug and green potted plants everywhere. A bank of wood-framed windows that descended almost to the floor provided all the light an artist could want. Her studio, which consisted of a drawing board, a stool and a desk, occupied another sunny corner, while a three-paneled Oriental screen, hand-painted by Lizzy's cousin, concealed the bedroom and bath.

The pièce de résistance, as she liked to call it, and the first thing that caught a visitor's eye as he or she entered the loft, was a large color drawing of Kitty Floyd on a far wall. With her fiery-red hair, long eyelashes and shiny red mouth, the comic-strip private investigator was as much a part of the surroundings as Zoe herself.

On a side table were old family photographs—her maternal and paternal grandparents, all of whom were now gone; her mother, still beautiful at fifty-eight, and her late father, an insurance salesman who had been killed in a car accident as he was driving back from a client's house. Only three when he died, Zoe could no longer remember him or the move from Philadelphia to New York she and her mother had made right after the accident, but the man she had called Daddy for three wonderful years still occupied a special place in her heart.

Aware that Zoe missed having a father, especially in

the early years, Catherine Foster had kept Henry's memory alive with photographs and stories of their life together. A fashion editor with the magazine *Trends* at the time, she had set her own hours so she could see Zoe off to school every day, and be home when she got back. She had even turned down a marriage proposal once, because Zoe, then seven, had declared with all the contempt she could muster, "I don't want him here. He's not my daddy."

Later, when Zoe had been old enough to realize that her mother probably longed to have a man in her life, she had been the one to bring up the subject of marriage. Catherine had brushed her daughter's concerns aside with a laugh. "My life is complete just as it is, darling," she had told Zoe. "So stop worrying."

Far from upsetting her, the memories lifted Zoe's spirits. Feeling better, she slipped out of her coat and hung it on the entry rack, resisting the urge to fish the ruined heel out of the pocket and take another look at it. She didn't need the added aggravation right now. Hopefully, Lizzy's uncle, who was a shoemaker, would be able to salvage the pump.

In her stocking feet, she walked over to the refrigerator and took out a small bottle of Vittel before making her way to the living room.

With a sigh of contentment, she sank into one of the easy chairs and propped her feet on the coffee table, knowing that she didn't have to worry about nosy neighbors. The building across the street was brightly lit, but the offices were empty, offering her complete privacy.

Her phone rang before she could take a second sip of her water.

"Zoe, it's E.J. The woman you described is not one of our employees. Maureen did invite the two new secretaries to the party, but both declined because of a previous commitment."

Zoe was glad for E.J. He had worked hard to make the *Herald* a success, and in spite of all that hard work and the millions of dollars he had poured into the publication, he had come close to bankruptcy, not once but twice. Now that the paper was finally starting to make some serious money, it was natural that he wouldn't want anything to jinx it.

"That's great news, E.J."

"I'll talk to you on Monday, kid. Get some rest."

After she hung up, Zoe's mind went back to the events of the past hour. Reluctantly, she found herself agreeing with the two police officers. The woman *could* have attended a holiday party, just as Zoe had. It was also possible that she had overindulged, as many did at this time of year. But that's where her concessions ended. No matter how much Zoe tried, she could not imagine that same woman deciding to sleep off a few drinks too many in a filthy alley. Someone had lured her there and killed her. Or she could have been pushed out of a window, but which one? The *Herald* occupied the building's first ten floors. The other six were leased to three companies, all of which had promptly closed their doors at five o'clock.

Her lips pursed in concentration, she stood up and walked over to her drawing board. Kitty Floyd's last case had just ended and Zoe was already working on the next mystery series, which would be introduced to her fans on Monday morning. Except for a few finishing touches, all four frames were ready to be sent to the paper.

She had come up with her Kitty Floyd character a little more than a year ago, hoping that the strip would be picked up for syndication so that she could quit her low-paying job as a children's-book illustrator. Unfortunately, newspapers were reluctant to sign up unknown, untested cartoonists, no matter how talented they might be. Only E.J. had been smitten enough with Kitty Floyd to give her a try.

Twelve months later, the intrepid P.I., who lived and worked in Manhattan, was a hit in all five boroughs. And while syndicates were not beating down Zoe's door just yet, she could now devote all her time to doing what she loved most—getting Kitty Floyd in hot water.

Without bothering to sit, she picked up her pen—a Rapidograph she preferred over a brush—and started drawing the face of the dead woman, using her memory as a guide. It took several minutes and three tries to get it right, but when the sketch was finished, it bore an amazing resemblance to the woman in the alley. Underneath the sketch, she wrote: "The *New York Herald* needs your help in locating this woman. If you have any information, please contact us at 555–7100."

Satisfied, she picked up her phone and dialed E.J.'s cell number. In the background, she heard someone give directions and guessed that the publisher was answering a question from the limo.

"I've just finished a sketch of the mystery woman," she said excitedly. "If it's okay with you, I'd like to put it in tomorrow's paper. There's plenty of time to e-mail it to Sal in the press room. All I need is your approval."

There was no reply. If it hadn't been for the background chatter, Zoe would have sworn they had been cut off.

"E.J.? Did you hear me?"

"Yes. I'm sorry, Zoe. I was temporarily distracted."

"Do you want me to repeat—"

"No, no, I heard you."

"Well, what do you think? Do I have your okay?"

"Yes, of course. It's an excellent idea. I'll call Sal and let him know the sketch is coming."

By the time Saturday morning came around, the snow had turned to gray slush, the Manhattan skies were a cloudless blue and the sun poured into the loft from every window. If it weren't for the outside thermometer registering a frigid twenty-nine degrees, Zoe would have thought that spring was just around the corner.

Wearing a blue-striped nightshirt, she padded to the front door to retrieve her copy of the *Herald.* She didn't have to look far to find her sketch. Sal, the production manager, had put it on the front page, probably as per E.J.'s instructions. With any luck, someone would recognize the woman before the day was over.

A little after twelve noon, Lisa, the weekend switchboard operator at the *Herald,* called to say that so far she had received seven phone calls in response to the sketch. Unfortunately, all were from pranksters who apparently saw humor in the situation and couldn't wait to have a little fun.

Zoe was beginning to lose hope when Lisa called again, shortly after four. A man by the name of Buddy

Barbarino had called to say that he was the woman's agent.

Zoe grabbed pen and paper from her desk. "Give me the number, Lisa."

She scribbled it down, hung up and immediately started dialing again. "Mr. Barbarino?" she said when the man at the other end answered with a lazy "Buddy here." "I'm Zoe Foster. I understand that you are acquainted with the woman in the sketch I drew?"

"Yeah. Name's Lola Malone. I'm her agent."

Lola Malone. Why was that name familiar? "Is she an actress?"

"Nightclub singer."

"I see." Zoe was still trying to place the name.

"What's this all about?" Buddy Barbarino asked. "Why is Lola's picture on the front page of the *New York Herald?*"

Then she remembered! A week or so ago, Sylvia, who ran the *Herald* switchboard Monday through Friday, had handed Zoe a stack of phone messages. One of them was from a Lola Malone. Because she had left no message, Zoe hadn't bothered to return the call, or the other two that had followed.

"I think we should talk, Mr. Barbarino," she said, not addressing his question. "Where can we meet?"

"Well, let's see. I've just finished some business on Seventh Avenue and I haven't had a thing to eat all day. I was thinking of grabbing a bite at the Carnegie Deli. Can you meet me there? I'm wearing a green jacket."

"I'm on my way."

Four

Carnegie Deli, on Fifty-fifth Street and Seventh Avenue, was the quintessential kosher-style delicatessen that served staggering portions of classic deli fare gussied up with celebrity names.

Zoe didn't have too much difficulty spotting Buddy Barbarino sitting alone in a back booth. He was a broad-chested man with a balding head, soft, puttylike features and, judging from the loud green-plaid jacket he had mentioned, terrible taste in clothes.

He was already working his way through a gargantuan sandwich when Zoe approached his booth. "Mr. Barbarino?"

He gave her a quick up-and-down glance but didn't bother to stand up or offer his hand. "Call me Buddy." He kept on chewing. "You must be Zoe." He waved at the seat across from him. "Care for a sandwich? I'm having a tongue, corned beef and Swiss with Russian dressing." Some of the dressing trickled down his fingers, but instead of wiping them off on his napkin, he licked them, one by one. "They call it Tongue's for the Memory." He laughed. "Get it?"

The name was derived from "Thanks for the Memories," Bob Hope's well-known sign-off song. Zoe had no idea whether or not the famous comedian had ever set foot in the deli, but judging from the signed celebrity photographs on the walls, he probably had.

When Buddy pushed a menu in her direction, she shook her head. "I don't care for anything, thank you."

"You don't know what you're missing." He looked up as he took another bite. "Anyone ever told you you've got a face made for the camera?"

Zoe felt her dislike for the agent grow. He was the type of man who gave New Yorkers a bad name, not only because of the loud jacket and brassy personality, but because there was something sleazy about him that put Zoe instantly on guard. "No. And if you're about to tell me that you can make me a star, forget it."

"Too bad. Freckles are in. So's red hair. What do you weigh? About one-ten?" He must have caught her exasperated look because he finally stopped talking and got busy with his sandwich again. "Tell me about Lola," he said with his mouth full.

A waitress stopped by their table and Zoe ordered a bottle of mineral water. The girl raised an eyebrow. "That's it?"

"That's it." Anxious to get this meeting over with, she told Barbarino how she had discovered his client, but did not mention Lola Malone's three phone calls to the *Herald.*

His pudgy face registered instant shock. He actually

stopped chewing and put the rest of his sandwich down. After a long silence, which Zoe respected, he found his voice again. "You're pulling my leg, right?"

"No, I'm not."

"But you said the cops don't believe you."

"That's because they work with facts, evidence and eyewitnesses, none of which I could produce. Nonetheless, I know what I saw and I stand by it."

"Lola lives uptown. What would she be doing in the East Village at that time of night?"

"I was hoping you could tell me that."

He shook his head. "I've no idea. Lola and I do business over the phone, and now that she has a steady gig, I never hear from her." He gave a disdainful snort. "Broads. They're all the same. When they need you, they're all over you. When they don't, you might as well be dirt."

"And where would this new gig be?"

"At one of those snooty nightclubs that charge an arm and a leg to get in. You may have heard of it—Blue Moon?"

Zoe pressed her back against her seat and tried to keep a poker face. Almost everyone in New York had heard of the upscale nightclub, Zoe more than most. For a couple of years, she had spent all her spare time there, and for good reasons.

The owner of Blue Moon was none other than Rick Vaughn, her ex-husband.

It had been at least four years since Zoe had allowed herself to come within a hundred yards of Blue Moon.

Just a glimpse of it as she rode by every now and then was enough to bring a flood of memories. Some good, some not so good, all of which she had tried hard to forget.

So what was she doing here, walking up Lexington Avenue where the plush nightclub was located, with all her thoughts once again focused on Rick Vaughn? To say that she hadn't thought of him since their divorce six years ago would be a lie. You didn't have a passionate affair with a man, elope to Vegas with him a month later and then live the two most exhilarating, tempestuous, frustrating years of your life without the experience leaving its mark.

So, yes, she had thought of Rick a few times in the last six years, probably more than she should have, considering they hadn't seen each other since the divorce. He was like an addiction, she had once told Lizzy. A habit you want to kick but can't.

She had met him at the birthday bash of a mutual friend. Tall and devastatingly handsome, he had been surrounded by a half-dozen women when Roseanne, the birthday girl, had taken Zoe by the hand and led her to the group. "Rick, there's someone here I'd like you to meet."

As six pairs of hostile eyes turned to her, Rick Vaughn smiled and shook her hand while Roseanne made the introductions. They had spent the rest of the evening together, talking about their respective careers—hers as a children's-book illustrator, his as the new owner of his late brother's nightclub.

"I'm still not sure why he left it to me," he admitted

candidly. "I was in the marines at the time of Simon's death, planning on a military career. Now I'm running a nightclub and actually enjoying it. Go figure."

His charm, combined with a genuine interest in Zoe's artistic talents, had won her over. By the time he called the following afternoon, she was a basket case, pacing up and down her apartment, willing the phone to ring.

He invited her to go horseback riding in Connecticut, where he owned a lakeside home. They made love that night, not in front of a crackling fire with Nat King Cole on the CD player as might be expected, but in the stables, where a sudden downpour had caught them by surprise.

It was that unconventional, impulsive side of Rick that she had found most endearing. He was a man who knew how to turn an unexpected moment into an unforgettable experience. A month later, during a visit to the Central Park Zoo, he had proposed. Under the unruffled gaze of a colobus monkey, Zoe had screamed her answer before he'd had a chance to finish his proposal.

Much to her mother's dismay, Zoe and Rick had shunned the idea of a traditional wedding and eloped to Las Vegas. Everyone around them was thrilled to see them so happy, but there were a few reservations. The strongest came from Zoe's mother. Catherine Foster knew her strong-willed, twenty-five-year-old daughter too well to believe that such bliss would last a lifetime. She admitted that Rick, six years older than Zoe, was a good man, caring, honest and hardworking. But for all his virtues and sophistication, he possessed old-fashioned values she believed would eventually clash with Zoe's free spirit.

It wasn't long until her fears were confirmed. Unable to understand why Zoe needed to work now that she had him to take care of her, Rick suggested that she spend more time at the club where she had already started to make important changes. But as much as Zoe loved Blue Moon, she feared that working full-time with her husband would damage their relationship.

There had been other clashes, during which Zoe had accused Rick of trying to run their marriage the way he ran his club. He retaliated by telling her that she was stubborn, immature and selfish. Two years after they'd eloped, they'd agreed to call it quits.

Zoe had waited an entire year before dating again, but although she had met a handful of interesting men, none possessed Rick's charisma, his sincerity or his ability to make her laugh when she least expected it.

And now, here she was, standing across the street from Blue Moon's frosted door, her heart beating much too fast, her throat dry, her palms moist. In an attempt to calm down, she reminded herself that she was here for Lola Malone and not because she had a sudden yearning to see her ex-husband.

After checking her reflection in the window behind her, Zoe squared her shoulders. Then, her step firm, she crossed the street and headed for the familiar door.

Five

The club was still the same, small and elegant in an understated way. With its subdued lighting, mahogany tables and hardwood dance floor, it was reminiscent of the supper clubs made famous during the Prohibition era when men like Bugsy Siegel and Al Capone had dominated the nightclub scene. Skeptics had predicted that without Simon Vaughn at the helm, Blue Moon would collapse like a deck of cards. Rick had proven them all wrong.

It was a little after six, too early for the evening crowd, but Lenny, a marine-turned-bartender and an old friend of Rick's, was already behind the bar, polishing glasses. The last six years had added a few pounds to his middle and turned his hair pewter gray, but the face was still the same, and the broken nose he had suffered during a marine versus air-force boxing match was still the first thing you noticed.

"You left a spot," she said, approaching the gleaming bar.

He turned around and as recognition dawned, his face split into a huge grin. "Zoe. Son of a gun." He threw the towel over his shoulder and hurried around the bar. Before she had a chance to draw a breath, he had wrapped his beefy arms around her and was giving her one of his famous bear hugs. "It's really you."

"In the flesh." She made a small choking sound. "What's left of it, that is."

He laughed as he released her. "I could never curb my enthusiasm around you." Then, after a long, appraising look, he added, "How are you, doll?"

"No complaints. You look well, Lenny. As handsome as ever."

"But you still won't marry me."

It was her turn to laugh. That gentle banter between the two of them had been a constant delight in her life years ago. She looked around. "The place looks good."

"It's not the same without you."

Instead of a reply, she stole a quick glance toward the back where a short hallway led to Rick's office and a couple of storage rooms. "Is the boss around?"

"He just got in."

She gave his hand a pat. "Don't bother to announce me. I'll surprise him."

"Are you still fond of Sloppy Joes?" he asked as she started to walk away.

Memories of the three-liquors-and-fruit-juice concoction made her smile. "Only if they come in a glass."

He grinned. "I'll bring one in."

In front of the door marked R. Vaughn, Zoe took a deep breath and knocked. Likely thinking it was Lenny,

Rick responded with a question, "Since when do you knock?"

Zoe opened the door and just stood there as the sight of Rick's broad back bent over his desk sent a little jolt of awareness through her system. He had the same light brown hair, long enough in the back for the ends to curl up against his neck. She had called it his bad-boy hair. As her gaze moved over the rest of him, she couldn't suppress a smile. No one wore a tux the way Rick Vaughn did.

"Hello, Rick."

He turned around, and although he did a fairly decent job of keeping whatever he was feeling in check, Zoe caught the look of surprise in those light hazel eyes. She remained just as controlled, taking in the strong jaw, the steady gaze, the well-defined mouth.

"Zoe." He cleared his throat, started to say something, then, with an "oh, what the hell" kind of gesture, he closed the distance between them and embraced her. "What a pleasant surprise."

He let her go but not completely, holding her at arm's length. "Success becomes you, Red," he said, using the nickname he had given her long ago. "You look terrific."

"Thank you."

"How long has it been?"

As if he didn't know. "Five years?" Just to test him.

"You were always lousy in math. Six." He gave her arms one last squeeze before letting her go. "I've missed you."

"You've survived."

"And you've become a household name."

"Not quite but thanks for saying that. Do you read the strip?"

"Seven days a week. I'm a huge fan of *Kitty Floyd*. Maybe because she reminds me of you."

He was the second person to tell her that in less than twenty-four hours. "Really? How so?"

"Well, let's see." The hazel eyes shimmered. "She's smart, gutsy, beautiful and sassy."

Zoe laughed. "Still the flatterer, I see."

"You make it easy." He peeked behind her shoulders. "You wear your hair in a braid now?" He was good at noticing little details other men missed.

She ran her hand over the tightly woven tress. "I wanted something new."

He didn't tell her whether or not he liked her new do, but simply wrapped an arm around her waist and led her to a grouping of comfortable blue armchairs overlooking East Seventy-second Street. "Can I get you anything?"

"Lenny is bringing me a Sloppy Joe."

"Excellent."

"You must be wondering why I'm here."

He took the chair across from hers. "You finally realized that you couldn't live without me?"

She burst into laughter. "Oh, Rick."

"Sorry, I couldn't resist. Yes," he said more seriously. "I was wondering."

There was a rap on the door and Lenny walked in carrying a red drink in a stemmed cocktail glass in one hand and a martini with three olives in the other. Knowing that he was waiting for her to taste her drink, Zoe took a sip and nodded approvingly. "Nobody does it better, Lenny. Thanks."

Once they were alone again, Zoe came straight to the reason for her visit. "I understand that a woman by the name of Lola Malone works for you."

Rick raised an eyebrow. "You know Lola?"

"No, but our paths have crossed, so to speak. Does she? Work for you?"

"Not anymore. She quit about a week ago."

"How come?"

He took a couple of seconds before answering. "Let me ask *you* a question. How exactly did your and Lola's paths cross?"

She told him, and this time she didn't leave anything out, as she had with Buddy Barbarino. Rick's first expression was one of shock, then she saw the skepticism in his eyes grow as her story became more and more bizarre.

"Let me see that sketch of yours," he said when she was finished.

Zoe took the drawing from her purse and handed it to him.

He studied it for several seconds. "It *could* be Lola. I wouldn't swear to it, though."

"Buddy Barbarino says it's Lola."

"Buddy Barbarino doesn't know his ass from his elbow."

"You don't like him?"

"The man's a sleaze."

"Then why did Lola keep him as an agent?"

"Buddy helped her get started years ago, and Lola remained loyal to him, not to mention generous."

"She gave him money?"

"From time to time. In spite of his claim that he's one of the hottest agents in the city, Buddy isn't very successful. If you've seen him, you know why."

"You still didn't tell me why Lola quit her job at Blue Moon."

"She was tired of the routine, the hours. She wanted to get away for a while, maybe travel to one of those exotic places in the South Pacific. She brought a few brochures to show me—Sydney, New Caledonia, Tahiti."

"Was she planning to leave anytime soon?"

"That's the impression I had."

"Doesn't that seem a little sudden? I mean, one moment she has a successful singing career, and the next she's planning to fly to the other end of the world?"

"She had been talking about a trip for a long time. I guess that day finally arrived."

"And now she's dead."

"You don't know that. Some people have pulses you can barely feel. Unless you're a doctor, or a trained—"

"I don't need a medical degree to know that the woman I saw and touched was dead. The only concession I might have been willing to make at the time was that she died a natural death. But the fact that her body disappeared changed all that. She was murdered, Rick. And whoever murdered her removed her body while I went for help."

He studied her for a moment. "What exactly do you want from me?"

"Tell me all you know about Lola Malone. Where she lives, the names and addresses of her friends and relatives. Was she married? Did she have a boyfriend?"

But Rick was already shaking his head. "I can't do that."

"Why not?"

"Because my employees' private lives are just that—private."

"Don't you want to find out what happened to her?"

"Not until I'm certain that something *did* happen."

He was as difficult as she remembered. "Would you at least let me talk to your employees?"

"No."

She felt a flush rise to her cheeks. "What's wrong with talking to Lola's co-workers?"

"I don't want my people upset and my club disrupted. And I certainly don't want rumors going around that my singer was murdered. News like that can destroy a business."

That was the second time in as many days that she had heard that comment. "That's why you won't help me? Because your business could suffer?"

"I didn't say that—"

"It was always the club, wasn't it, Rick? Blue Moon first, no matter what."

"I see that you are as stubborn as ever. You still refuse to see someone else's point of view. Your way is the only way."

She jumped out of her chair, spilling some of her drink on her tweed slacks. "That is so not true!"

Rick took a white handkerchief from his back pocket and handed it to her.

She yanked it out of his hand and wiped up the spill.

"Look," Rick said in a softer voice. "Why don't you

wait a few days? Knowing Lola, if she went on a trip, she'll start sending postcards by the dozen. In the meantime, *if* she is truly missing, someone will report it to the police."

"And what if they don't? What if nobody cares?"

"I care. I'll wait a couple of days and then I'll go talk to her concierge. He knows me."

"In a couple of days the trail to her killer will have gone cold."

He smiled. "That sounds like something Kitty Floyd would say."

He wasn't taking her any more seriously than Officers Curtis and Barnes had. She dropped the handkerchief on the table. "I see that I'm wasting my time here." When he started walking around the coffee table, she raised a hand. "Don't bother to show me out. I know the way."

"Come on, Zoe, don't walk out of here mad."

"It wouldn't be the first time."

She was at the door, one hand on the knob, when he called, "Hey, Red."

She should have kept right on walking, but some inexplicable, uncontrollable force made her turn around.

"I like you better with your hair down."

Six

"She hasn't changed one bit, has she?" Lenny watched Zoe march out of the club. "She's still as full of piss and vinegar as ever."

Rick remained silent as he, too, watched Zoe's departing back. She was one of the few women he knew who looked as good leaving a room as she did entering it.

Lenny was right. She hadn't changed. She still had that same fiery temper, and that same hard head. Once she got hold of an idea, good or bad, she didn't let it go until every facet of it had been examined. As for the outside, she was simply stunning, even with that severe braid hanging down her back. At least she hadn't changed the color of her hair. He'd heard that some women did that after a divorce. They either cut it all off or they dyed it some ungodly color. Zoe had done neither, and he was glad. He loved her hair, a deep natural auburn that contrasted sharply with her pale, freckled skin. How many times had he sunk his hands into that rich, curly mane? Or kissed those freckles, one by one? Or listened to Zoe's smoky, sexy voice whisper, "Don't stop."

"She must have thrown you for a loop, showing up like that."

Rick had almost forgotten that Lenny was still here, behind the bar. "Which reminds me," he said. "You could have warned me."

"Aw, come on, boss. What would be the fun in that?"

"And I'm sure you enjoyed every minute of it."

"I admit that it was kinda nice seeing her here, like old times, like she never left. Funny, ain't it? How some people can make their mark on a place? The kid walks in after six years and—"

He'd had about all he could take. "Can it, Lenny, okay?"

Lenny chuckled. "Sorry. I didn't mean to reopen old wounds."

"You didn't."

"If you say so." Lenny opened the cash register, took out a roll of quarters and banged it against the edge of the drawer. "So what did she want?"

"She found a dead body."

"Someone we know?"

Rick put Zoe's sketch on the bar.

Lenny's mouth opened. "Lola?"

"You think it looks like her?"

"Yeah, a lot. Lola is dead?" He sounded as if he was about to cry, which was about as Rick had felt a moment ago.

"Zoe thinks so, but you know what an imagination she has." He repeated what she had told him before picking up the sketch and slipping it back into his tux jacket. "It's probably a misunderstanding. Or a case of mistaken identity. Didn't I read somewhere that we all have some-one who looks exactly like us?"

"What did she want you to do?"

"Let her talk to the employees, dig into Lola's life."

"And from the way she stormed out of here, I'm guessing you said no."

"What did you expect me to do? Turn the club over to her? Let her play Nancy Drew with my people?"

Lenny closed the register. Then, resting his arms on the counter, he looked straight into his old friend's eyes. "As well as I know you, there are times when I can't figure you out."

Even though Zoe was long gone, Rick kept his eyes on the door. "What can't you figure out?"

"Why a smart guy like you keeps making all the wrong choices."

Rick gave him a dark look. "Is this one of your deep observations I can never understand?"

"I'll put it in layman's language for you. You've just ruined any chance you may have had of getting Zoe back."

Rick turned away from the bar and headed back to his office. "Who said anything about wanting her back?"

From the cab that was taking her home, Zoe called E.J. "You can take the sketch out," she told him. "The mysterious woman has been identified."

"Who is she?"

"Her name is Lola Malone. Until a week ago, she was a singer at Blue Moon."

There was a short silence before E.J. spoke, "Wasn't that your ex-husband's nightclub?"

"Still is. I went there to talk to Rick but didn't get any-where. He won't cooperate." She could hear the bitter-ness in her own voice.

"He gave you a reason?"

"He's worried that the adverse publicity will hurt his club. And," she added reluctantly, "he doesn't believe that she's dead. He said that she had been meaning to take a trip to the South Pacific and that's what she prob-ably did."

"He could be right."

Zoe rolled her eyes. Men. They oversimplified every-thing. "I thought you were on my side." She realized how childish that remark sounded and corrected herself. "I mean, I thought you believed me."

"I do, but at the same time, I can't ignore the fact that if Lola Malone worked for your ex-husband, he knows her a lot better than you ever will."

"I hate it when you turn practical on me."

He laughed but his heart wasn't in it. "I've got to go, Zoe. Keep me informed?"

"Sure."

The cab had come to a stop in front of her building. She paid the driver and ran up the stairs to the second floor where she stopped abruptly. NYPD Detective Joe Santos, her best friend next to Lizzy, sat on the last step. Al-though he was attached to the fraud and white-collar crime division and worked out of a midtown precinct, he had friends everywhere and had probably heard about last night's incident.

She and Joe had met in September 2001, soon after the 9/11 tragedy. Zoe was helping Lizzy deliver food to the rescuers at Ground Zero. Joe Santos, then a rookie officer, had come to national attention a few days earlier when he ran into one of the towers and pulled two women away from the building moments before it had collapsed.

As they became better acquainted, Zoe had realized that Joe's feelings for her went much deeper than mere friendship. The problem was, Zoe didn't return those feelings. She loved him dearly, but not in a romantic way. Although the truth had been painful, Joe had accepted her decision and had agreed to remain friends.

He was, without a doubt, one of the most handsome men she had ever met. He had inherited his parents' Puerto Rican good looks—black, wavy hair, intense dark eyes and a smile that seemed to radiate from his very soul.

Although he had never married, he was what Zoe called a true family man; totally devoted to his mother, now a widow, his four sisters and his six nieces, all of whom adored him.

"Hi, beautiful," he said, kissing her cheek.

She sniffed the brown bag he was carrying. "Is that your mom's *sancocho* I smell?"

"And a thick slice of Puerto Rican rum cake. After hearing what you went through, she thought you needed some nourishment."

She did. Zoe hadn't had a bite to eat since her morning cornflakes. "Your mother is an angel." She walked into the loft and headed straight for the kitchen. "So are you, for coming all the way here."

"And don't you forget it." He took Maria Santos's Tupperware container out of the bag while Zoe retrieved bowls, spoons and a ladle from a drawer. He declined her offer to join her, but filled her bowl with the fragrant Caribbean soup. "So, what kind of trouble did you get yourself into now?"

She took a spoonful of the rich soup. "You don't know?"

"Oh, I know. I'd like to hear your version."

She winced. "How many versions are there?"

He chuckled. "It depends on who you talk to."

Zoe repeated the story she practically knew by heart. Well trained in the art of listening, Joe pulled up a stool and didn't interrupt her. When she slid Lola Malone's sketch toward him, he looked at it but made no comment until Zoe was finished.

She looked at him anxiously. "Say you believe me."

"Let me put it this way. I know you too well to think that this story is just a figment of your imagination."

"Is that what they're saying at the precinct? That it's a figment of my imagination?"

"Put yourself in their places, Zoe. They have no body, no murder weapon, no eyewitness and no evidence of foul play. They've even sent a lab team to go over the alley. They found nothing."

"What about the neighbors?"

"They were questioned. No one saw or heard anything."

"And I assume no one has come forward to report the woman missing or I would have already heard."

"Sorry."

Zoe ate in silence, wondering if she should mention

her visit to Blue Moon. She decided that if she wanted Joe's help, she had to level with him. "I found out who the woman is."

He looked surprised. "You did?"

Zoe nodded. "Someone called the *Herald* after seeing the sketch. Her name is Lola Malone. She's a singer. Until a week ago, she performed nightly at a club, right here in Manhattan—Blue Moon."

She saw the shock in his eyes. "Your ex's place?"

"I was surprised, too. As it turned out, Lola quit her job at Blue Moon a week ago." She gave him a brief summary of her conversation with Rick. "Apparently Lola had been meaning to take a trip and that's what Rick believes she did."

"A trip where?"

"He's not sure—somewhere in the South Pacific."

"Did you talk to anyone besides Rick?"

She let out a bitter laugh. "He wouldn't let me. Didn't want to hurt his precious club."

Joe laughed. "You two went at it again?"

"You could say that."

"Hmm."

She debated whether or not to have more soup and decided she wouldn't have room for dessert if she did. She reached for the rum cake. "What's that look for?"

"Nothing. It's the cop in me thinking."

"Come on, Joe, don't clam up on me, too. I need help here."

"Well…" He scratched his head. "Could Rick and Lola be involved with each other?"

"You mean romantically?"

"That could be the reason he doesn't want you to pry."

Zoe shook her head and didn't tell him that the same thought had passed through her mind but she had quickly dismissed it. "He would have told me."

"Are you sure? A liaison is hardly something you confess to an ex-wife you haven't seen in six years. Especially one who reenters your life ready for battle."

"That's not the impression I wanted to give."

"But that's how he took it."

When she remained silent, he lowered his head a little, forcing her to look up. "May I make a suggestion?"

She shrugged. "You're going to make it whether I want it or not."

"True, so here it is. Stop making yourself crazy and drop the whole thing."

"I can't do that."

"Why not?"

"I feel a certain responsibility toward this woman."

"Because she was trying to contact you?"

"That's right."

"Come on, Zoe. She could have been anybody, maybe even a deranged fan."

"She didn't look like a deranged fan."

"And Ted Bundy didn't look like a serial killer."

After a silence that Zoe didn't know how to break, Joe let out a resigned sigh. "Okay, here's what I'll do. I'll put her name in the police database and see what I come up with. Are you happy?"

Zoe's spirits lifted. "What if she doesn't have a record?"

"You don't need to be a criminal to be in our database. If she witnessed an accident, reported a barking dog, was fingerprinted for employment purposes or applied for a driver's license, we'll have the information."

"Thank you, Joe."

"Don't mention it." He climbed down from the stool. "I'll let you know what I find out. Right now, I've got to run. I start on my night shift in about thirty minutes. Will you be home tomorrow?"

"As far as I know. I need to work on my new story-line."

He kissed her on the cheek. "You look tired. Go to bed."

She snapped a sharp salute. "Yes, sir."

"Smart-ass."

Seven

Instead of taking Joe's advice and going to bed, Zoe took a soothing bath, slipped into a clean nightshirt and wandered back into her living room to call Lizzy at the restaurant. Her friend would be winding down by now. After a seventeen-hour day, most people would be ready to drop. Not Lizzy. The Chinese-born American was so full of energy that she needed a couple of hours every night in order to unwind before she could even think of going to bed.

She and Zoe had met at Northwestern University where Lizzy had been studying, of all things, computer science. After finding out that her new friend's true love was cooking, Zoe had encouraged her to follow her heart. Six months later, Lizzy had dropped out of college and returned to her native New York where she enrolled at the French Culinary Institute. The next ten years were spent working for some of the best chefs in Manhattan and perfecting her craft. Then, three years ago, the Min family had pooled their resources together and opened Lotus in the heart of Chinatown.

"Hello?" Lizzy sounded as cheerful at ten o'clock at night as she did in the early morning hours.

"It's me."

"Hi, you. How was the Christmas bash?"

"Different. I found a body."

"In your Christmas stocking?"

"In an alley." Zoe went through the drill one more time.

"It sounds like one of your Kitty Floyd stories."

"I'm afraid that's what the cops think, too."

There was laughter in Lizzy's tone. "So how was it to once again be in the presence of the hunk?"

Lizzy had always had a soft spot for Rick. "Irritating, what else?"

"What I meant was, did any of the old feelings resurface? After all, didn't you tell me once that no man you had ever met could measure up to Rick Vaughn?"

"That's before he and I lived under the same roof." She walked around the kitchen, rinsing bowls and setting them into the dishwasher. "Believe me, the man is as much a bully now as he was then."

"I'm not sure he was ever a bully. Unwavering, perhaps, but then, so are you."

"He called me stubborn."

"The cad."

"You're not helping, Lizzy." But Zoe found herself smiling. "Rick's lack of cooperation doesn't matter anyway," she continued. "If Joe gets me the information I need, I'll never have to set eyes on Rick Vaughn again."

"Does that make you feel better?"

Did it? "You bet."

Then, because it was high time to steer the conversation away from her annoying ex-husband, she said, "I broke the heel of one of my new shoes—the ones I wore at the Christmas party?"

"Not your new Manolos."

"Yes, my new Manolos. An air vent chewed it to bits before spitting it back. The shoe's a mess. I was hoping your uncle could take a look at it."

She could hear Lizzy's soft laugh. "You know he will. Why don't you bring it to the restaurant tomorrow and I'll take it over to him. Unless you want to hop in a cab and come down now."

"I'd better not. I need to work on the new strip."

"I'll let you go then. I heard a crash that I should probably investigate. Come tomorrow, okay? I'll make you some lunch."

Still awake, thanks to the four cups of coffee she had ingested over the last couple of hours, Zoe walked over to her drawing table where *Kitty Floyd and the Case of the Child Prodigy,* her next adventure series, was waiting. As she had last night, she sat down, flipped to a new page and picked up her pen. Her fingers seemed to move without prompting as they traced Kitty's familiar outline within a three-by-two-and-a-half-inch frame.

After a few minutes Zoe stopped, aware that the scene she had just sketched was totally unrelated to *The Case of the Child Prodigy.* In this frame, Kitty was dressed to the nines and walking out of a swank Manhattan hotel after attending a friend's Christmas party. Her arm was raised as she hailed a cab.

Zoe bit on the end of her pen, studying the drawing, which so closely mirrored last night's events. This wasn't a bad idea at all. Instead of having Kitty investigate the child prodigy mystery, Zoe would give the New York P.I. a case similar to the disappearance of Lola Malone. It would be a blend of fiction and reality, depending on how much information she could unveil.

She continued to follow her muse, moving to the second frame where Kitty's gaze was drawn to something shiny in the alley next to the hotel. Zoe drew Kitty's open mouth as she spotted the body of a beautiful woman lying on the ground. The third frame showed Kitty crouched beside the woman, trying to wake her up. The fourth and last frame contained a distraught Kitty running back into the hotel and asking the desk clerk to call the police.

Zoe worked for another hour, adding internal thoughts and dialogue. When she was finished, she started on the Tuesday strip, updating the story and adding more information. She wouldn't have to worry about Wednesday's and Thursday's strips until tomorrow. Because her work appeared in only one newspaper, her lead time was sharply reduced. Instead of the usual four-to-seven days, Zoe often worked with a two- to three-day lead and sent the strip to the *Herald* electronically, or dropped it off at the paper herself.

At the top of the strip, beside *Kitty Floyd, P.I.,* she wrote her new subtitle: *Who Killed Mona Gray?* It wasn't very original, but it had the impact she wanted. The names and professions of the principal characters had been changed. Lola Malone was now Mona Gray, a popular soap opera actress. Rick, alias Nicholas Simms, had become the show's handsome director, and instead of an agent, Zoe had given Mona an ex-husband with traits similar to those of Buddy Barbarino.

When she was finished, she went over both strips, changed a word here and there and put her pen down. It was ready.

Now all she had to do was sell the idea to E.J.

The one place where Zoe was sure to find E.J. on a Sunday morning was the indoor running track on Third Avenue, near Cooper Square. Fond of his wife's home-made cannoli, he made up for his indulgence by running four miles three times a week, although he often said that no matter what he did, the cannoli were winning the battle.

Zoe waited until he had turned the corner of the inside track before moving into his line of vision. Looking surprised, he waved and slowed down before coming to a complete stop.

"Zoe." He bent, both hands on his knees, and took a few shallow breaths. "What in God's name are you doing here?"

"Looking for you, what else?"

He glanced at the manila envelope she held. "What have you got there?"

"The Monday and Tuesday strips. I want you to take a look at them."

"You already sent the Monday and Tuesday strips."

"This is a new story." She opened the envelope and pulled out a sheet of paper with the eight new frames.

A frown creased E.J.'s perspiring forehead. "What's that?"

"Lola Malone's disappearance, slightly altered."

"What about the child prodigy?"

"We shelve it, for now, and run the Lola Malone story instead."

"Why?"

"Because I need to get closer to her, into her skin, so to speak. Working on the story every day will enable me to focus on what I may have missed."

The publisher gave her a worried look. "You talk as if you were planning on investigating her disappearance yourself."

"What else am I supposed to do? No one will take me seriously." She didn't wait for him to protest. Whatever he had to say she had already heard, from Rick and from Joe. "The story will generate huge interest. After Buddy Barbarino called the paper, several people from the *Herald* wanted to know everything about Lola. The newspapers haven't picked up the story yet, but when they do, readers will draw the parallel between Mona Gray and Lola Malone and become completely involved in her disappearance."

E.J. studied each frame again. "You certainly hooked me, I'll give you that."

"There's more." She talked rapidly now, caught up in the excitement of her own little brainstorm. "I'm going to ask readers to help Kitty solve the mystery by e-mailing the *Herald* daily clues. Every few days, I'll select the best one and use it as part of Kitty's investigation." Worried she may not have sold him entirely, she added, "Just think what this new twist will do for your circulation. If you need more convincing—"

E.J. laughed. "All right, all right, you win. We'll go with *Who Killed Mona Gray?*"

Zoe placed a noisy kiss on his cheek. "Thanks, E.J. You're the best."

Lotus Restaurant was one of those Chinatown gems a food critic had discovered by accident a couple of years ago and given a four-star billing. The high mark was well deserved. Lizzy was both talented and imaginative. While she had kept many of her standard dishes on the menu, she had also incorporated dishes that were complex and truly unique.

The experiment was a hit. By the time the restaurant's first anniversary arrived, Lotus was *the* place to dine. Booked solid weeks in advance, the popular eatery buzzed with activity from eleven-thirty in the morning, when it opened its doors for lunch, to about midnight when it closed.

The atmosphere was as much a part of Lotus as the food itself. Lizzy's brother, Jimmy, worked in the kitchen, side by side with Lizzy. Her mother, Lao, manned the cash register, and Lizzy's two younger sisters, Suzie and Judy, waited tables. It was a harmonious combination—most of the time. On those few occasions when tempers flared, Lotus became high theater with everyone talking at once, in English and Chinese, and gesturing wildly.

Madame Min, as everyone called the family matriarch, spotted Zoe the moment she entered. She was a diminutive woman with short black hair and a face that had weathered much too prematurely. A broad smile deepened the lines around her eyes as she waved at Zoe from behind the cash register.

"Come here and give me a hug," she said in her sing-song voice. "How are you, girl? Lizzy told me what happened. Don't worry, okay? The police will find your friend."

Before Zoe could tell her that Lola wasn't exactly her friend, Madame Min touched Zoe's hair, which had always fascinated her. "You wore your hair down. I like it."

"I didn't have time to braid it." Which was a lie.

"Are you hungry?" Madame Min was always worried that Zoe didn't eat enough. "Lizzy made those cold noodles you like. There's plenty left."

"I'm not hungry, but thanks just the same. If you don't mind…" She pointed toward the kitchen.

"Go. She's waiting for you."

The usually noisy kitchen was relatively quiet, as the lunch hour was coming to an end. Lizzy sat on a stool, her eyes closed, her hands resting on her knees, fingers touching. Her chest moved slowly as she breathed evenly. A strong believer in the benefits of meditation, she often took short breaks throughout the day in order to reconnect with what she called her inner self. The mental exercises enabled her to go through her working day with maximum efficiency.

She was a lovely girl, with her mother's sleek black hair, almond-shaped eyes and delicate features. She'd had many suitors over the years, some who had even earned Madame Min's approval. Lizzy was too busy to get involved in anything more than a passing romance.

"Is this any way to run a kitchen?" Zoe asked as she walked in.

Lizzy's eyes popped open. In spite of the sudden interruption, she looked as refreshed as if she had just awakened from a two-hour nap. She slid off her stool, graceful as a swan. "You think you can do better?"

"Maybe in my dreams." The two women kissed.

"How about some lunch?" Lizzy asked. "I made those noodles you like. And we have half a Peking duck left over."

Zoe laughed. "You are your mother's daughter."

Lizzy was already reaching for a plate. "What will it be? Noodles? Peking duck? Both?"

"Neither. I'm not hungry. I'd love a cup of tea, though."

Jimmy, who looked enough like Lizzy to be her twin, gave them a gentle nudge toward a small table in the back. "As much as I love having two beautiful women in my way, unless you want to be put to work, you'd better sit over there." He smiled. "And I'll be glad to bring you a pot of tea, my dear lady."

Lizzy rolled her eyes. "Don't mind him. He's in love."

"Jimmy! Who's the lucky girl?" But Jimmy was already out of earshot.

"He's not telling, not even our mother, which irritates her to no end. You know what a control freak she is. You look tired," she added after they were both seated. "Are you still worrying about that woman?"

"No one else seems to."

"The police still refuse to investigate her disappearance?"

"They can't do anything until someone reports her missing."

"What about her agent?"

"He doesn't count. He hasn't seen her in months."

Jimmy was back, carrying a tray with a pot of tea, two delicate china cups and matching saucers. He didn't believe in mugs or tea bags. "You might as well drink straw juice in a can," he had told Zoe once.

"Thank you, Jimmy. It smells heavenly."

Pleased, he bowed and disappeared.

"What exactly are you planning to do?" Lizzy asked as she poured.

Zoe told her about the new strip, but instead of her friend's approval, all she got was a shake of her head.

"I don't know, Zoe. What if you're right and Lola *was* murdered? And the killer is out there, reading your strip, worrying about being exposed?"

"What is he going to do? Go after Kitty?"

"Or you."

"He's not that stupid. Right now, he believes that he has committed the perfect crime. He's not going to mess that up by giving himself away so easily." Then, because she didn't want the conversation to get too heavy, she took her broken heel from her tote bag and set it on the table.

"Now here's a real challenge." Lizzy took the heel and turned it around in her hand. "Lucky for you, my uncle An is not only a shoe repairman, he's a magician."

Jimmy came back, this time with a plate of noodles,

which he put in front of Lizzy. "Mother's orders," he declared. "You don't eat, I don't leave this establishment alive."

Eight

"What did you do to be so popular all of a sudden?"

At the sound of Lenny's voice, Rick looked up from a stack of invoices on his desk. "Who wants to see me now?"

"Detective Joe Santos of the NYPD."

"Don't know him." Rick returned his attention to his bills. Then, because he couldn't very well ignore a visit from one of New York's finest, he asked, "What does he want?"

"Didn't say, but he made himself comfortable at the bar and ordered a Coke, so I'm guessing he's going to stick around until you come out."

"In that case, tell him I'll be right there."

Even in civilian clothes, Joe Santos had cop written all over him. His dark hair was neatly trimmed, his handsome face freshly shaven and that powerful physique could only belong to a man who worked hard at keeping fit. The name suggested an Hispanic background and his looks confirmed it.

"Mr. Vaughn." The detective offered his hand, which

Rick shook. "I appreciate you seeing me. I know you're a busy man."

"No problem. I didn't forget to make my yearly donation to the Police Athletic League, did I?"

Santos laughed. "No, sir, you didn't. In fact, your contribution was more than generous."

"You checked?"

"I like to know as much as I can about a man before I talk to him."

Rick gestured behind him. "In that case, would you like to talk in my office?"

"Right here is fine." The detective's gaze swept over the club's main room, in semidarkness at this time of day. "Maybe we could sit at one of the tables?"

"Sure." Rick glanced over his shoulder. "Lenny, bring Detective Santos another Coke, and a Sprite for me."

"Sure thing, boss."

After the two men were seated, Rick saw the detective take an appreciative look around him. "This is quite a place you've got. Classy without being intimidating, if you know what I mean."

"I know exactly what you mean, and all the credit for what you see goes to my late brother. His intention was to create the kind of club that was both glamorous and comfortable. A few skeptics thought the idea would never fly. Simon knew better." He waited until Lenny had put their drinks on the table before saying, "You look familiar. Have we met?"

Santos shook his head. "No, but you may have seen me on TV a few years ago. After 9/11? I was part of a search-and-rescue team working at Ground Zero."

Memories of a highly publicized rescue jumped into Rick's mind. "Of course. You're that cop who ran in one of the towers just before it collapsed. You pulled two women from the rubble. That was very brave of you."

"Anyone on my team would have done the same thing."

Brave and modest. A very likable combination. Rick leaned back in his chair. "What can I do for you, Detective?"

"Actually, the favor I came to ask is not for me but for a mutual friend."

"We have a mutual friend?"

"Zoe Foster."

Rick held back a laugh. The little wench. She hadn't gotten anywhere on her own so she had sent the fuzz? How much did she think *that* was going to accomplish?

"She didn't send me, in case you were wondering." Santos filled his mouth with an ice cube and started chewing it.

"Yet you're here."

"Normally I wouldn't butt in, but she's pretty upset over this Lola Malone mystery. She thinks that if she had returned your singer's phone calls, the woman would still be alive."

"That's nonsense. We don't even know if Lola is dead."

"True, but you know as well as I do how…determined Zoe is."

At the slight hesitation, Rick almost smiled. The policeman had been about to say "stubborn."

"I offered to check our database," Santos continued.

"Unfortunately, I came up empty. Lola Malone never applied for a driver's license, never registered to vote and never filed a single complaint."

"So you're buying Zoe's story?"

"Aren't you?"

"My main problem is that I can't imagine what Lola would have to discuss with my ex-wife that she couldn't mention to me. And to chase her all the way to a Christmas party in the East Village? In the middle of the night?" He shook his head. "That doesn't sound like Lola."

"What if she thought that going to that Christmas party was the only way she could get to talk to Zoe?"

Rick watched the detective in silence. He didn't seem to have a problem believing Zoe. Why was that? What did he know about her that Rick didn't? "May I ask how you know Zoe?" He kept his tone casual.

"We met at Ground Zero. She was helping her friend Lizzy deliver food to the rescuers."

Rick nodded, remembering how restaurants from all five boroughs had come together, generously giving of their time and talents to feed the exhausted men and women on the site of the tragedy.

"And you and Zoe are just…friends?"

The two men's eyes met and held. "Why do you want to know?"

Rick had always possessed a high level of perception. The look of challenge in the young cop's eyes was barely noticeable, but it was there and Rick saw it. "I'm just curious. If you don't want to answer—"

"We're just friends."

"And that's how you want it?"

This time Santos laughed. "Zoe didn't tell me you were so nosy. You almost sound…"

"What?"

"As if you're still in love with her."

"I want to see her happy."

"That's all?"

"We could play this game all day, but I don't think that's why you came to see me, is it?"

"No, and since you've been honest with me, I'll be honest with you. Being *just* friends with Zoe isn't my idea. I love her. If I had my way, I'd marry her tomorrow. Unfortunately, she's not ready to commit just yet and I'm respecting her wishes."

In other words, the handsome detective's advances had been turned down but he wasn't giving up. Good for him. Zoe was worth fighting for. Rick wished he had realized that when their marriage had started to go south.

He wondered if Santos's decision to contact Rick was self-serving. Was he here to help a friend? Or to score points?

Careful, Ricky, old boy, you're starting to sound like a jealous husband.

"And now, Mr. Vaughn," Santos continued, "for the real reason that I'm here."

"Call me Rick."

"All right, Rick. I came to ask you to reconsider your decision not to help Zoe. All she wants is a little information on Lola Malone, just enough to help her make some sense out of what happened the other night. Is that so hard to understand?" When Rick didn't answer, he pushed a slip of paper across the table. "That's Zoe's address, in case you wanted to stop by."

Rick glanced at it. "She shouldn't be playing cop. She could get hurt."

"I'll make sure she won't."

Although Rick wasn't particularly fond of cops, he liked this one. Joe Santos wasn't pushy or patronizing, and he didn't pretend to be someone he wasn't. He genuinely cared about Zoe and wanted to do something nice for her.

Jenny, his interim singer, walked in at that moment and headed for the stage for a quick rehearsal. Her arrival reminded him that he needed to talk to her about her song selections. He pushed his chair and stood up. "I'll give your suggestion a thought. How's that?"

Santos offered his hand and Rick shook it. "That's all I ask. Thanks, Rick."

Nine

After leaving Lotus, Zoe had returned to the loft and immersed herself in her work. She was drawing the Manhattan Bridge outside Kitty's office window, when her front doorbell rang. She ignored it. Only Joe and Lizzy dropped by unannounced and since she already knew it couldn't be them, anyone else could come back some other time. Right now she needed to finish this frame.

But apparently her visitor had no intention of going away. He or she rang again, this time more insistently. Zoe blew out a breath, turned off her CD player where Josh Groban's love ballads had kept her inspired, and climbed down from her stool.

"All right," she shouted as she crossed the room. "I'm coming already." She opened the door and just stood there, unable to hide her surprise. "Rick." After the way they had parted yesterday afternoon, finding her ex-husband on her doorstep was the last thing she had expected.

His amused gaze traveled from her hair, which she

was still wearing loose, to the washed-out jeans and bare feet. "Am I interrupting something?"

"I was working." Her earlier resentment vanished, she let him in. "It can wait."

He looked handsome and casual in a brown tweed jacket, a tan turtleneck and cord trousers. He smelled good, too. She recognized the scent—Hermès aftershave. She hadn't noticed it last night. Had he worn it today, hoping to evoke a few memories? If so, he had succeeded.

"Are you sure it's safe for me to come in? You don't have a machete hiding behind your back, do you?"

She smiled. "I guess you'll have to take your chances."

"I'm good at doing that."

As he walked in ahead of her, she stole a quick glance at the small mirror in the entryway. In her haste to catch E.J. at the gym, she hadn't bothered to put any makeup on, not even lipstick. Oh well, too late to do anything about it now.

"Wow."

Her looks forgotten, Zoe came to stand beside Rick. He stood in the center of the loft, his gaze sweeping around, taking in every nook and cranny.

"This is a great place," he said, walking in. "How in the world did you find it?"

"The previous owner, a candy maker, was one of Lizzy's customers. When he told her he was relocating to Brooklyn and selling the factory, she took me to see it. I wasn't in the market to buy, especially something that needed so much work, but the price was right and

Lizzy said she'd help me renovate, so I took the plunge and became a homeowner."

He made no mention of the studio apartment he had signed over to her at the time of the divorce. She hadn't been able to afford the mortgage and had sold it six months later.

"You did a great job," he said. "This is truly spectacular." He looked at Kitty's larger-than-life drawing on the wall. "And better still, it is you."

"Thank you. My mother helped with the decorating."

"How's Catherine?"

"Very well. She moved to Cape May and opened a bed-and-breakfast." Zoe motioned toward the kitchen. "I just made coffee. Would you like some?"

She saw him hesitate and remembered the awful stuff she used to brew. "I've gotten better at it," she said, taking mugs from a cabinet.

She could feel his eyes on her as she poured. "I'm sorry about yesterday," he said suddenly.

Rick apologizing? That was a first. "What about?" Might as well make him grovel a little.

"You're going to make me say it?"

She gave him an innocent look. "Say what?"

He laughed. "Okay, I'll play. I was a jerk. An asshole. A total idiot."

She handed him one of the mugs. "Don't let me stop you. You're on a roll."

"I didn't realize how much finding Lola meant to you."

"And that realization came to you overnight?"

"Not exactly." He added a few drops of milk to his coffee and stirred it. "A friend of yours came to see me."

Zoe raised an eyebrow. "Lizzy?"

"Joe Santos."

Her cheeks burned with sudden embarrassment. "Joe? Why?"

"He was concerned about you. He thought you were taking this thing much too hard."

"He had no business interfering."

"I'm glad he did." He took something out of the bag he carried and set it on the counter.

She looked at the videotape. "What's that?"

"Two hours of Lola Malone doing what she does best—entertain. This is a copy of a video that was made at the club about a month ago, in preparation for a Broadway audition."

"She *was* an actress, then?"

"Aspiring. She didn't get the part. She never does, but she's a real trouper. She doesn't let a few rejections get her down." He glanced down at the tape. "A TV reporter was in the audience the night of the taping and she interviewed Lola after the show. I pasted the interview at the end of the tape so you could have an insight into what she's all about."

Zoe looked from the tape to Rick. "I don't know what to say."

"Say you won't do anything crazy, like hunting down potentially dangerous people."

"Was Lola acquainted with dangerous people?"

"Not to my knowledge."

"Was she married?"

"No, but she was seeing someone. I don't know who," he said as though anticipating her next question. "Lola wouldn't talk about him."

"Was it someone she met at the club?"

"Possibly, although she had enough spare time out-side the club to have met him elsewhere."

"Did anyone in the audience seem to pay particular interest to her?"

Rick laughed. "Zoe, every man who came to Blue Moon was totally captivated by her, including your boss."

Zoe slowly put her mug down. "E.J.?"

"Yup. Elijah himself. I recognized him from a photo-graph. He came fairly regularly for a while, then he stopped. He didn't tell you?"

Stunned that the publisher hadn't mentioned know-ing Lola Malone, she shook her head. "No. How long ago was that?"

"Oh, four or five months ago."

Bits and pieces of that first night when she had dis-covered the body flashed through her mind, demanding attention. E.J.'s concern that the woman in the alley was someone he knew. His unusual silence when Zoe had de-scribed her to the two officers. His hesitation when she had asked him to run a sketch of the dead woman in the *Herald.* None of it had meant anything at the time. But now…

Rick was watching her. "You're not suspecting your boss of anything, are you? He seems like a nice guy, but he's hardly Lola's type."

"What *is* her type?"

He seemed to think for a moment. "She's crazy about George Clooney."

Who wasn't? "What else can you tell me about her?"

"Let's see. She's an only child. Her parents died when she was eleven and she was raised by an aunt who now lives in a nursing home in upstate New York. You may have heard of her—Frieda North?"

"The Broadway actress? Three-time Tony winner?"

Rick gave a nod. "That's the one, although you'd hardly recognize her these days."

"What's wrong with her?"

"Dementia. Except for an occasional moment of lucidity, she doesn't remember anything. Her illness has hit Lola hard."

"Does Lola visit her often?"

"Every Saturday. They talk for a couple of hours, although it's mostly Lola who's doing the talking."

"What do they talk about?"

"Anything Lola feels might trigger a response—the past, her job at Blue Moon, the auditions she goes to."

"The man she loves?"

"Possibly."

"Could you arrange for me to see Frieda? I'd love to talk to her."

Rick shook his head. "Lola wouldn't want that. Frieda gets easily distraught these days. A visit from a stranger could put her over the edge."

"But Frieda could be the only person who knows the identity of her niece's mysterious boyfriend."

"She's off-limits, Zoe," Rick said sharply. Then, as if realizing he had spoken *too* sharply, he added, "Why don't you talk to Annie instead?"

"Who's Annie?"

"My head waitress. She and Lola were good friends."

"You think Lola would have confided in her?"

"I don't know. It's worth a try. She gets in at six-thirty to set up the tables."

"Thank you." She refilled his mug. "I guess I'd better thank Joe, as well."

"Speaking of Joe." Rick's eyes filled with humor. "Are you aware that the man is crazy about you?"

"You two talked about me?"

"I was curious. Did he ever propose?"

"Not that it's any of your business, but yes, he did. Twice."

"Why did you turn him down?"

"What makes you think I turned him down?"

"I don't see an engagement ring on your finger."

"For your information, I came very close to saying yes. Joe is a good man. He's caring, supportive and smart. His family adores me."

"So what's wrong with him? Smelly feet? A roving eye? He turns into a pumpkin at midnight?"

"He has his faults. I overlook them."

"In other words, you like him a lot."

"Yes, I do." She watched him as she sipped her coffee. "What about you? Why haven't you remarried?"

He looked at her for a long moment before replying. "Oh, I don't know. I guess I never found the right woman. Or maybe I'm just not the marrying kind."

Not the marrying kind? When had he come to that conclusion? After their divorce? Did those two years with her leave such a bad impression that he had sworn off matrimony forever?

He glanced at his watch. "I'll let you go back to

work." He lifted his cup before taking it to the sink. "Thanks for the coffee. You were right. You've greatly improved. Juan Valdez would be proud."

She walked him over to the door. "Thanks for the tape. And for your invitation to talk to Annie. I'll take you up on it."

"You do that." He gave her a quick kiss on the cheek and then he was gone.

Ten

Standing at the window, Zoe watched Rick exit the building and walk down Wooster. She touched her cheek where he had kissed her goodbye.

It had felt good being around him again, having him here in her surroundings, drinking coffee together, laughing the way they used to. She had forgotten how charming he could be and how quickly she could fall under his spell. She would have to be careful. Just because they had enjoyed each other's company for an hour or so was no reason to fall in love again. *That* aspect of their relationship was in the past. Over. Finito.

Besides, hadn't he said it himself? He wasn't the marrying kind.

When Rick had disappeared, Zoe pulled away from the window, walked over to the video recorder and inserted Lola's tape. Then, from the comfort of her favorite chair, she pressed Play on the remote control and settled back to watch and listen.

As the image of a shapely blonde appeared on the

screen, Zoe felt a small jolt of recognition. Until now, she'd had no definite proof that the woman in the alley and the nightclub singer were one and the same. But now, watching her on tape, Zoe knew with absolute certainty that the search for the dead woman's identity had ended.

Lola Malone was even more beautiful on tape than she had been in death. From the first moment she appeared on Zoe's TV screen, it was clear that the singer had cultivated a 1940s bombshell look that had made a handful of actresses of that era superstars. The face was exquisite, with delicate features, large blue eyes and that big, shiny red mouth Zoe had glimpsed in the alley. The long blond peekaboo hairstyle was pure Veronica Lake, while the raw sex-appeal was a cross between Sharon Stone and Halle Berry.

Her voice was not remarkable in itself. It was the smoky, sultry way she sang that held the audience spellbound. Even the women couldn't take their eyes off her. She sang tunes that could only be described as torch songs—"Fever," "Embraceable You," "Somebody Loves Me," "I've Got You Under My Skin." From time to time, she would lighten up the mood with swingy numbers such as "Let's Misbehave" and "Come On To My House" as she walked through the audience, microphone in hand. She ended the two-hour performance with the club's signature song, "Blue Moon."

On the night of the taping, Lola had worn a shimmering black gown and black elbow-length gloves. Strapped around her left wrist was the gold cuff.

Zoe leaned forward. There was something attached to the bracelet, a charm of some sort. As the singer brought her left hand to the microphone and the camera zoomed in, Zoe took a closer look. It was a little golden cupid, wings and all. In his hands, aimed at lovers everywhere, was a bow and arrow. Zoe was certain it had not been on the bracelet the night she had found Lola.

So where was it?

The interview at the end of the tape allowed Zoe to see a side of Lola she wouldn't have known otherwise. As the reporter questioned her about her singing, her dream of becoming an actress and her hopes of landing a role in the current Broadway hit *Wicked,* Lola spiced up her answers with humor and charisma. When the reporter mentioned Lola's famous aunt, however, the singer quickly and effortlessly shifted the conversation in another direction.

Zoe smiled. *Well done, Lola.* Not too many people could make a pushy reporter back off, but Lola had. Zoe found herself liking the woman and wishing she'd had a chance to know her. They might even have been friends.

When the tape ended, Zoe watched it a second time. As the camera went in for a close-up at the end of the show, Zoe studied the beautiful features. "Who killed you, Lola?" she murmured. "Whose face did you see before you closed your eyes forever?"

Annie Baker was an attractive girl with blond hair tied behind her head in a classic chignon, and intelligent brown eyes. Already dressed for her shift, she wore the same ankle-length black dress the other four waitresses were wearing. She went from table to table, pulling a cart holding small, festive pots of red poinsettias.

"Annie?"

The young woman turned around. "Yes?" After a brief look at Zoe, she smiled. "You must be Zoe Foster. Rick described you perfectly."

Zoe would have loved to hear how he had described her but refrained from asking. "Then you know that I'm here to talk to you about Lola."

"Yes." She centered one of the pots on a table. "Do you really think it was Lola in that alley?" Her eyes misted as she met Zoe's gaze.

"I *know* it was Lola."

"How can you be so sure?"

"Rick brought me a tape of her singing." As Annie gave a somber nod, Zoe added, "I'm sorry. I know you and Lola were friends."

Annie picked up another pot and moved to the next table. "I can't believe she's dead. I talked to her a couple of days earlier."

So she had still been in town and not on a trip. "Do you remember what you talked about?"

"Pretty much the same things as we always did. Her aunt, whose condition is deteriorating, the television shows Lola could watch now that she didn't work nights, the trip she was planning to take."

That trip again. "Did she say where or when she was planning to go?"

"No, only that she had decided on Tahiti."

"Was she going alone? Or with her boyfriend?"

Annie let out a brittle laugh. "Her boyfriend would have had a difficult time explaining a trip to the South Pacific to his wife."

"He was *married?*" She hadn't thought of that. A married man. That put an entirely different perspective on the relationship. It even opened a door on a possible motive—blackmail.

Annie nodded. "Lola never really came right out and admitted it, but all the signs were there—her dark moods, the occasional tears in the ladies' room after a phone call, the way she had erected this wall of secrecy around the man, a wall that no one, not even me, could penetrate."

An insidious thought crept into Zoe's head. E.J. was married. "So you know nothing about him? His age, what he does for a living, how they met?"

"No, but I can tell you this." She dragged the cart behind her. "He was making her miserable. Over the last couple months, the cheerful, happy Lola I knew turned into a sullen, moody bitch. Except when she stepped behind that microphone."

Annie's gaze drifted toward the spotlight in the center of the small stage. "Up there, she was able to leave her troubles behind and become the performer everyone expected to see. She was wonderful in that respect."

"That couldn't have been easy, to have so much on her mind and still entertain an audience every night."

"I couldn't do it, but Lola pulled it off every time, without anyone knowing how badly she felt, not even Rick."

She had to have confided in *someone,* Zoe thought. No woman goes through a difficult relationship without experiencing the need to talk to a good friend. If not Annie, then who?

"What can you tell me about Lola's relationship with

her aunt?" she asked casually. At the same time, she cast a quick look around to make sure Rick was nowhere around.

"They adored each other. Frieda raised her, you know."

"Yes, Rick told me."

"Lola was devastated when Frieda was diagnosed with dementia. Frieda insisted on moving into a nursing home right away, before she could become a burden to her niece, even though Lola practically lived at the Belvedere by then."

"The Belvedere on Eighty-seventh Street?"

Annie nodded and bent to straighten a bow around one of the little pots. "Frieda put the apartment in Lola's name and gave her a power of attorney, then together, they found a nice nursing home, not too far from the city. Lola didn't drive, so she either took the bus, or I drove her to Sagemore. Sometimes Rick did."

"When did Frieda stop recognizing Lola?"

"Six or eight months ago. The spells were short at first, then they got longer and longer. Now, she's out of it most of the time. Occasionally, she'll recognize Lola. On those rare occasions, you would think that Lola had just won the lottery."

"Would she have confided in her?"

"About what?"

"Her boyfriend."

Annie was thoughtful for a moment. "She may have. Frieda wasn't in a position to offer any kind of advice, but Lola could have poured her heart out to her without feeling she was betraying her man."

Zoe glanced at the stage, imagining Lola up there, one hand on the mike. "On the tape Rick brought me, I noticed a small gold charm attached to her bracelet, a cupid?"

Annie nodded. "Her boyfriend gave it to her. I know because she told me about it."

"When was that?"

"Four month ago. He gave it to her for her birthday on August twenty-first. Lola never took it off after that."

"So at that time, things were going fairly well between the two of them."

"I think so. The relationship didn't start deteriorating until a couple of months ago. That's when she started looking so depressed."

A man in blue overalls was on the stage, checking the lighting. "Do you have a new singer?"

Annie's tone turned sarcastic. "Jenny Figuerosa is filling in."

"Did somebody say my name?"

Turning around, Zoe saw an attractive young brunette with a duffel bag swung over her shoulder and a defiant look in her eyes.

"Telling lies about me again, Annie?"

"I wasn't talking about you, Jenny. Or *to* you."

The girl's challenging gaze came to rest on Zoe. "Who are you?"

"Zoe Foster."

She pursed her lips and gave Zoe a quick appraisal. "Oh, yeah. Rick's ex. You're here to find out about Lola."

"If you have anything—"

She put up her hand. "Keep me out of this. Unlike

some, I'm not the gossipy type. Besides, as Blondie here will tell you, Lola and I weren't exactly bosom buddies."

"Does that mean you didn't like each other?"

"It means," she said, shifting her bag over her other shoulder, "that she left me alone and I did the same. Does that answer your question?"

"Not exactly, but thanks just the same."

Jenny stood there for a moment, looking at Zoe as though trying to figure her out. Then, with a shrug of dismissal, she turned sharply and walked away.

"Wow," Zoe said after she was gone. "Is she always this friendly?"

"Pretty much. She's had a chip on her shoulder ever since she and Lola came to audition and Lola got the job."

"Is she a waitress?"

"God, no. She would turn this place into a boxing arena. She's the coat-check girl."

"If she's so unpleasant, why is Rick keeping her?"

"Because he has a good heart. He knew she needed the money and felt sorry for her, so he offered her the job of coat-check girl, with the understanding that whenever Lola was away, on vacation or whatever, Jenny would fill in for her."

"Does Jenny have *any* friends?"

"Not that I know of. We just don't trust her. She's rude, arrogant and self-centered."

"Has she ever been antagonistic toward Lola?"

"Not really. She knows Rick would never put up with that kind of bickering between employees. But she has this lazy, good-for-nothing boyfriend who is pushing her to be more aggressive, to 'stand up for her rights,' as he put it." Annie shook her head. "He is a terrible influence on her. Right now he's pissed off because Rick wants to see how Jenny connects with the audience before he decides to keep her as Lola's permanent replacement. Mike Brenner—that's his name—actually had the gall to come and see Rick the other night and tell him he'd be a fool to let Jenny slip through his fingers. He didn't quite say it like that, if you know what I mean."

Zoe chuckled. Rick wasn't the kind of man who could be pushed around. "How did that go?"

Annie smiled. "Not well for Mike."

Zoe caught Annie glance at her watch and realized they had been talking for nearly half an hour. "Thanks for your time," she said, picking up her purse from a chair nearby. "You've been very helpful." She let a couple of seconds go by before asking casually, "By the way, where did you say Frieda's nursing home was?"

"Nyack, in the Hudson Valley."

Eleven

It was a little past noon on Monday when Zoe stepped out of the cab that had taken her to Sagemore in the lovely, snow-covered village of Nyack.

The nursing home was a series of small buildings, Victorian in style and all beautifully landscaped. Miniature golden lights were strewn around the trees and shrubs, adding a festive touch to the surroundings.

Zoe followed the sign to the reception area, where a huge Christmas tree greeted visitors. A woman in a crisp white uniform sat at the front desk. A small blue tag on her pocket read Nurse Mendoza.

"Good morning." Zoe smiled. "My name is Zoe Foster. I'm here to visit Frieda North. My friend, Lola Malone, is out of town for a few days and she didn't want the week to end without her aunt having a visitor."

"That's nice." The nurse took a visitor's pass from a box and slid it across the counter. "You'll need this." She pointed down a hallway on the left. "Frieda's in room 111. Did Lola explain that her aunt gets easily agitated?"

"Yes. I'll be very careful."

Zoe walked away, her heart pounding at the bold way she had lied to the nurse.

Room 111 was open. Zoe peered in and saw a small, tidy room, with old photographs displayed on a dresser, half a dozen Madame Alexander Dolls lined up on the window seat and a twin bed with guardrails on each side.

Frieda sat by the window, a frail-looking woman with rounded shoulders and gray hair held back with a barrette. A colorful quilt covered her legs.

"Hi, Frieda," Zoe said softly as she approached.

Vacant blue eyes turned in her direction. It was difficult to believe that this diminutive woman had once dominated the American stage, dazzling audiences from coast to coast. "Who are you?"

"My name is Zoe Foster. I'm a friend of Lola's."

Bony fingers started toying with the quilt on her lap. "Who's Lola?"

"Your niece." Zoe pulled a chair and sat down, being careful not to crowd her. A picture of the singer sat on the dresser and Zoe pointed at it. "That's Lola in that picture. She is very beautiful, isn't she?"

"I don't have a niece." Her tone had turned belligerent. "I don't have anyone. Didn't they tell you that?"

"You have Lola. She comes to see you every week."

The old woman's attention returned to the snow-covered lawn outside. "It snowed last night. And the night before. I don't like snow. It makes everything white. I don't like white."

"What's your favorite color?"

"Not magenta. I hate magenta."

Zoe smiled. "Not too many people like magenta."

"I like red. I used to wear a lot of red."

"Was that when you were on the stage?"

A small spark flashed in her eyes. "Red is the color of hell," she said in a more forceful tone. "Hell is Satan's lair!"

Gently, if not skillfully, Zoe steered the conversation back to the woman's beloved niece. "Did Lola ever talk to you about her boyfriend? A man she cared about very much?"

Instead of answering, the woman fastened her gaze on the gold box on Zoe's lap. "What's that?"

"Chocolates." Taking a chance that everyone, young and old, liked chocolates, Zoe had picked up a box of Godivas from the candy shop down her street before coming here. She handed it to Frieda. "I thought you might like them." She smiled encouragingly. "Go ahead, take them. They're for you."

"Why are you bringing me presents? I don't know you."

"I'm a friend of Lola's."

"Are you trying to poison me?"

"No, of course not."

"Yes, you are. Satan sent you! He sent you to poison me!"

Dismayed, Zoe pulled back from the screaming woman.

"Help!" Frieda's body stiffened as she gripped the arms of her chair with both hands in an attempt to stand. "Help, she's trying to poison me!"

A nurse ran in. "What's wrong, darling? What's all the commotion about?"

Zoe stood up to make room for the nurse whose name tag identified her as Nurse Valgram. "I was just trying to give her a box of chocolates," she said, feeling miserable.

The nurse gave her a stern look. "Who are you?"

"Zoe Foster. I'm a friend of Lola Malone—"

"She's come to kill me!" Frieda shouted, clearly distraught now. "They've all come to kill me. Get them out of here." She grabbed the nurse's collar. "Quick, before they kill you, too."

"It's okay, honey. No one's going to hurt you." As the screaming continued, two men in white ran in to help the nurse.

"You'd better leave," she told Zoe. "We need to calm her down."

"I'm so sorry. I didn't mean…"

"It's not you. It happens all the time. We never know what's going to set her off."

As Zoe was about to leave, another man in white walked into the room. The tag on his pocket read Dr. Keefer. "What's going on? Who are you?"

Zoe wanted to disappear. "I'm Zoe Foster. Lola is away, so I came to see Frieda."

"Did you call first?"

"I wasn't aware that I had to."

"Frieda has been having a rough time lately. If you had called, I would have told you to hold off your visit."

At a loss for words and more upset than she could say, Zoe started to make her way toward the door.

"What did you say your name was?" he asked as Zoe moved past him.

"Zoe Foster."

"Where's Ms. Malone?"

"On a trip." Oh, God, how much longer would she have to lie to these people? She knew now that coming here had been a costly mistake. Not only had she not learned a thing, but she had upset a sick old woman.

The doctor gave a curt nod. "Good day, Miss Foster."

Zoe was still experiencing feelings of guilt and low self-esteem over the incident at Sagemore when her cab pulled up in front of the *Herald* building. She had called the nursing home twice during the thirty-minute ride, but no one had been able to give her an update on Frieda's condition. She would try again from home. Right now she had another unpleasant task to face.

E.J. was in a great mood when she walked into his office. "Your idea to have readers help Kitty solve her mystery was a stroke of genius," he crowed, rubbing his hands together. "The e-mails are pouring in, and convenience stores in all five boroughs ran out of copies of the *Herald* by nine this morning."

Zoe tried to say something but he wasn't letting her put a word in edgewise. "We'll need to increase circulation *and* notify our advertisers. They're going to love this."

As he talked, Zoe took out a sketch she had made in the cab and put it on his desk. She watched his face closely as he looked at it.

"What's this?" he asked, looking puzzled.

"A charm that Lola Malone wore on her bracelet."

"You didn't say anything about a charm when you described the bracelet to the police the other night."

"That's because it wasn't there. The head waitress at Blue Moon told me Lola never took it off, so it's fair to assume that it came off in the alley, maybe during a struggle with her killer."

"Why are you showing it to me?"

"I want to put the sketch in the *Herald.*"

"Why?"

"Just as Buddy Barbarino recognized Lola, someone might recognized the charm and lead me to the man who gave it to her, a man no one seems to know anything about—Lola's mysterious lover."

"Take it to Sal, then."

"You don't mind?"

"Of course I don't mind. Why do you even ask? Haven't I fully cooperated with you so far?"

"Yes, but…" Now she was thoroughly confused. Either E.J. was a master of deception, or Rick was mistaken.

"But what, Zoe?"

"E.J., I know…I know that you were a regular at Blue Moon for a while."

This time she didn't have to search for a reaction. It was plainly visible. His complexion paled a little and he fell back against his chair. Several seconds passed before he could speak again. "I was afraid you'd hear about that sooner or later."

"So it's true."

He let out a heavy sigh and nodded. "How did you find out?"

"From Rick. He recognized you." She watched him pick up a pencil and play with it, turning it around and around on his ink blotter. "Why didn't you tell me? Why did you pretend you had never heard of her?"

"I was afraid that if I said anything and my wife found out…"

"Found out what? What did you do?"

"Nothing! I just went there to watch Lola sing." He let the pencil drop. "It all started very innocently, back in the spring when two of my advertisers were in town. They had heard of Blue Moon and asked if I would take them there."

When he stopped, she prompted him to continue. "But you went back afterward, many times, alone."

"I know how that sounds, but believe me, it was nothing more than a foolish old man wishing he was young again."

"Why did you stop going?"

He shrugged. "I don't know. I guess I got tired of the act. Or maybe deep down, I realized that I was beginning to enjoy watching Lola Malone a little more than I should."

"And you never told your wife?"

"God, no. Peggy would never understand."

Zoe wasn't sure she did, either, but she wasn't here to judge the eccentricities of an aging man. What mattered was that E.J. was not Lola's mysterious lover.

"I'm sorry I didn't say anything to you sooner," he continued. "I didn't think it had any bearing on her disappearance."

"It doesn't." Zoe took the sketch from his desk and

threw him a reassuring smile. "Why don't we forget we had this conversation and I'll take this down to Sal."

"Thank you, Zoe."

Twelve

Night had fallen over Manhattan and a nasty wind was blowing in from the East River by the time Zoe walked out of the *Herald.* Fortunately, the blizzard that had been predicted never materialized, making the city at rush hour a lot more manageable than it would have been in a major snowstorm.

Zoe joined the crowds as hundreds of office workers poured out of surrounding buildings, heading for home, department stores or the subway. Now that E.J. was no longer on her mind, she could devote all her thoughts to her disastrous visit to Sagemore, and Frieda, whom she hoped had recovered from her episode.

Once in the lobby of her building, she took out her phone and dialed the nursing home. "My name is Zoe Foster," she said. "Is this Nurse Mendoza?"

"Nurse Mendoza is gone for the day. I'm Nurse Miller. May I help you?"

"I was there earlier, visiting Frieda North, and I'm afraid I got her upset. I called to find out how she is doing."

"One moment, please. I'll transfer you to Nurse Val-gram. She's still here."

Within a few seconds, she was connected to Frieda's nurse. "Yes, I remember you, Miss Foster. Frieda is rest-ing comfortably. She had to be sedated but she should be fine by morning."

"I feel so awful."

"I understand. An outburst like that is always difficult, even more so for first-time visitors."

"Does she get like that often?"

"Oh, maybe every couple of weeks or so." Zoe heard the nurse being paged over a loudspeaker.

"I have to run," she said. "Was that all, Miss Foster?"

"Yes. Thank you."

Feeling only marginally better, Zoe walked over to her drawing board, hoping to find comfort in her work. But when Kitty stared back at her, waiting to be brought into action, Zoe dropped her pen. The muses had abandoned her, at least for tonight.

Maybe she needed to unwind, she thought. Not with a cup of tea, but with something physical, something ex-erting—like a good workout.

Her mood lifting, she ran to change into a pair of old sweats, threw on a jacket, then, her gym bag slung over one shoulder, she walked out.

"Mr. Vaughn?"

"Speaking."

"This is Dr. Keefer at Sagemore. I've been trying to reach Ms. Malone but I haven't had any luck. Is she there by any chance?"

Rick had met Dr. Keefer during one of his visits to the nursing home. He was a pleasant, compassionate doctor for whom Lola had high regard. "Ms. Malone no longer works at Blue Moon." He put aside a review of Blue Moon in a New Jersey paper. "Is there a problem? Is her aunt all right?"

"Not exactly, which is why I'm calling. Frieda had a visitor earlier today, a friend of Ms. Malone. During the visit, Frieda became highly agitated. It took us nearly an hour to stabilize her heart rate. I wanted her niece to know that from now on, the only visitors who will be permitted to see Frieda are those who are accompanying Ms. Malone. No exceptions will be made."

"I'll be sure to pass the instructions along when I hear from her. May I ask who the visitor was?"

"A woman by the name of Zoe Foster. Do you know her?"

Anger, swift and hot, flared up, but Rick managed to keep his annoyance in check, for the doctor's sake. "As a matter of fact, I do."

"Then please relay my message to her, as well."

"I will. Thank you, Doctor."

After ending the call, Rick stood up. He blamed himself as much as he blamed Zoe. He should have seen this coming. He knew her, perhaps better than she knew herself. And because he knew her so well, he should have realized that she would try to find out the information she was after, one way or another.

That obsession to find Lola's killer, if there was a killer, was no longer amusing. Not only was she putting herself at risk, she was now harming innocent people. It had to stop. From now on, she would have to keep her cloak-and-dagger act within the confines of her comic strip.

He picked up the phone and dialed the number Zoe had given him. She answered on the fourth ring, sounding out of breath.

"Where are you?" he asked curtly.

"Spring Street Gym. Why?"

"I'll tell you when I get there."

Zoe cupped the basketball between her hands, aimed and went for the shot. The ball flew into the basket, barely touching the rim. Pleased, she caught the ball on the rebound and dribbled gently across the court.

She came to the Spring Street Gym a couple of times a week for the sole purpose of shooting hoops. Although the gym closed at 8:00 p.m. each night, the manager, Danny, let her use the court until the cleaning crew arrived at nine. In exchange for the favor, she made a generous yearly contribution to the Special Olympics team Danny had been coaching for the past five years.

Shooting hoops was her only form of exercise. In high school, she hadn't excelled at any sport except basketball. Although she had been the shortest player on her varsity team, her talent, along with a 3.8 grade-point average, had earned her a four-year scholarship at Northwestern University, where she had graduated with a degree in art.

Every now and then, Danny tried to get her to join the local women's league he coached every winter, but Zoe always turned him down. At thirty-three, she wasn't sure she could keep up with the twentysomethings who raced up and down the court without so much as breaking a sweat.

She went for another shot, but this time she missed. Rick's call had broken her concentration. He hadn't sounded happy, and it didn't take a genius to figure out why.

She was dribbling furiously when the doors opened and Rick walked in. One look at his expression and she knew her instincts had been right on the money. He had found out about her visit to Sagemore.

She caught the ball and went to meet him, picking up a towel from her bag on the way. Wiping her face, she stopped in front of him. "Hi." Anything more was unnecessary.

"I had a call from Dr. Keefer," he said, not wasting any time in civilities. "I believe you've met him?"

"Rick, listen—"

"No, *you* listen. I came to you in good faith. Thanks to that cop you've managed to bamboozle into doing your dirty work, I actually believed that I had acted like a heel."

"I didn't know Frieda was going to go off on me."

"I told you how fragile her condition was, and how quickly she could get upset. I also made it plain that I didn't want you to go up there. But did you listen? Of course not. Instead, you found out the nursing-home address, probably from Annie, and then you went to Sagemore under false pretenses and created total chaos. I hope you're proud of yourself."

She tried to offset his anger by remaining calm. "May I say something now?"

"What could you possibly say in your defense?"

"I'm sorry."

The apology seemed to throw him off.

"I was wrong to go there." She pushed a damp strand of hair away from her forehead. "I thought I could learn something."

"From a woman who has lost all contact with reality?"

"I was hoping to catch her in a good moment. Annie said—"

"You have become obsessed with something that has nothing to do with you, Zoe, and you've got to stop."

There was no point in arguing with him. She wouldn't win. Not tonight. "How many times do I have to say that I'm sorry?"

"Did you tell Frieda that Lola was missing?"

"Of course not! I'm not a monster, Rick. I have ethics."

He let out a sarcastic laugh. "They're not exactly shining through right now, are they? What you did today was irresponsible and selfish."

Oh, how she hated it when he called her that. She lifted herself as high as her five-foot-six frame allowed, but still had to look up to meet his eyes. "Selfish?" She almost choked on the word. "All I want is to find out the fate of a woman no one seems to care about. And you're a fine one to talk about selfishness," she continued, all wound up now. "If memory serves, all you wanted during our two-year marriage was to satisfy *your* ambitions."

"Where is *that* coming from? Why are we suddenly talking about me?"

"What about my own ambitions?" she forged on. "You could never get it through your head that I had dreams, too. I was a person before I married you, Rick. An independent, talented, ambitious person. But you wanted to stifle all that. You had this warped image of what a wife ought to be and you made no compromises."

"That's not true. You had all the freedom of expression you wanted."

"Yes, with Blue Moon. Big deal."

"So that's it? That's how you decided to get back at me, six years later? By nearly killing an innocent woman?"

"Oh." Zoe's voice trembled. "That's low, Rick."

"You think so? Frieda has high blood pressure and an irregular heartbeat in addition to her dementia. She could have died. Talk to Dr. Keefer if you don't believe me. Oh, and by the way, you're no longer welcome at Sagemore, in case you were thinking of a return visit."

When she remained silent, he turned around and walked out.

Thirteen

Rick was still in a foul mood when he returned to Blue Moon, and not up for a confrontation. Unfortunately, that's exactly what was waiting for him when he stepped into his office. Jenny Figuerosa was pacing like a caged animal.

She barely gave him time to close the door before pouncing. "I just found out that you've been holding auditions."

"Is that a problem for you?"

"You're damn right it's a problem for me. I thought the job was mine. That's a valid assumption, isn't it? Considering the audience loves me?"

What a *few* customers seemed to enjoy was Jenny's tight-fitting gowns and plunging necklines. "Your style isn't right for my club, Jenny."

"What's wrong with my style?"

"Your repertoire, for one thing. Your modern ballads don't fit our theme. You and I talked about that. We even went over your numbers, then last night, in the middle of your set, you threw in Celine Dion."

"So, I'll cut Celine Dion."

Rick shook his head. "I've already hired someone else. She starts next week."

"You bastard," she hissed.

"You're out of line, Jen."

"You stuck me in that hellhole for three years," she shouted, pointing at the door behind her. "I hated it, but I stayed because you promised me that if Lola ever left, the job was mine."

In spite of his intention to remain calm, Rick's voice rose. He hated liars. "I never promised you a permanent job. As for that 'hellhole,' you've made out pretty well or you wouldn't have stayed, so don't throw that in my face. And for the record, I didn't have to give you a job. I did it because you were going through a rough time and I wanted to give you a break."

"Pity?" She almost spat the word. "You kept me out of pity?"

"You're not listening, Jenny."

"Am I fired?"

He was tempted to say yes. The girl was trouble, all of it of her own making.

But there was something about this kid, a vulnerability combined with a string of bad luck that wasn't unlike what *he* had gone through during his early years. Then the Vaughns had taken him in and his life was changed forever.

"Your job at the coat check is still yours. I'll even give you a raise."

"Don't bother." She stormed by him, her heavy perfume enveloping him like a bad omen. "I quit."

Rick winced as she slammed the door behind her. This was not how he had wanted to end it with Jenny, but he wasn't about to run after her. Hopefully, after she'd had time to think, she would realize that what he was offering wasn't such a bad deal. Right now, he had a problem of his own to solve—how to find an interim singer on short notice.

Rick stood at the bar, watching Chandra van Doren delight the crowd with her renditions of Billie Holiday's greatest hits. After answering his urgent call earlier, his newly hired singer had come over and gone over her numbers with the piano player without seeming the least bit ruffled. Rick had introduced her to the audience, and although the applause had been a little less than cordial at first, the moment she started to sing, the atmosphere in the room had improved considerably. By the end of her first show, Chandra was a hit.

He was listening to the opening number of her second show, when his cell phone rang. "Hello?" He started toward his office.

"Rick?" The voice was a mere whisper.

"This is Rick Vaughn. Who is this?"

"Me." Another whisper, a weak one. "Jenny."

He walked into his office and closed the door. "Jenny, what's wrong?"

"I need some help. I didn't know who else to call."

"Are you sick?"

A short silence. "I'm hurt. I don't know how bad. Mike beat me up."

"Jesus Christ, Jen." Then, because this was no time for criticism, he asked, "Where are you?"

"Home."

"You're still at West Forty-first Street?"

"Yes. Fourth floor."

"I'll be right there."

He found her in the bathroom, huddled between the toilet and the vanity. Her face was bloodied and her right eye badly swollen.

He crouched down and took her battered face between his hands. "Did he hit you anywhere else?"

"No. He always goes for the face."

Always. Meaning he had done it before. Trying not to think of what he'd like to do to Mike Brenner, he took a washcloth from the edge of the sink, ran it under the faucet and then squeezed it.

"Look up," he said when he was once again eye level with her. She obeyed and he wiped the blood away as gently as he could. There was a cut on her left cheekbone, but it wasn't deep enough to require stitches. She would have a nasty black eye in the morning, but that, too, looked worse than it was. He disinfected the cut with alcohol he found in the medicine cabinet before covering it with a Band-Aid.

When she was all patched up, he helped her stand. "Can you walk?"

"I'm fine. He's careful not to hit me in a way that could land me in the hospital."

He sat beside her on the sofa. "Why do you stay with him, Jenny?"

Her eyes glistened with tears. "He said he'd kill me if I ever left him."

"So you let him use you as a punching bag?"

"He's not always like that."

"What set him off this time?" But he already knew.

"He got angry when I told him I quit my job. He was laid off a month ago from the garage where he worked and—"

"And he hasn't bothered to look for another job."

She looked at him through her good eye. "He's had some bad breaks, too."

"Don't defend him, Jenny. Not after what he did to you. There is no justification for a man hitting a woman."

She looked away. "I know."

"Are you ready to do something about it? Put a stop to that nonsense?"

"How?"

The fact that she asked was promising. "Leave him."

"This is his apartment. I have nowhere to go."

"I know a place."

"He'll find me."

"Not where I'm going to send you."

He took out his cell phone and dialed Blue Moon. When Lenny answered, he asked to be transferred to Stretch. The six-foot-five bouncer, whose real name was Marcus Finch, had come with the club and was as devoted to Rick as he had been to Simon.

"Stretch," Rick said when the bouncer came on the line. "I need you for a little specialized work. Could you come to Jenny's apartment?"

"Sure thing, boss. Where does she live?"

That was what he liked about Stretch. He never asked any questions. "201 West Forty-first Street. Fourth floor."

"When do you need me?"

"ASAP."

"I'm there."

When he hung up, Jenny was crying. "I hope those tears aren't for that sleaze of a boyfriend. I haven't touched him yet."

She shook her head. "I can't believe you're doing all this for me after the way I treated you earlier. I knew Mike would be pissed off that I didn't get Lola's job, but I shouldn't have taken it out on you."

"Forget it. I have a thick skin." He looked at the mess around him, the lamps that had been knocked to the floor, the overturned tables, a spilled bottle of beer. "You'll stay with Stretch for a few days, but afterward, we'll have to find you a new place to live. Do you have any relatives?"

"My parents are dead. I have a cousin in New Orleans. Her name is Rosa."

"Are you on good terms with her?"

"I guess. We talk on the phone from time to time."

"Does Mike know about her?"

Her expression seemed to brighten. "No. He never showed any interest in my family, so I never mentioned her."

"Good. Tomorrow, you call Rosa and ask her if she could take you in until you get back on your feet. In the meantime, I'll make some calls to nightclubs in the New Orleans area and see if I can get you a few auditions."

She started crying again.

"Now what?"

"No one has ever been this nice to me before."

"Call me a sucker for damsels in distress."

That made her smile.

"Now," he spoke calmly, "I need to know where I can find Mike."

She looked alarmed. "Why? What are you going to do to him?"

"Where is he, Jenny?"

She shook her head. "He'll know I told you."

"It doesn't matter. He won't hurt you ever again."

For a while, as she remained stubbornly silent, he thought she was going to stand by her man, like so many battered women chose to do. Then she surprised him by raising her head up high. "He likes to hang out at a bar on Thirty-fourth Street called Ralph's."

Fourteen

Ralph's was packed with a rowdy crowd watching a wrestling match on TV when Rick walked in. He had left Jenny with Stretch, with instructions not to leave her alone for one minute.

After a sweeping glance across the crowded room, Rick spotted Brenner sitting at the bar. He was alone, staring into his beer and not paying attention to the action around him.

Rick shouldered his way to the bar. "Let's you and me step outside for a minute," he said into Brenner's ear.

Mike turned on his stool. He was short but muscular, with broad shoulders and thick hands. His eyes were bloodshot from too much beer, but alert enough to spot trouble. "What the hell do you want with me?" he asked.

Unceremoniously, Rick knocked him off his stool and gave him a shove toward the door. "You're about to find out."

Once outside, Rick didn't waste time in lengthy explanation. Holding Mike with one hand, he backhanded him across the face. The kid staggered, hitting the wall, but managed to stay on his feet. "That's for beating up Jenny."

"You son of a bitch." A tough guy who didn't know when to quit, Brenner took a swing at Rick, and missed.

"It's not so easy fighting a man, is it, punk?"

Without warning, Brenner's foot shot out, catching Rick on the chest. Rick retaliated with a blow to the man's chin that knocked him flat on his back. After a couple of seconds Brenner sat up. Blood gushed out of his mouth as he spit out a handful of teeth.

"I'll kill that bitch."

"Your grievance is with me, Brenner, not with Jenny."

With a dark expression in his eyes, the wounded man pressed the back of his hand against his bleeding mouth. "She'll get her due, whether you like it or not. And when I'm finished with her, I'll go after that hot little redhead of yours. She won't be so pretty after one of Mike Brenner's workovers. How's that for a lesson?"

The missing teeth made him slur his words, but Rick heard them, loud and clear. He grabbed Brenner by the collar and yanked him to his feet. "You lay one finger on Zoe Foster, or Jenny, for that matter, and I'll break your legs. You got that?"

"I'm shaking in my boots, marine."

"You ought to. You don't know what I'm capable of." He brought his face close to his. "Consider yourself warned."

Lizzy, bless her heart, had a way of dropping by when she was needed the most. It was as though she had a crystal ball that allowed her to know exactly when her best friend was in trouble or needed comfort. She showed up bearing cartons of Chinese dishes, which, as far as Lizzy was concerned, was the ultimate comfort food.

"Who's holding the fort?" Zoe asked as she retrieved chopsticks from a drawer.

"Jimmy. You know how he loves to play boss." She looked up from her task of opening the cartons. "You look bummed out. Something happened?"

Zoe started digging into one of her favorites—ginger chicken with broccoli. As she ate, she told Lizzy about her visit to Sagemore and Rick's reaction when he had found out.

"Go ahead and say it."

Lizzy sank her chopsticks into a carton of Cantonese shrimp. "There's nothing to say. You made a mistake and you've apologized. What more can you do?"

"Rick says I'm meddling and I should stop."

"What do *you* want to do?"

"I want to find Lola's killer. And if she's not dead, as some people seem to believe, then I want to find out what happened to her. I feel a connection to that woman, Lizzy. I don't know how or why, but it's there. I can feel it."

"Does Rick know that?"

"Rick doesn't give a rat's ass what I feel."

"That's not exactly true, is it? He's been a huge help. You said so yourself." When Zoe didn't answer, she added, "He's angry right now. Give him a couple of days."

Zoe reached for the pan-fried noodles. "Can we

change the subject? Talking about Rick gives me indigestion."

Lizzy's eyes twinkled. "That's an improvement, isn't it? He used to give you hives."

Zoe laughed, remembering how she had accused Rick of giving her hives one day before realizing that she had developed a sudden allergy to strawberries. "All right, I agree I wasn't always fair to him."

"And he always forgave you. He will again."

"I don't know. He was more than angry, Lizzy. He was disappointed."

Lizzy put her chopsticks down and reached into her bag. "Maybe this will put a smile on your face." She set Zoe's Manolo Blahnik pump on the island counter.

Zoe took it and turned it around in her hand, marveling at the exquisite craftsmanship. "Oh, Lizzy, the velvet is a perfect match. It looks like a brand-new shoe."

"I told you my uncle An was a magician."

"I'll call him to thank him personally. In the meantime, how much do I owe you?"

"Please. He'd be insulted if you tried to pay him."

"I want to do something for him."

"I tell you what. His daughter Cassie is a big fan of Kitty Floyd. Why don't you autograph one of your strips for her? That would make An very happy."

"It's done. In the meantime, be sure to thank him for me."

Well fed and now alone, Zoe sat at her desk, going over the stack of mail she had picked up from Maureen earlier today. She read each letter carefully, setting aside those she found most intriguing. When she was left with only five or six possibilities, she read them again before selecting one from a reader calling himself Lonesome Me.

Maybe the understudy did it.

That was not a bad idea at all. Like every major cast member in a soap opera, Mona Gray had to have an understudy, someone who rehearsed the lines as she did and could step into the role on a moment's notice. The understudy could be jealous enough to want Mona out of the way, like in the movie *All About Eve,* where a cunning assistant schemes to take over the actress's job, her husband and her friends.

Jenny, who was presently filling in for Lola, seemed like the perfect model for the new character. Zoe didn't know her well enough to form an opinion, but the girl's abrasive personality and dislike for Lola Malone had been hard to miss.

The note still in her hand, Zoe walked over to her drawing table and started sketching the understudy, whom she named Lynn. In the first frame, the woman, blond and pretty, watched herself in the mirror. Above her head, Zoe wrote, *"At last, my dream has come true. I'm going to be a star."* In the second frame, she put Lynn on set, hiding behind a piece of scenery as she watched Nicholas discuss a shot with two other actors. The look in Lynn's eyes left no doubts about her feelings for the handsome director, and neither did her thoughts. *"Stop talking about Mona as if she's coming back, Nicholas. She's not. And soon, very soon, you, too, will be mine."*

Zoe worked until the clock on the kitchen wall bonged twelve times. Then, as fatigue tugged at every muscle, she finally put her pen down and went to bed.

Fifteen

The Belvedere, in the Upper West Side, was a prewar, nineteen-floor building that boasted twenty-four-hour security, a rooftop garden and a spectacular view of Riverside Park. Standing outside the locked street door, Zoe peered into the well-lit lobby. She could see a peach marble floor, exotic potted plants and upholstered furniture in neutral beige. In the center of the space was an antique-looking desk where a uniformed concierge sat reading a newspaper.

Zoe pressed the bell. The concierge raised his head and gave a dispassionate glance before pressing the release button. At the click, Zoe pushed the door open and walked across the slick floor, stopping at the reception desk.

"Hi," she said to the attendant. "My name is Zoe Foster. I wonder if you could give me some information on one of your tenants—"

The man didn't let her finish. "We don't give information about our tenants."

"But I haven't told you who—"

"Don't matter. No information." He picked up his paper again and gave it a sharp snap. "Good day, ma'am." He started reading again. The conversation was over.

Frustrated, Zoe walked out and stood looking around her. The street was partly residential and partly commercial, with the latter consisting of a couple of restaurants, one Indian, one Thai, and various businesses. Two doors down from the Belvedere was a nail salon. A woman in a pink cover-up stood in the doorway, smoking a cigarette and looking bored. The name Martha was embroidered on her pocket.

Zoe walked over to her. Bartenders and hairdressers were notoriously chatty. She prayed that nail-salon employees fell into that category, as well.

"Good morning." Zoe smiled engagingly. "I wonder if you could help me. I'm trying to find out information about Lola Malone, who recently disappeared. Would you happen to know her by any chance?"

"Know her?" Martha dropped her cigarette on the sidewalk and crushed it with the point of her white sneaker. "She's my best client. Has her nails done here all the time." She looked up. "Is there any news about her? I saw a drawing of her on the front page of the *Herald,* and a notice asking for information."

"We're still looking for her."

"You don't look like a cop."

"I'm not. I'm Zoe Foster. I drew the sketch you saw in the *Herald.*"

The name didn't spark any recognition, as it had with

Officer Barnes. "It was a pretty good likeness. I recognized her right away. I even called the paper, but they told me that someone had already come forward."

She *was* chatty. *Thank you, God.* "That was her agent."

Martha made a snorting sound. "That one."

"You know him?"

"Once in a while, when Ms. Malone doesn't feel like coming down, I go up to her apartment. I was there one day, setting up my table in the kitchen, when he arrived. Moments later, they started arguing."

"What were they arguing about?"

"He wanted her to do a porn movie. Apparently he had already contacted a producer who was willing to pay Miss Malone a big fee. She said no, but this guy, Buddy, kept pressuring her, telling her this was a golden opportunity, the ground floor to bigger and better things. When he realized that she wasn't budging, he called her a name I won't repeat and stormed out." She looked troubled. "You think something bad happened to her?"

Zoe wondered if Buddy should be investigated, although he looked more like a con man than a murderer. "I hope not," she said in answer to Martha's question. "Did you ever see her with anyone else? A friend? A relative? A boyfriend?"

Martha shook her head. "I don't know about any relatives. The man who owns Blue Moon comes here, although not often. So does one of the waitresses."

That would be Rick and Annie. "That's it?" Zoe was disappointed. "No boyfriend?"

"She had a boyfriend but I never saw him."

Zoe's heart gave a thump. "Can you tell me anything about him?"

"Well…" She let out a girlish laugh. "He was a real romantic. I used to kid Miss Malone about him. I told her that whenever she was tired of him, she should introduce me. I'd take him, sight unseen. A man who sends a girl a dozen red roses every week is my kind of guy."

"Every week?"

"Every Monday, like clockwork. The delivery truck would pull up right there." She pointed at the curb in front of the building. "Double-parked, if he had to."

"Are the roses still coming?"

"No, I stopped seeing that truck, oh, sometime in August. When I asked Miss Malone what happened to Mr. Romance, she said, 'Nothing lasts forever, Martha.'"

"And there was no one after him?"

"No one that I know of. Miss Malone is what you'd call discreet."

"Do you remember the name of the flower shop?"

The woman pursed her lips and squinted, deep in concentration. After a few seconds, she shook her head. "There was something written on the side of the van, but I'm drawing a blank. I'm sorry."

"That's all right, Martha. You've been very helpful." Zoe took a business card from her purse. "Would you call me if you remember?"

The woman read the card. "Sure thing, Zoe."

Twenty minutes later, Zoe was back home and working on her strip, which she had been neglecting far too long. She didn't stop until she had two days' worth of

Kitty Floyd completed. Stretching, she glanced at a new stack of e-mails on her drawing board. One was from Lonesome Me, the same person who had given her the clue about the understudy. This time, he wanted Kitty to search Nicholas's office for proof that Mona had dumped him and he was out for revenge.

She wasn't going to use his clue. With the amount of mail she received every day, it wouldn't be fair to choose the same person twice. Everybody deserved an equal shot.

Instead, she drew Kitty at home, puzzling in front of the big wallboard where she had written the names of all the suspects—the handsome director who loved Mona, the ex-husband who exploited her and the understudy who envied her.

In the first frame, Kitty stood looking at the board, her arms folded across her chest, her index finger curled around her mouth, her pretty face creased in concentration.

"Come on, Kitty," Zoe murmured as she filled the frame with details. "Inspire me. Send me a sign."

As if on cue, the phone rang, startling her. She put her pen down and went to answer it.

"Zoe, it's Maureen. We just heard from a man who recognized the cupid charm," she said excitedly. "His name is Rudy Goldberg. He owns a pawnshop on Worth Street in lower Manhattan, two blocks from the subway station. He said he'll be there until six."

Zoe walked back to the drawing board and started scribbling. "I got it. Maureen, do me a favor, will you? Call Rudy Goldberg back and tell him I'm on my way.

If he could just hang around in case I'm late, I would be very grateful. Beg him if you have to. Identifying that charm could be a huge break in the case."

After hanging up, Zoe glanced at her watch. She had promised Joe she'd have dinner with him before he started his night shift. Luckily, Worth Street wasn't far from the loft. She would have plenty of time to talk to Mr. Goldberg and come back here in time for Joe to pick her up.

Sixteen

Rudy's Pawnshop was a small, dingy storefront that smelled of sweat and motor oil. At the back of the room was a cage with half a dozen shelves displaying an assortment of objects for sale—a saxophone, power tools, silver candleholders, an espresso machine. Zoe saw no jewelry or weapons. Those items were big business with pawnbrokers and were kept locked away.

A muscular man in a sweatshirt with the sleeves rolled up to the elbows sat in the cage. At the sound of the doorbell, he looked up, his expression blank. "Can I help you?" he asked when Zoe approached.

"I'm Zoe Foster."

His face lit up and he stood. "Zoe Foster, son of a gun. You came."

"You seem surprised."

"I thought you'd send the cops. In my business, the less I see of our boys in blue, the better off I am." He gave her a quick appraisal. "Anybody ever tell you you look like Kitty Floyd?"

Him, too. It must be the hair, which she continued to wear loose. "Are you familiar with the strip?"

"My wife is. She's the reader in the family. That's how she saw the charm in the newspaper. She recognized it right away."

"May I ask where she got it?"

"A homeless guy walked in a few days ago and wanted to sell it. I gave him twenty bucks for it and gave it to my wife for her birthday."

"Tell me about the man who sold it to you. Have you ever seen him before? Did he have identification? Did you—"

Rudy put up a hand. "Whoa, lady, slow down. First of all, in my business, we don't ask for ID. You bring the goods. I check it out. If it's something I can sell, I'll give you a fair price for it. No questions asked."

Zoe felt her hopes deflate. "So you don't know where the charm came from?"

"Nope."

"And the man?"

He shook his head. "Sorry."

"Don't you keep a record of what you buy and sell?"

"Not if I'm planning to keep the item for myself. Why is it so important? Was it stolen or something?"

There was no way out of this. If she expected him to hand over the charm, she had to tell him the truth. "I don't know if it was stolen, but it could be evidence."

"Evidence of what?"

"The woman who owned the charm was…has disappeared. The charm, if it's hers, could lead the authorities to her abductor."

Rudy let out a groan. "The authorities. I'll have to talk to the cops?"

"Most likely. There is also a possibility that the charm will not be returned to you for a while."

"Me and my big mouth."

Zoe gave an understanding nod. "Could you bring it to the shop tomorrow?" She would ask Annie to come along. She would know if the charm was Lola's.

The pawnbroker let out a long sigh. "My wife's gonna kill me."

Zoe was pleased as she headed back toward SoHo. Locating a charm that everyone at Blue Moon could confirm never came off Lola's bracelet might be enough to convince the police to start an investigation.

She was about to cross Broadway, when she heard the gunshot.

Frozen in place for a moment, Zoe looked around, not sure the sound, a resonant pop, was in fact a gunshot. It could have been a car backfi—

A second shot sent half a dozen people screaming and running for cover. A woman flattened herself to the ground and started crying while another made a beeline for a nearby electronics shop. Coming out of her trance, Zoe followed her.

"It's a sniper!" a man inside the shop shouted, pointing at the roof across the street. "Look, he's getting away!"

"Did someone call the police?" another customer asked.

The clerk behind the counter, barely eighteen and

white as a ghost, was already on the phone. When he hung up and spoke, his voice shook. "The police are on the way. They want everyone to remain inside the store."

Zoe ventured near the open door. Out on the sidewalk, people stood in small groups, as though seeking comfort from one another. All kept looking at the roof of a six-story building with a fire escape running up the side.

"He came down the fire escape," a woman was saying. "And no one stopped him."

Within minutes, three police cruisers pulled up, sirens blaring, followed by an ambulance. Uniformed officers jumped out, hands on their weapons. When it was apparent that the immediate danger had passed, four officers started questioning the crowd outside while two walked inside the electronics shop.

The one with the gray hair spoke first. "I'm Officer Sharkey," he said. "And this is Officer Mead. First of all, is anyone hurt?"

All six people, three men and three women including Zoe and the clerk, shook their heads. Then, as if a button had been pushed, all started to speak at once. Officer Sharkey stopped them. "Let me ask the questions, okay? And you answer one at a time."

All agreed that the shots had come from the building across the street, which prompted Officer Sharkey to call his precinct and request that a unit be sent to search the building.

When it appeared that the interrogation was over, Zoe glanced at her watch. It was a few minutes before eight. Joe would be knocking at her door any moment now. "May I make a phone call?" she asked.

Officer Sharkey nodded.

Joe answered on the second ring. "It's me," she said, trying not to sound too panicky. "Where are you?"

"I'll be up in a minute. I'm circling your building looking for a parking space."

It would never enter his mind to use his clout as a cop and double-park. "I'm not at the loft." She told him what had just happened. At the word *sniper,* he blew up.

"Where are you?" he shouted loud enough for the officer sitting across from her to hear him.

"Electronic City on Broadway and Canal."

The officer shook his head. "I'm sorry, miss. This is a crime scene. No one will be allowed in until we're through."

"Joe Santos is a detective with NYPD."

On the other end of the line, Joe asked, "Is that a cop? Let me talk to him."

Zoe handed Officer Sharkey the phone. "He wants to talk to you."

The policeman took the phone and walked away, out of earshot. When he came back a few minutes later, he handed the phone to Zoe. "Detective Santos is on his way."

Zoe was relieved. "I figured that much."

Seventeen

The moment Joe walked into the electronics shop, Zoe ran to him. "I've never been happier to see your face."

He gave her a worried look. "Officer Sharkey says the shots were meant for you? Is that true?"

"That's what one of the witnesses says, but the area was crowded with holiday shoppers. The sniper could have been aiming at anyone."

"Let me have a word with Sharkey. Which one is he?"

Zoe pointed him out, then watched from a distance as the two men spoke in low tones. From time to time, the uniformed officer would point at the building across the street. Joe would follow his gaze and nod. She was glad he was here, not only because he had taken charge of a situation that was totally foreign to her, but because through it all he remained solid as a rock.

After a conversation that lasted about five minutes, Officer Sharkey turned back to the other five people inside the store. "All right. You're all free to leave, but you'll need to come to the First Precinct at Ericsson

Place sometime tomorrow morning and make formal statements. Anyone here need directions?"

Only the clerk raised his arm. Zoe started to do the same, but Joe stopped her. "I'll take you."

He waited until they had reached his car, an unmarked Ford Crown Victoria parked down the block, before he asked, "What were you doing out? I thought you were home, waiting for me to pick you up."

"I had a call from E.J.'s secretary about Lola's charm."

"What charm?"

She realized that she hadn't had a chance to tell him about her latest findings yet. "Lola had a charm on her bracelet," she said once he was behind the wheel. "On the night I found her, the charm wasn't there."

"Then how did you know about it?"

She told him about Rick's change of heart and the tape he had left with her. "That's when I decided to do a sketch of the charm and put it in the *Herald*. A pawnbroker on Worth Street called the newspaper and said he had it and I went there to talk to him."

Joe drove into a small side street and started looking for a parking space. "So if the sniper *was* waiting for you, he must have known about your visit to the pawnbroker."

"I guess so."

"How many people knew that you were headed for the pawnshop?" Joe asked.

"Not many. Maureen, from the paper. She's E.J.'s secretary. And Rudy Goldberg. That's the pawnbroker. He knew I was coming because Maureen asked him to wait, but why would he—"

"Who else?"

"I think that's it."

"Your boss didn't know?"

"E.J.?" She thought for a moment. "I don't know. He may have." The thought of the publisher standing on a rooftop with a rifle in his hands brought out a chuckle.

"You think that's funny?" Joe didn't look amused. "Someone may be stalking you, Zoe. Someone who seems to know your every move."

"You're exaggerating."

"Am I? If those shots were meant for you, he knew you were going to Rudy Goldberg's pawnshop, then home. How do you explain that?"

"I don't," she snapped. "I'm not the detective, okay? *You* are."

Her frazzled nerves were finally beginning to crack. She had never been the type to scare easily, or worry unnecessarily. She left that duty to her mother, who was a perpetual worrier. But being shot at was a new experience, and the thought that whoever had fired those shots might try again was enough to shake her confidence.

"I'm sorry, Joe. I shouldn't have snapped at you."

Always in tune with her feelings, Joe threw her a quick, apologetic look. "I snapped first." He slid into a vacant space. "Are you sure you feel up to having dinner? If not, I'll just order some takeout and we'll go back to your place."

She thought of the twelve-hour shift he was about to pull, and of the way he had rushed to help her. He never complained, never asked for anything in return. He was right, she didn't feel like being out in a crowded restaurant. She wanted to be home, where she felt safe. But Joe had probably been looking forward to this evening, and she didn't want to let him down.

"Are you trying to welsh on your promise of a good dinner, Detective Santos?"

He laughed. "I guess I have my answer."

Moments later, they stepped into Tarantella, a small, busy neighborhood restaurant in the heart of Little Italy. Zoe waited until she and Joe were seated before she asked, "Do you think they'll catch him? The sniper?"

Although Joe's expression remained somber, he nodded. "It may take a while, but they'll catch him. Someone is bound to have seen him well enough to describe him. A man with a rifle, coming down a fire escape, is not something you see every day, even in New York City."

"I hope you're right." But as she spoke, she thought about the two Maryland snipers who had terrorized the Washington, D.C., area a few years ago, and the conflicting descriptions the police had received. New Yorkers had had their share of tragedies in recent years and the thought of a sniper on the loose in Manhattan, especially during the busiest season of the year, made her blood run cold.

"Zoe?"

She dunked a piece of Italian bread into a small plate of olive oil. "Hmm?"

"I've had some time to think."

"Uh-oh."

"We need to talk about what just happened."

"I know what just happened."

"Right. A sniper fired two shots at a sidewalk full of people and didn't hit a single person."

"We were lucky."

A waitress brought out their drinks—a glass of Ruffino for Zoe and club soda for Joe, who never drank before starting a shift.

When the waitress was gone, he leaned forward. "Let me ask you this. What do all snipers have in common?"

"A desire to exert control over others?"

"Besides that."

"I don't know."

"They're excellent marksmen."

"What are you saying?"

"Nothing that the detective who will be assigned to the case won't corroborate. Our sniper had no intention of shooting anyone."

"So what were his intentions?"

"To scare you?"

She put her glass down. "Do you think the sniper is Lola's killer?"

"It's something to consider, along with the possibility that you've become a threat to him."

"Are you trying to scare me?"

"Yes, and I hope it's working, Zoe. Because next time you might not be so lucky."

"Next time? I thought you said the police would catch this guy."

"But in case they don't, did anything I've said sink in?"

"Yes. Someone, possibly Lola's killer, wants me to back off. What happened today is just a warning."

"That's my girl."

"I'm not backing off."

Joe's face turned an angry red. "Why not?"

"Because now I'm mad. I don't like to be spied on. And I don't like to be scared. That sniper, whoever he is, has trespassed on my rights. He used whatever talents he may have as a marksman to terrorize me and I won't play his little games."

Joe was unimpressed. "You want those words engraved on your tombstone? Or would you prefer them included in an eulogy?"

"Laugh all you want. Until someone takes me seriously and begins to look into the disappearance of Lola Malone, I'm not backing off."

Joe was silent for a moment. When he looked as though he had made a decision, he gave a nod. "All right then. I'll get someone to investigate Lola's disappearance."

"You can do that?"

Instead of answering her, he glanced at his watch, then with a nod, he dug into his pocket and came out with a handful of bills. "Come on. If we hurry, we'll catch him before he goes home."

"Who?"

"A friend of mine at the Ninth Precinct." He dropped the money on the table, apologized to the waitress who was coming to take their order, and grabbed Zoe's hand.

Eighteen

Detective Jack O'Bryan turned out to be much less of a skeptic than the two officers Zoe had first talked to. He listened to her story, which she had to tell from the beginning, took copious notes and didn't speak until she was finished.

Although he hadn't had time to hear about the sniper incident officially, he agreed with Joe that the shooter may only have wanted to scare Zoe off, although he couldn't guarantee that she would be safe if she took the hint. At any rate, a detective would be assigned to the sniper case and they would be able to get more information from him.

Because Zoe was now certain that E.J. had nothing to do with Lola's disappearance, she had left him out of her story entirely, but she had told Detective O'Bryan everything else, from her first meeting with Buddy Barbarino to her recent discovery that Lola's mysterious boyfriend had sent her roses every week. The simple task of passing over the information and letting an authority take over was a huge weight off Zoe's shoulders. She hadn't realized until now how deeply Lola's murder had affected her, emotionally and physically.

"So what's the verdict on O'Bryan?" Joe asked as they walked out of the police station.

"I like him."

"Will you take his advice and back off the case?"

"After he threatened to throw the book at me if I interfered in an ongoing investigation?" She laughed. "You'd better believe I'll take his advice. Something tells me that Detective O'Bryan is not a man you want to tangle with."

"He's a good cop, but he likes to do things his way." Joe pulled the Ford in front of her building but kept the engine running.

"Do you have time to come up?" she asked. "I feel bad that you missed dinner. I have some hot dogs in the freezer."

He made a face. "Tempting as that may be, I'd rather grab something on the way to the station. Besides, we're shorthanded again. I told the captain I'd be in early."

"Rain check, then?"

"Absolutely." With no warning, he pulled her to him. "Don't you dare try to stop me this time," he said in a husky voice.

She almost did. But the events of the past couple of hours had mellowed her considerably. And there was no denying that Joe's strong arms around her, his warm breath brushing her face and that hard body pressed against hers were more than any red-blooded American girl could take.

She raised her face to him. "That was the furthest thing from my mind."

As his lips crushed hers, she returned the kiss with all the passion she could muster.

When both needed to come up for air, he released her. "Wow. Aren't you full of surprises."

She licked her wet lips. "What did you expect? A peck on the cheek?"

"Or a knee in the groin."

She winced. "Don't remind me. I consider the day I did that to you one of the lowest points in my life."

"You more than made up for it tonight." He kissed her again, this time on the tip of her nose. "Go on, get out of here before I decide to play hooky."

"Dear God, Zoe," her mother said the second Zoe answered the phone. "What happened? Are you all right? Why didn't you call me? I'm your mother. Don't I have a right to know when my daughter is almost shot?"

When her mother finally came up for a breath, Zoe calmly climbed on a kitchen stool and put both elbows on the island counter. "Which question do you want me to answer first?" she asked.

"That's right, be flip with me."

"I'm sorry, Mom. I guess I'm still a little rattled."

Catherine's voice turned motherly again. "Of course you are. My poor darling, what did you get yourself into? Who is Lola Malone?"

"A nightclub singer."

"I *know* that, Zoe. Just as I know that she sang, coincidentally, at Blue Moon, but that's another story. What I meant is what is she to *you* that you've become so involved?"

"I didn't know her, if that's what you're getting at."

"Then why are you putting yourself at risk?"

"Because I have to, Mom. I don't expect you to understand, but that's how it is. Lola had been trying to see me. I ignored her calls and now she's dead."

"Oh, honey, you make it sound as though it was your fault." Catherine made an impatient sound with her tongue. "Look, why don't you come down and spend a few days with me. You can do your strip from here, can't you? And you could help me decorate the inn. I'm on the Christmas house tour again this year. I didn't want to be, but Helen Frankel at the chamber of commerce insisted."

"You would have been insulted if she hadn't."

Catherine's cascading laughter resonated through the miles. "You know me too well. Say you'll come down, Zoe," she added in the same breath. "I want to see for myself that you're in one piece."

"I can't get away now, Mom. I have too much to do. But I'll come down on Christmas Day as planned."

There was a small sigh of resignation before Catherine said, "All right. I won't pressure you. Will you be bringing Joe?"

"Joe is having Christmas with his family." Her mother knew that but kept trying every year.

"How are things between the two of you? Have you come to your senses yet?"

Zoe rolled her eyes. That was her mother's not-too-subtle way of telling her that she was a fool to let a catch like Joe Santos slip through her fingers. Because of that,

Zoe thought it best not to mention "the kiss," at least not until she had had a chance to decide what, exactly, that kiss had meant to her.

"You're incorrigible, Mom."

"You didn't answer my question."

"I would, if I had time, but I don't. I'm behind with my strip. Stop worrying, okay? I'll see you soon." She blew her a kiss, not giving her a chance to say another word, and hung up.

The phone conversation with her mother had left Zoe with a vague sense of guilt, not about her mother, but about Joe. Catherine wasn't the only one who wished the relationship between him and Zoe would turn into something more romantic. She did, too. She would have to look far and wide before she found a man more devoted to her. Even Rick, in his best days, hadn't been at her beck and call the way Joe was. That last incident with the sniper had proved it. He had dropped whatever he had been doing and rushed over without a second's hesitation. That's the way he was. For the past four years, she had relied on him, confided in him and admitted to herself over and over that he was probably the best catch in the entire city. With Joe, she felt safe. She felt respected. She felt good. Every now and then, mostly when she was home and feeling a little bit lonely, she found herself fantasizing about her and Joe living together as husband and wife. What would it be like to be Mrs. Joe Santos?

How different would it be from being Mrs. Rick Vaughn?

Annoyed that once again she had allowed her ex-husband to intrude in her thoughts and spoil the moment, she went into the kitchen to see what she could make for dinner. The choices were meager—leftover Chinese, a six-pack of assorted yogurts, a half-dozen eggs and a quart of milk.

She settled for a bowl of cornflakes.

Nineteen

The first thing Rick saw on Wednesday morning as he opened the *New York Herald* was a photo of Zoe on the front page. Underneath was the headline: *Close Call for Popular Cartoonist.*

He didn't bother to finish reading. As soon as he realized that someone had taken a shot at Zoe, he was on the phone, dialing the number Joe Santos had left with him.

It took several minutes for him to answer. When the detective finally picked up, his voice sounded gruff. "Santos here."

"I thought you were going to keep Zoe out of harm's way," Rick barked into the phone.

"Jesus Christ, Vaughn, I can't be with her 24/7!"

"So you let her get shot?"

"She didn't get shot. The bullet didn't even come close."

"Who did the shooting?"

"The police don't know yet. The general feeling is that whoever fired those shots may have missed on purpose. In other words, in case you don't get it," he added sarcastically, "someone tried to scare Zoe into backing off from the Lola Malone case."

"I got it, Santos." Rick took a calming breath. "How is she?"

Santos must have taken a deep breath as well, because it took a couple of seconds for him to answer. "She's fine." His tone turned sarcastic again. "Am I to understand that you haven't talked to her yet?"

"You understand correctly."

"How come?"

"None of your damn business."

"Just trying to be helpful."

"Yeah, you're a real Boy Scout."

"My, my, did we get up on the wrong side of the bed this morning?"

The detective's attitude was starting to get on Rick's nerves. "Why don't you cut out the bull and tell me what the police have on the perp."

"What am I? An information booth?"

"Come on, Santos."

"There are no leads at this point."

"Why the hell not?"

Rick heard the sigh of exasperation at the other end of the line and felt a tug of satisfaction. "Because we don't work miracles. Finding a suspected killer takes time." He waited a beat. "Everything happened too fast. The shooter was gone before anyone could react. The police are trying to get a description from a couple of people who claim they saw him, but there was a lot of panic at the scene and we're getting conflicting reports."

Joe had told him far more than Rick would have if the circumstances had been reversed, which meant that an apology was probably in order. "Thanks for talking to me," he said.

"You're welcome."

"And Joe?"

"What now?"

"I'm sorry about the outburst earlier."

The detective just hung up.

Rick had kept in contact with Stretch throughout the morning before calling Jenny a little after noon. Physically, she was still a mess, but emotionally, she was much better and getting stronger. She had already talked to her cousin in New Orleans, who had told her to get on the first plane. Jenny wasn't too crazy at the thought of traveling in the condition she was in, but she was anxious to put as much distance as possible between her and Mike. There was a flight at seven o'clock tomorrow morning and she had decided to take it.

Rick sat at his desk, drumming his fingers and thinking about Zoe. The irritation he had felt toward her the other night had been replaced by another emotion, one he couldn't control as well—fear. In spite of Santos's reassurance, Zoe could still be in danger. The girl had a nose for trouble and a gift for burying herself neck deep into it. And with a killer still on the loose, he wasn't about to take any chances.

He picked up his phone again and dialed Lenny's number. "Lenny," he said when his army buddy answered. "I need a favor."

"Name it, boss."

"I'd like you to switch places with Stretch until Jenny leaves tomorrow morning. I need him for something else."

"You want me to babysit that brat?"

"She's changed, Lenny."

"I'll believe that when I see it."

"Well, now's your chance. Will you do it?"

Lenny muttered something Rick chose not to understand, then asked, "Who will tend bar?"

"I thought I'd ask Annie. She's been dying to give bartending a try."

Fortunately, Lenny liked Annie. "When do I report for duty?"

"Right away. And tell Stretch to come straight to my apartment. I'll explain when he gets there."

"Come on, baby, get in here."

Huffing and puffing, Zoe tried to drag the Douglas fir she had carried for four and a half blocks through her front door. Why had she bought such a huge Christmas tree? Every year, she vowed to go smaller and every year she walked into the outdoor lot on Sullivan Street and ended up taking home the biggest tree.

She should have asked one of the many visitors she'd had earlier to stick around and help get this beast inside. Her loft had been a beehive of activity all afternoon. Friends and neighbors had stopped by, bringing flowers, food and good wishes. Joe's mother had brought a big pot of Zoe's favorite *sancocho,* not only because soup could cure everything, but because Maria believed it chased away the evil spirits she sensed were surrounding Zoe.

Unfortunately, she was alone at the moment, with this damn tree that didn't want to budge. She gave one last yank and stumbled backward as it finally came through. "Good boy."

She dragged it to the window where the tree stand was already waiting. It took her almost half an hour to get the trunk into the ring and tighten the bolts, but she did it.

She was about to go into the bedroom for the box of ornaments she kept on top of her wardrobe, when she stopped. On the television screen, a picture of a heavyset woman in a blue parka had suddenly popped up. She was surrounded by a small crowd and was crying softly as she spoke into a microphone. At the lower right corner was a snapshot of a man. Zoe recognized him instantly.

"Rudy!"

The woman's voice shook as she talked. "What kind of world is this where a gunman can come into your own home in the middle of the night and kill your husband in cold blood? And for what? A few dollars, a ten-year-old watch and a necklace that was worth less than a hundred dollars."

Zoe's hand went to cover her mouth. Rudy was dead. Someone had killed him.

"Rudy didn't deserve this." The woman took the handkerchief someone handed her. "He was a good man. His job may not have been the safest in the world, but when he was home, he was supposed to be safe."

"You didn't see the intruder?" the reporter holding the mike asked.

The woman shook her head. "I was in the bathroom. I don't think I was gone for more than five minutes." She started to cry again, prompting the man standing next to her to wrap his arm around her shoulders and lead her away.

The reporter turned back to face the camera. "That was Anita Goldberg, the wife, widow now, of Rudy Goldberg. Mr. Goldberg was shot at close range in his bed last night as he slept. Although the motive appears to have been robbery, nothing of great value seems to have been taken."

"Sheila," an unseen news anchor said, "are the police saying why the robber shot Mr. Goldberg, since he was sleeping?"

"They're not positive that he *was* sleeping. The drawer in his bedside table, where he kept a 9 mm Beretta, was partially open, suggesting that he may have caught the intruder in the act and had gone for his gun."

"Thank you, Sheila." The anchor appeared on-screen. "That was Sheila McKnight, reporting from Worth Street. Stay tuned for more—"

Zoe sank into a chair, her hands still covering her mouth. Rudy had been murdered. As much as she wanted to believe that it was just a terrible coincidence, one of those infamous random acts of violence for which the city was known, she could not. Why Rudy? And why now?

Reluctant to ask for Joe's help, she called Detective O'Bryan at the Ninth Precinct and let out a small sigh of relief when he answered. He didn't sound overjoyed to hear from her and sounded even less amiable when she told him the reason for her call.

"Ms. Foster, that murder is out of my jurisdiction."

"Not necessarily. If the sniper incident is connected to the Lola Malone case, and you agreed that it could be, then Rudy Goldberg's murder could be, too."

"How do you arrive at that conclusion?"

"Simple. With Rudy dead, there is no one to identify the homeless man who sold him Lola's charm, the same man who could tell us where he found it."

"Lola Malone could have lost that charm anywhere."

"I realize that. But what if he found it in the alley where Lola died? What if he *saw* what happened that night? I know it's a long shot, but can you really afford to ignore it?" When he didn't reply, she added, "All I want to know is if the necklace that was stolen from the Goldbergs' home had the charm on it. That's not too much to ask, is it, Detective? You can get the answer with one phone call."

"I'm glad you have that much confidence in me, Ms. Foster."

His tone was heavy with sarcasm, but she let it go. Now was not the time to be overly sensitive. "Will you do it?"

"I'll make a couple of calls."

"And you'll let me know?"

"Will that get you off my back?"

"Yes," she lied.

Twenty

Ray Dougherty stood at his kitchen window, sipping coffee and gazing at the blue, glittering San Diego Bay. After more than twenty years in this idyllic city, he still couldn't get enough of the relaxed lifestyle, the perfect weather and the many events that took place throughout the city all year long.

It made him glad that he had no one to answer to but himself. Selling hardware might not be the most glamorous profession in the world, but there was a lot to be said about owning your own business. For one thing, it allowed him to do what he wanted when he wanted. He could just take off, as he had today, and take part in any of his favorite activities—bowling, deep-sea fishing or just playing a game of canasta with his best friend, Lou Agnelli—without having to justify his actions to anyone.

The business had also made it possible for him to buy a condo with one of the best views in town, although the view wasn't the only reason he had bought the property. He also liked the privacy and anonymity a city apartment provided. The building, located on Island Avenue, was occupied mostly by young professionals who were too busy to pay much attention to the fifty-plus tenant on the twenty-second floor.

If they had, they would have been surprised to learn that Ray Dougherty's real name was Tony Marcino and that he had once been a member of a powerful Philadelphia crime family. And that he used to be the proud father of a beautiful three-year-old little girl and the devoted husband of a lovely woman, both of whom he still loved deeply.

In those early days in Philadelphia, Tony would have done anything for his family, but he couldn't do the one thing his wife wanted most—to leave the mob, move back to New York and find a job they could all be proud of.

It was a request Stephanie had made often, and the only one Tony couldn't grant. Members of a crime family did not leave the organization—except on a stretcher. To try would be like signing your own death warrant. That's why he had kept his job as attorney for Frank "the Whale" Scolini, hoping that in time, Stephanie would see the wisdom behind his decision.

He hadn't been that lucky. On Angie's third birthday, Frank was arrested and charged with crimes ranging from racketeering to murder. A few days later, Frank's second in command was executed by a rival mob, days after he had announced his appointment as the organization's new boss. Terrified that the same fate awaited Tony, Stephanie had given her husband an ultimatum: leave the mob or she would file for divorce. She preferred to leave him than to see him being shot down in front of their house the way Rocco was.

Tony knew her as a loving woman who would never break up their family, and he assumed the threat was just that—a threat. He couldn't have been more wrong. That same day, Stephanie filed for divorce, and three months later, she and Angie moved to New York, changed their names and never looked back.

Shortly after losing his family, Tony was arrested. To everyone's surprise, he agreed to turn state's evidence in exchange for immunity and a chance to start a new life under the witness protection program. Many of his friends in the syndicate thought he was insane. He'd never get away with it, they warned him. Frank would find him and have him killed.

Tony didn't care. He was so despondent over the loss of his wife and child that he didn't give a damn whether he lived or died.

As he was escorted out of the courthouse after his testimony, a dark sedan drove by and sent a volley of bullets in Tony's direction. Although badly wounded, Tony survived. To keep him safe, however, the FBI put the word out that Tony Marcino had died on the way to the hospital.

While there, he underwent extensive plastic surgery. His jaw was widened, his nose narrowed, his freckles removed and his prematurely receding forehead was made full again through hair restoration.

The transformation was so dramatic that Tony, who now went by the name of Ray Dougherty, had asked the FBI agent in charge of his case to relocate him to New York City where he could be close to his daughter.

Agent Fay had explained that to be in such proximity to his former family was much too dangerous for him, and for his wife and child. They sent him to San Diego instead. A month after his arrival in the southern California town, Ray had found a job as a salesman in a hardware store. To his surprise, he had liked not only the job but his boss, as well. Ten years ago, eager to retire, Mel had offered to sell Ray the store at terms that were too attractive to pass.

Throughout the years, Ray had kept a low profile. His only close friend, and the only person who knew his true identity, was Lou, a private investigator he had met shortly after arriving in San Diego. Lou had helped him, discreetly, to locate his wife and daughter. Over the years he had provided him with regular reports, photographs and the latest happenings in their lives.

His little Angie had done well for herself. Of course, she wasn't little Angie anymore. She was all grown up now, and beautiful….

The doorbell interrupted his thoughts. That would be Lou. He was always early on bowling day, partly because he carried a hundred and eighty average and couldn't wait to beat the competition's ass, and partly because the activity, along with his job, helped him get over his wife's death a year ago. Handy with tools, Lou helped Ray at the store whenever he needed him, and when both men were out at the same time, as they were today, Ray simply closed shop.

Ray opened the door. Older than Ray by a couple of years, Lou bore his sixty-one years well. Reasonably attractive, he had succeeded in making himself totally forgettable, which, in his job, was an asset. Should someone need to describe him, they would be hard-pressed to say anything other than average height, average weight and brown hair touched with gray. No distinguishing marks. The description could have fit millions of Americans and that suited Lou just fine.

The two men were so different from one another, they could have starred in a remake of *The Odd Couple*. Ray tended to be relaxed about housekeeping, what went into his stomach and how often he saw a doctor, which was never. Lou was meticulous, a health freak and a hypochondriac. Yet in spite of their differences, the bond between them had become stronger with each passing year.

"You're early," Ray said as he let his friend in.

Lou set his bowling bag down on the foyer floor and followed Ray into the kitchen. "I have news I thought you'd want to hear."

"I'm listening." Ray headed for the kitchen. "How about some coffee?"

"Forget the coffee. Sit down, Ray."

The firm tone and the grim look on Lou's face alerted him that what Lou had to tell him was serious. "Is it about Angie?"

"Before I tell you, give me your word that you won't go ballistic on me."

"You know I hate it when you start a sentence like that."

"Give me your word."

"Okay, I give you my word."

"You know that I've just returned from New York."

"You went there to check on that jewelry heist your brother-in-law was involved in. Yes, I know."

"He wasn't *involved,* Ray. He was just—" He waved an impatient hand. "Never mind. What I want to tell you is that two nights ago, on a Manhattan street, a sniper on a rooftop took a shot at Angie."

"What?"

"She's okay. She wasn't hurt. And she's in good hands."

"Whose?" Ray asked suspiciously.

"That friend of hers, Joe Santos."

"The cop?"

Lou nodded. "He's watching her like a hawk. And so is her ex-husband."

Ray's fears subsided a little. "How do you know all that?"

"I read it in the papers. Angie has become big news."

"Why didn't you call me right away?"

"I didn't want you to do something stupid, like jump on the first plane and go to New York."

Ray sat down. "Jesus, Lou. Who would want to kill Angie?" Although he now thought of himself as Ray, he had never gotten used to the name Zoe.

"No one knows." Lou shrugged. "Maybe it was one of those random shootings you hear so much about, and she was caught in the cross fire."

Eyes narrowed, Tony studied Lou. He knew him much too well to fall for that innocent look. "What aren't you telling me?"

"Nothing."

"You're a lousy liar, Lou. Now come clean or I'm getting the truth out of you in ways you don't even want to think about."

Lou muttered something under his breath, before heaving a long sigh. "Last week, Angie, I mean Zoe, was involved in an incident. The shooting two nights ago *could* be a result of that incident."

Ray listened as Lou told him how Angie had discovered the body of a singer in an alley. While Angie went to get help, someone had removed the body. With no corpse and no evidence of foul play, the police had done little except question the people who lived near the alleged crime scene. That's when Angie had started her own investigation.

Restless, Ray started pacing the living room. "So, all of a sudden, the random-shooting theory isn't holding up so well. Is that what you're telling me?"

"The police are checking out every possibility."

"Cops." Ray made a derisive sound. "They'll find zilch. And in the meantime my little girl is an open target."

He went to stand by the mantel and took down one of the pictures Lou had brought back from New York eight months ago. His friend had kept him well supplied over the years. Whether it was a piano recital, a swim meet, a basketball game or a graduation, Ray had been able to follow his daughter's transformation from schoolgirl to career woman every step of the way.

When he learned that Zoe had eloped, he had asked Lou to find out everything he could about Rick Vaughn. An ex-marine himself, Ray had felt an instant connection to the young man and was saddened to hear two years later that he and Angie had divorced.

He kept looking at the photograph. She was so beautiful. She had inherited his red hair and freckles. But the rest of her, the beautiful blue eyes, the perfect cheekbones, the full mouth—all that belonged to Stephanie.

He waited until the familiar ache in his gut receded before putting the photograph back on the mantel. Then, he calmly announced, "I'm going to New York."

Lou rolled his eyes. "Aw, Ray, no. That's crazy."

"What would you have me do? Sit on my ass while someone uses my daughter for target practice?"

"I told you, she's in good hands."

But Ray was no longer listening. The bowling game forgotten, he headed for his bedroom where he took a suitcase from the closet and put it on the bed.

Lou followed him. "You're not doing this. I won't let you do this. It's suicide."

Ray took a stack of shirts from a dresser drawer and threw them into the suitcase. "You think I'm stupid? You think I'm going to put myself in a situation that could cost me my life? Or worse, the life of my daughter?" He picked up a pair of old boots and tossed them in with the shirts. "I'll be a business owner on vacation in the Big Apple. What could be more innocent?"

"What if Frank has Stephanie and Angie under watch?"

"After thirty years? Don't make me laugh."

But when Lou was all wound up, nothing could stop him. "What? You think you're safe just because he's in prison? Even from behind bars, the man wields tremendous power. And he doesn't forget, either. Men like him don't like to lose face. It's bad for their reputation. If he has the slightest notion that you're still alive, he'll move heaven and earth to find you. He'll kill you for sure, but first he'll kill Angie and make you watch. That's the type of man he is."

Ray continued to fill the suitcase. "You're not telling me anything I don't know. I was his *conciglieri*, remember? I know him. I know how he operates, and what he is capable of. That's why I can beat him at his own game. So stop worrying, okay?"

"Tell me how you're going to beat a man like Frank Scolini at his own game."

"I have friends in New York. People who can find out what cops can't."

"Friends you knew thirty years ago. They could all be dead by now."

"Will you stop being such a pessimist? Instead of bitching, why don't you go and pack."

"For what?"

"You're coming with me."

"No way, Ray. I want no part of this. I won't have your blood on my hands."

Ray zipped the suitcase shut and set it on the floor. "Suit yourself."

Twenty-One

It wasn't the Ritz, but it would have to do.

In his first-floor room at the Select Hotel in mid-Manhattan, Ray Dougherty set his suitcase on the bed. While he unpacked, he went over his plan. As he had told Lou, he had a few friends in New York, all of whom dated back to his school days. Whether or not they were still his friends would remain to be seen. Right now, Guiseppe, whom everyone had called Peppe, was his best bet. They had met in the fifth grade, and between the two of them they had accumulated more detention hours than the rest of the two fifth-grade classes put together.

After graduating from high school, Tony had gone off to college and then law school, while Peppe chose to work with his father in the family trash-collecting business in Queens. Like his father, and his grandfather before that, Peppe was one of the most connected men Ray knew. He was on a first-name basis with the area's most notorious mob bosses, and rumor had it that if he wanted a favor done, all he had to do was ask.

He had been arrested twice, for allegedly providing stolen weapons to the Pantano crime family, a local organization that had been cited for a number of felonies. Peppe had beat the rap both times. Or maybe he was innocent as he'd claimed. Ray still wasn't sure, even though Peppe was the one who had introduced him to Frank Scolini.

They had kept in touch, even after Tony had moved to Philadelphia. Then Tony had "died" and all contact was broken.

There were a couple of other old pals—JoJo, who had become a barber; Manny, the number cruncher, and Deano, who ran the Bronx Zoo. Ray would have to track them down as well, if they were still around.

And if they could still be trusted.

But before he contacted old compadres, he had to see his daughter, even if it was from afar. He had often entertained thoughts of flying to New York and posting himself outside her apartment building until she came out. Each time the fear that Frank's thugs could be watching her had stopped him.

He no longer felt that way. The attempt on Angie's life had made him realize how quickly things could change. What if she had been killed? What if his precious daughter had died before he could even set eyes on her? That was simply not going to happen. First, he was going to find the son of a bitch who had taken those two shots and then, if he wanted to see his daughter, he would do so. He would just have to come up with a plan that would keep them both safe.

He walked to the bathroom to empty his shaving kit,

only to see that there were no towels. Grumbling, he walked over to the phone and dialed housekeeping.

"We'll send someone right up, sir," the clerk assured him

Ray hung up and checked out his little notebook. Lou had given him the name of some of the places where Angie went regularly. First there was Lotus, the Chinatown restaurant her best friend, Lizzy Min, owned. And there was the pizza place on south Broadway where she and Joe Santos went occasionally. Ray also knew that she bought her groceries at Ellis's Market on Canal Street, had her hair cut at Tresses and took her cleaning to Speedy Cleaners just down the street. The *Herald* was in the East Village, a fifteen-minute walk from her apartment, and the gym where she shot hoops a couple of times a week was about the same distance.

He would have plenty of opportunities to see her. And while even a glimpse of her would bring him a great deal of pleasure, what he *really* wanted was to take her in his arms and tell her how much he loved her. He wanted to talk to her until the sun came up. He wanted to see where she lived, the mementos she surrounded herself with, the food she ate, the books she read. And he wanted to see her work.

He hadn't been surprised to learn that she had made art her career. She may have inherited her good looks from Stephanie, but her talent for drawing had come from him. While he hardly considered himself an artist, he had worked his way through college by waiting tables and selling caricatures he made of people.

The knock at the door pulled him out of his reverie and he went to open it.

Instead of a maid with an armful of towels, Lou stood there, a carry-on bag in one hand and a suitcase in the other. He wore his favorite sour expression.

"Well, are you going to let me in or do you plan on standing here like an idiot all morning?"

Ray moved aside. "What the hell are you doing here?"

"What does it look like?"

"What happened to 'I don't want your blood on my hands'?"

Lou set his luggage on the floor and looked around. "I changed my mind."

"You *want* my blood on your hands?"

"Oh, enough with your stupid questions already. You know damn well why I'm here."

"Yeah, I do. In fact, I half expected you to show up on my flight."

"I tried. It was full."

Ray grinned. "You're a good friend, Lou. I don't think I tell you that often enough." He looked down at the suitcase. "Just one thing, though. You don't expect to bunk with me, do you?"

"Hell, no, you're too damn messy. My room wasn't ready so I told the desk clerk I'd leave my stuff here for now. I'm just one floor up—room 203."

He glanced in the mirror and gave a tug to his necktie. Always dapper, he had dressed to the nines for the trip—shirt and tie, a green and brown argyle sweater and a tan trench coat. "Now what do you say we go grab some lunch? Before all those exhaust fumes ruin my appetite."

* * *

Perched on top of a ladder, Zoe stretched herself as tall as she could and gently set the Victorian angel on the top branch of the Christmas tree. After climbing down, she took a step back.

"Fabulous," she declared. "Good work, Zoe."

She was carrying the ladder back into the kitchen, when her phone rang. She was surprised to find out that it was Detective O'Bryan, sounding rather subdued.

"That charm you told me about," he said. "It *was* part of the necklace."

"I knew it." She tried not to sound as though she was gloating. "What now?"

"The theft could be purely accidental. The robber grabbed the necklace and the charm happened to be attached to it."

"Or it could have been intentional. Either way, it's worth investigating, don't you think?"

This time he laughed, not mockingly, but with good humor. "I'll definitely look into it."

"Thank you, Detective."

"You can show your appreciation by donating a toy for our toy drive. There's a box right here in our lobby."

"I'll be sure to do that."

She walked back into her studio, her thoughts on the little cupid, which seemed to be getting more and more significant as the investigation progressed. But without the homeless man, tracing the charm to the killer wouldn't be easy.

Unless they could tempt him to come forward on his own.

Encouraged by the idea that had crept into her mind, she picked up the phone and dialed E.J.

"E.J.," she said when he answered, "would you mind running the sketch of that charm for a few more days? This time I'd like to post a reward."

"Wait a minute," he protested. "Didn't you say that you were staying out of police business? Haven't you learned your lesson?"

"I'm not interfering, E.J. Whatever information we get, I'll pass it on to Detective O'Bryan."

"Do I have your word on that?"

"Yes."

"All right. What do you want to say?"

She thought for a moment. "How about 'A hundred-dollar reward will be given to anyone who can provide information about the charm pictured above.'?"

She could hear him scribbling on his pad. "A hundred dollars isn't much money."

"To a homeless man, it's a fortune. And we can always raise the ante later. Will you do it?"

"It's done."

Satisfied she had done all she could for Lola, she walked back into her studio where another stack of mail from her growing list of fans was waiting for her. As always, it included a clue from Lonesome Me.

This time he or she wrote, *Maybe Mona was blackmailing someone. A former lover?*

Another excellent suggestion, considering that it was now almost certain that Lola was dating a married man. Zoe tossed the note in the wastebasket. She would deal with the blackmail issue another time and in some other way. Flipping through the stack, she spotted a letter from a Paula Smith in Brooklyn. *Have the police search Mona's apartment?*

She would go with that clue. Most likely, Detective O'Bryan had already gone through Lola's apartment with a fine-tooth comb. He hadn't told her what, if anything, he had found, and she doubted that he would. He had been very clear about his practice of not sharing information during an ongoing investigation. And anyway, she couldn't call him twice in one day and run the risk of truly aggravating him. She'd wait until *after* she had dropped off her gift for the toy drive. He might be in a more receptive moved by then.

With Paula Smith's suggestion in front of her, Zoe started to draw.

Twenty-Two

Rick had driven Jenny to the airport himself. After handing her two thousand dollars to tide her over until she found a job, he had made her promise to keep in touch and call if she needed anything. Much stronger, physically and emotionally, she had managed to hold back her tears until she turned to wave one last time before entering the jetway.

Later that afternoon, Rick was back at his desk, reading the *Herald*'s headlines. Nightclub Singer Vanishes.

Now that the story was out and an official investigation had begun, the press hadn't wasted any time in making Lola, and the fact that she was the niece of a Broadway legend, the news of the hour. A half-dozen reporters had descended on Blue Moon earlier today and although Rick had been tempted to throw them out, he had reconsidered. A little cooperation would get them off his back quicker than a kick in the rear.

This wasn't exactly the kind of publicity Lola had dreamed of all her life, but if the screaming headlines and her picture in the papers brought her back safe and sound, then it would be worth it. A Detective O'Bryan had stopped by less than an hour ago and had questioned Rick extensively about Lola. Suspecting a three-way connection between Lola's disappearance, the sniper incident on Worth Street and Rudy Goldberg's murder, O'Bryan had been curious about anyone who may have had a grudge against Zoe.

Even though Rick didn't think Jenny's boyfriend had it in him to climb on a rooftop and start shooting into a crowd of people, he had told the detective about his confrontation with Brenner and the young man's threats against Zoe.

"I'll check it all out," O'Bryan had said. "But from now on, it might not be a bad idea for you to let the police handle domestic disputes, or any kind of dispute. As much as Brenner deserved what he got, that kind of practice could get you in a heap of trouble. You understand what I'm saying?"

Rick had understood perfectly, and promised to be a model citizen from now on. As he kept reading the *Herald,* he saw that his ex-wife had received her share of headlines, as well. To the press's chagrin, Zoe had turned down all requests for interviews, stating that the focus should be on Lola Malone and no one else.

"Good for you, Red," Rick murmured as he read her comment.

He was still looking at Zoe's picture when the phone rang. It was Stretch. From the sound of his voice when he said, "Hi, boss," Rick guessed he had bad news. "Don't tell me that Zoe spotted you," he said.

"No."

Stretch was a man of few words. "Then what's the problem?"

"Some dude is tailing her."

Rick sat up straight. "Who?"

"I don't know. I lost him."

"You lost him?"

"I told you I wasn't good at this kind of stuff. I can toss a man across the room, but when it comes to trailing people, I suck. You should have asked Lenny."

Rick ran a hand through his hair. "Can you describe the guy?"

"I couldn't see much of him. He wore a trench coat with the collar up. From the back he looked to be of medium height and medium weight."

"That's not much help."

"I know. I'm sorry...."

"How did you lose him?"

Stretch sounded embarrassed. "He pulled an old classic. He entered a department store through the front entrance and went out the back."

"Where is Zoe now?"

"At the loft. I just saw her going in."

"And there's no sign of the tail?"

"No."

"All right, forget the surveillance. Go home, Stretch. I'll see you tonight."

Rick hung up. He sat at his desk for a while, then he stood up, grabbed his overcoat and walked out.

Knowing he wouldn't find a parking space in SoHo at this time of day, Rick took a cab, asked the driver to drop him off at the Nancy Hoffman Gallery on West Broadway, and walked the rest of the way. SoHo was a part of town he had always enjoyed and rarely found the time to explore. The area had undergone an amazing transformation since the 1960s, when it was just another Manhattan neighborhood filled with superb but badly run-down buildings. Now a major art gallery district, SoHo also boasted some of the best restaurants and boutiques in Manhattan.

It was a cloudy afternoon and the lights were on in Zoe's loft. Rick looked around him, trying to spot the man Stretch had described. The area was teeming with students from nearby NYU and shoppers. Picking out one man wasn't easy. For all he knew, the stalker wasn't even here. Having spotted Stretch, he had probably run for cover.

An art gallery with bizarre sculptures in the window and a bench outside the front door stood directly across from Zoe's building. Rick stayed out of sight and waited.

After a few minutes, a man came around the corner, hesitated for a moment, then walked over to the bench and sat down.

He was in his late fifties and wore a trench coat with the collar pulled up. He just sat there, seemingly content to watch people go by.

Rick observed him, wondering if he was the man Stretch had spotted, or if he was just a weary shopper resting his feet.

A shopper with no shopping bags?

When the man's gaze suddenly shot up to Zoe's window and stayed there for a few seconds, Rick threw the weary-shopper theory out the window. "All right, pal," he murmured, taking out his cell phone. "Let's find out who you are and what you want with Zoe."

Positioning himself so the man wouldn't see him, he dialed Zoe's number.

Her voice was soft and mellow, like a warm blanket. "Hello?"

"Hi, Red."

The warm blanket turned into a thin layer of frost. "What do you want?"

She was still mad. That was to be expected. He had been rough on her the other night. Justified, but rough. Apologizing would have taken too much time, so he went straight to the point. "I need you to do something for me."

"After the way you treated me the other day, I should do you a favor?"

"Actually, the favor is for you."

Silence. He could almost hear the wheels turning in that complex head of hers. What would she do? Slam the phone in his ear? Or give in to curiosity?

Curiosity won. "What's this all about?"

"I want you to go out and take a walk."

Another short silence. "A walk where?"

"Away from the crowds. Toward the river."

This time she laughed. "Are you out of your mind?"

He kept his eyes on the man on the bench. "No harm will come to you. I'll be right there. In fact, if you look out your window, you'll see me."

He saw her approach the window. He gave her a two-finger salute.

"What are you doing here?"

"A man is following you."

Instinctively, her gaze swept over the crowded street. "Who?"

"That's what I want to find out, but I need your co-operation."

"Where is he?"

"Outside the Fenwick Gallery. The man on the bench. Don't let him see you."

She fell back into the shadows. "He seems harmless enough. How do you know that he's following me?"

"Stretch told me."

"Stretch?"

"He's my bouncer. He does odd jobs for me. After reading about the sniper incident, I asked him to keep an eye on you."

"I'm no longer your responsibility, Rick. I can take care of myself."

"This has nothing to do with responsibility."

"What then?"

He let out an exasperated sigh. She could never be happy with a simple answer. She had to grill you until she knew every little detail. "We're wasting time, Zoe. Will you please do as I ask? We can talk later."

"I'll be right down," she said after a short silence.

She walked out two minutes later, wrapped in a red wool poncho. Her luxurious red mane was loose again, a brilliant beacon in the gray afternoon.

As she headed east on Grand Street, the stranger scrambled to his feet and started after her.

Rick let him go as far as Mercer. Then, quickening his step, he closed the distance between them in a few strides.

When he was within reaching distance, he grabbed him by the shoulder and slammed him against the wall of a building, hard. "Just what the hell do you think you're doing?" he asked.

Although surprised, the man didn't try to fight back. He didn't even appear to be afraid as he held Rick's hard gaze.

"Isn't it obvious?" he replied calmly. "I'm taking a walk. Is there a law against it?"

"There's a law against stalking women."

"You're mistaken, sir. I'm not stalking anyone."

Rick jerked his head in Zoe's direction. She had stopped and was watching them. Rick put his hand up, signaling her to stay away. "You've been following that woman all day. And when you're not following her, you're sitting on a bench across from her apartment, watching her window. When she came out of the building just now, you got up and went after her. In my language, that's called stalking." He tightened his grip around the man's collar. "Who are you? And what do you want with her?"

"My name is Ray Dougherty. I own a hardware store in San Diego. I'm in town for a little R&R. Would you like my serial number, too? I used to be in the marines."

Rick hated wise guys. "All right, Mr. Dougherty from San Diego, you've got five seconds to tell me what you want with that young woman over there. One more cute answer from you and I'll have you singing soprano."

"I'm sure you're quite capable of doing that, but I assure you it would be the wrong thing to do."

"What are you? Some kind of comedian?"

"I'm just being practical."

"You want practical?" Holding him firmly against the wall with one hand, Rick took out his cell phone. "I'll start by calling the cops. Is that practical enough for you?"

Bingo. This time, there was a flicker of mild panic in those calm brown eyes. Rick started to punch 911. He was about to hit the last digit when the man spoke.

"Don't do that, Rick."

Startled, Rick looked up. "You know me?"

"We haven't been formally introduced, but yes, I know you. Sort of."

Rick snapped his phone shut. "Who the hell *are* you?"

The man who called himself Ray Dougherty threw another look in Zoe's direction. "I'm her father."

Twenty-Three

Rick let the man go but stayed firmly planted in front of him, just in case he decided to make a run for it. "What did you say?"

The man straightened his collar. "I'm Angie's—I mean, I'm Zoe's father."

"Zoe's father died when she was a little girl."

"That's what everybody thinks." He cast a quick look at Zoe, who was beginning to show signs of impatience. "Look, I know you have questions and I'll answer them all, but not here. Someone could be watching me. Earlier today, I caught a man following me."

"And you lost him. I know. The man works for me."

The stranger looked at Rick with what seemed like renewed interest, even mild amusement. "You're exactly as I pictured you—resourceful, impulsive and impatient."

"And how would you know that?"

"Let's go somewhere for coffee and I'll tell you."

"You can tell me right here."

"Not with Zoe only a few feet away."

"Rick?" Apparently tired of waiting, Zoe started walking toward them.

"Let me go," the man said in a furious whisper. "Before she takes another step. I give you my word that I won't disappear. I'll meet you wherever you say."

Rick only had a split second to make up his mind. Oddly, he chose to trust this stranger. "Do you know where O'Brady's is?"

"It's been a long time since I lived in New York."

"It's on Broome Street. Directly across from the Kerr Museum. It's a five-minute walk from here. Meet me there in twenty minutes."

As the man hurried away, a hand came to rest on Rick's arm. "You let him go?" Zoe's eyes were wide with disbelief. "Why didn't you call the police?"

"I'll explain later."

"Explain what? Who is he? What did he want with me? How long has he been stalking me?"

"He wasn't stalking you."

"Then what was he doing watching my window?"

"I won't know that until I've talked to him."

"You can't talk to him. He's gone!"

"I'm meeting him for coffee."

She stared at him, mouth open. "You're socializing with my stalker?"

"I told you—"

"He's not stalking me, yes, I heard you. Now I want you to hear me. Wherever you're meeting this man, I'm coming, too."

Rick shook his head. "Absolutely not."

"Why? I'm the victim here, remember? I have a right to know why he's been following me."

"And you will. Later."

Zoe's sixth sense, which Rick had found so spooky at times, kicked in. "Why are you acting so strange? What are you hiding?"

"Nothing."

"Bull. You call me at home and tell me to go out for a walk so you can catch a man you claim has been following me. When you catch him, you let him go without asking him anything. Who are you kidding?"

"All you need to know right now is that the man you saw does not want to hurt you." He took her hand. "Come on, I'll walk you home. As soon as I'm done with him, I'll stop by and tell you everything."

"Promise?"

"Word of honor."

The suspicion in her eyes began to fade. She didn't fight him. In fact, she was almost docile as she walked beside him. Apparently, his word was still good.

"I'll be waiting," she told him at the door.

O'Brady's was nothing more than a hole in the wall with a neon beer mug in the window blinking on and off. A large selection of cheap food and drinks made it a favorite amongst NYU students, who packed the place night after night. As always, the crowd at the bar was three-feet deep with noisy young men drinking beer and checking out the girls.

The man who called himself Ray Dougherty had found a seat on a window ledge wide enough to accommodate his slender frame. Two bottles of Heineken, no glasses, were beside him. Did the man know that Rick drank only Heineken beer? And never in a glass but out of the bottle? Or was this just a coincidence?

That same amused smile pulled the corner of Dougherty's mouth as Rick squeezed into the seat. "Is the beer all right?"

"It's fine." Rick took a swallow. "How did you know?"

"When I learned that you had married my daughter, I made it a point to find out all I could about you." He leaned forward. "I know that you had a tough childhood, that you went from foster home to foster home and had several encounters with the law until the Vaughns adopted you and turned you around."

"All right, I'm impressed. Now, enough about me. I want you to give me proof that you are who you claim to be."

"Before I do, I must have your word that what I'm about to tell you will be held in strictest confidence. If anyone finds out that I'm alive, I won't stay that way for long. And neither will Zoe."

"Why Zoe?"

"I'll explain. Do I have your word?"

"I have to tell Zoe. There's no way I can avoid that. And don't ask me to lie to her, because I won't."

"No, I guess you wouldn't." Dougherty gave a de-layed nod. "All right. Do what you have to do."

Nothing had prepared Rick for the incredible story that followed. If Dougherty hadn't been so believable, Rick would have called the cops long ago. But the details of Zoe's life over the years were so clearly drawn, the dates of various events so precisely stated, that Rick had no choice but to believe him.

"So what do I call you?" he asked at last. "Ray or Tony?"

"Ray. Tony is dead. And he has to stay that way."

Rick was quiet for a while. "You really think you can find out who's after Zoe?"

"I can try. There can't be that many first-rate snipers in New York City."

"The guy missed in a street crowded with motorists and pedestrians. Why would you think he was a first-rate sniper?"

"Because he missed. A bad, or even an average shooter, would have hit someone or something. The fact that he didn't tells me that the miss was intentional."

"And the objective?" But he already knew.

"I know that Zoe is involved in some kind of investigation regarding the disappearance, and possibly the death, of your nightclub singer, Lola Malone." Ray took a sip of his beer. "Maybe my little girl is getting a little too close to the truth, and whoever took that shot—a hired assassin, or maybe the killer himself—wanted to scare her into backing off."

Rick shook his head. "It's a good theory but it doesn't hold water. Why scare her? Why not kill her?"

"Good question. One I intend to ask."

"What can I do to help?"

"Keep Zoe safe."

Rick laughed. "That's easier said than done."

"Is she that tough?"

"Tough, ornery, stubborn. She runs the gamut."

The next question came so fast, Rick never saw it coming. "Do you still love her?"

Rick swallowed a mouthful of beer. How the hell did he answer that? It wasn't a yes-or-no question. It was much more complicated than that. As complicated as Zoe herself.

"I think you do," Ray said. "A man doesn't get involved in his ex-wife's affairs the way you have without having strong feelings for her. Am I right?"

Rick gave a shrug that made the older man smile. "I'll take that as a yes. Which brings me to my next question. Why did you let her go?"

"Because we made each other crazy. We thought that loving one another would be enough, but in the end, all that fighting just wore us out."

"Marriage is hard work, son. Anyone who goes into it thinking it'll be a walk in the park is nuts." He was watching Rick closely. "Do you think things could be different now that you're both older?"

"If you mean is there a chance that Zoe and I will get back together, I honestly don't know. In the first place, I have competition."

"Joe?" Ray shook his head. "Don't get me wrong, Joe Santos is a fine man and he seems to love my daughter very much, but from what I've learned about Angie over the years, she's a woman who loves the unexpected, the unpredictable. Like you, she's impulsive, to the point of being reckless at times. Joe is exactly the opposite. He walks a straight line, and he follows orders. I'm not sure he's ever done anything even remotely impulsive in his life. That's why Angie will never love him the way she loved you."

"She's moved on, Ray."

"Six years have passed and she is still alone. What does that tell you?"

"I'm not sure I would want to disappoint her again."

"What makes you think you would?"

"Because there may be too much of the old Rick in me, the pre-Vaughn Rick. The bloodline isn't so great, you know."

"You had a sad childhood."

Rick looked down at his beer. "Yeah, I guess you could say that."

"If you feel like talking, I'm pretty good at listening."

For reasons he couldn't explain, Rick found it easy to talk to this man. "My father left my mother when she became pregnant and she never saw him again. Then my mom started drinking. She lost her job, couldn't pay the rent and eventually, she skipped town, too. Without me."

"How old were you?"

"Ten. That's when I entered the foster program. I hated it, hated my foster family, and they hated me back. I went through three more families, all very undeserving of the dysfunctional child the system had placed in their care. On my thirteenth birthday, I busted a liquor store. The judge gave me a choice—juvy or another foster home. The thought of teaming up with another family didn't thrill me, but it beat being locked up. It turned out the Vaughns were patient, loving people. They had to be, to put up with me."

"You couldn't have been that bad."

"I got better. My grades improved. I started making friends. I even made the varsity football team."

"And after you enlisted in the marines, you applied for Officers Candidate School and were accepted. Why didn't you go?"

"I didn't want to be an officer. I wanted to be a regular marine, you know, one of the guys. I was planning to reenlist when my brother, Simon, died and left me the club."

"You could have hired someone to run Blue Moon."

His marine buddies had told him the same thing. "I thought about it, but Simon cared a lot about that club, and to know that he trusted me to run it touched me more than I can say. I couldn't let him down."

"You did a good job."

Rick met the older man's eyes. There were only two other people who knew about his early life—Lenny and Zoe. "Thank you." He finished his beer. "Where are you staying?"

"The Select, room 123."

"I'll let you know how Zoe takes the news."

"What's your guess? You know her better than I do."

Rick laughed. "If there is one thing I learned during my two-year marriage to Zoe Foster, it was to never try to predict what she's going to do."

Twenty-Four

Zoe had been on pins and needles for over an hour. What was taking Rick so long? Why didn't he call?

At last, she heard the light knock on the door and ran to answer it. Rick walked in without saying a word.

"Well?" She followed him into the living room.

"First of all, the man doesn't want to hurt you."

"You said that already."

"I know. I'm just buying time."

"Just tell me."

"You may want to sit down first."

"I'm not some fragile little thing who's going to become all faint…"

"The man is your father."

She wasn't sure what she experienced first—shock, or anger at Rick for saying something so stupid. "Have you lost your mind?"

"I didn't want to believe it either at first, but once Ray—that's his name—started talking, I knew he was telling the truth. He knows everything about you, Zoe—

all the things you've done since you moved to New York from Philadelphia."

"Stalkers do that. They find out everything about the person they've targeted."

"He's not a stalker."

"Well, he's not my father, either! I told you, my father died!"

"He didn't die. He had to pretend that he did."

Rick's serious expression and his grave tone started to sink in. "My God, you really do believe him. What kind of tale did that man sell you?"

"It's no tale. Your father wasn't an insurance salesman. And he didn't die in an automobile accident. He faked his death, with the help of the FBI. Then he went under the witness protection program and changed his identity. He had to, in order to escape the mob."

The warmth in the loft vanished. Instinctively, she wrapped her arms around herself as a cold fist settled deep into her stomach and began to spread. She had difficulty processing what Rick had just told her. *FBI. Witness protection program. Escape from the mob.* The words hung over her like a dark, ominous cloud. She thought of the man whose photograph had sat by her bedside all these years. A handsome man with eyes you could trust and a smile that made you feel warm and safe.

Confused, she sank into the nearest chair. "Tell me what he said."

He did, with a tenderness and compassion she would remember later. Right now, she was too stunned to experience anything but shock.

By the time Rick was finished, tears were streaming

down her cheeks. She did nothing to stop them. Her father was alive. It was a wish she had included in her evening prayers every night for several years after his death. Three decades later, her wish had finally come true. The life she had led all those years was a lie. Even her name, Zoe Foster, a name she had always felt suited her like a second skin, was a lie.

Questions raced through her mind. She struggled to keep them in some sort of order. "My mother? Does she know?"

"No one knows except Ray's best friend, Lou Agnelli, who's a private investigator, the FBI, and now you and me."

"What did you think of him?" Half an hour wasn't nearly enough time to form an opinion, but Rick was exceptionally astute about people.

"He's a good man, Zoe. He made a wrong choice early in life and he has been paying for his mistake ever since." He hooked a finger under her chin and forced her to look at him. "And he loves you very much. That's why he came to New York. That's why he took such a huge risk."

She was silent for a long time, knees drawn up, arms wrapped around them. She stared out the darkened window, knowing that he was out there, alone, maybe wishing the same thing she was wishing.

At last she returned her gaze to Rick who hadn't taken his eyes off her. She cleared her throat so the words could be clearly heard. "I want to see him."

Rick gave a shake of his head. "Forget it."

"Rick, listen to me." She uncoiled her legs and leaned forward. "I know you think it may be dangerous—"

"There's no maybe about it. Why do you think your father has never approached you in all these years?"

"But if he doesn't look anything like Tony Marcino, what's the problem?"

"His friend Lou is convinced that Frank has had you and your mother watched."

"For thirty years?" She laughed. "Come on, Rick. Even a vendetta freak like Frank Scolini wouldn't waste his time doing something so stupid." She placed a hand on his. "It can be done, Rick. We could arrange something, an outing somewhere. A picnic in the country."

He smiled. "Ten days before Christmas?"

"We could go ice skating then, like old times. What could be more innocent?"

"Why, Zoe Foster. Are you suggesting that we pretend to be in love again? Because if you are…" His eyes shone with mischief. "We would have to make it realistic."

Feeling bold, she asked, "What did you have in mind?"

He stood up, braced his hands on her chair's armrests and leaned forward. "I don't know. I'm open to suggestions."

She felt his breath brush her face. Up close like this, she could see the little golden specks in his eyes. Something inside her stirred. Her gaze went to his mouth, and she was filled with a sudden and irresistible need to kiss him, taste him, touch him. The thought thrilled her and frightened her at the same time.

Before she could give in to the temptation, she pulled back, covering her confusion with a shaky smile. "Why don't you talk to Ray and see what he has to say. We'll take it from there."

He gave her a long, semi-amused, semi-serious look before he, too, pulled away. "I'll do that," he said. "Will you be all right?"

If she said no, would he stay? Instead, she stood up. Together, they walked to the door. "I'll be fine. Call me as soon as you've talked to him."

Twenty-Five

Veneti Disposal in Queens was a far cry from the small family business Ray remembered. For one thing, the original building had been torn down and rebuilt and was now twice the size. The fenced back lot had also been expanded, and contained more than twenty trash-collecting trucks instead of the three Peppe's father had owned.

Ray parked his rented Toyota in a visitor's space in front of the main entrance and walked in. A half-dozen glassed-in offices with dispatchers manning state-of-the-art computers lined one side. The rest of the space was used as a garage where mechanics in blue overalls were busy working on three trucks that had been pulled into the bays.

A female employee wearing jeans and a sweatshirt that read Love Me, Love My Trash, walked by. Ray stopped her and asked for the boss.

"You'll find him in that back office over there." She pointed at another glassed-in room at the far end.

Peppe was on the phone, gesturing the way he always did when he talked. Ray used to tease him that if someone tied his hands behind his back, he wouldn't be able to utter a single word.

Ray stayed out of sight, happy enough to observe his old friend. At fifty-nine, Guiseppe Veneti was older and grayer, but the years didn't seem to have affected his physique. He still looked as if he could pick up one of those trucks in the back lot all by himself.

Sensing perhaps that he was being watched, Peppe looked up, quickly ended the telephone conversation and waved Ray in. He gave him a quick appraisal before standing and offering his hand. "Hi, I'm Peppe Veneti. How can I help you?"

Ray's chest rose and fell with a sigh of relief. He had passed the first test. There hadn't been a flicker of recognition in those watchful brown eyes. Before Ray told him the truth, Peppe would have to pass a test of his own. "My name is Ray Dougherty," he said, hoping he wouldn't recognize the voice, "I'm trying to locate an old friend I was told you know well."

Peppe sat down, waving for Ray to do the same. "What's his name?"

"Tony Marcino."

Peppe looked at him hard. "Tony died thirty years ago."

Ray did his best to look dismayed. "Damn. What happened?"

Peppe replied with a question of his own. "How exactly did you know Tony?"

"We met in 'Nam. We were stationed at Da Nang together in '71. When he was sent back home at the end of his tour, we promised to keep in touch but didn't. You know how it is."

"No. I keep track of my friends."

Ray held back a smile. Peppe was never one to mince words.

Peppe continued to scrutinize him. "So, you lost touch with Tony after the war, and now, thirty-five years later, you decide to look him up?"

"I've had a few problems. Now that I have more time on my hands, I thought I'd do a little traveling and look up my old friends."

"Well, have a good time in New York." Assuming the conversation was over, Peppe stood up.

But Ray wasn't ready to leave just yet. "You didn't tell me how Tony died."

"He was shot."

"Shot? Jesus. Where? How?"

"It's a long story and I don't know you, so if you don't mind…" Peppe's legendary brush-off drove his point home. He wasn't going to say another word about his late friend.

"Of course. I'm sorry. But before I go." Ray took a scrap of paper from his pocket and glanced at it. "Tony had mentioned three other buddies—JoJo, Deano and Manny. Any idea where I can find them? I'd like to say hello."

"Deano retired and moved to Florida, and JoJo passed away about a year ago." His voice turned bitter. "I haven't seen Manny since the funeral."

Ray couldn't help a little dig of his own. "I thought you kept track of your friends."

"Only those worth keeping track of."

Point taken. Manny, for an unknown reason, was no longer part of the loop.

"Sorry I couldn't be more help," Peppe said. "Now, if you don't mind, I've got a business to run."

They stood face-to-face, the two forces that had held the mighty foursome together. It would be good to see the look on Peppe's face when Ray told him the truth.

He was trying to think of a way to break the news to him, when a man in blue overalls came rushing in.

"Peppe, we need you out there. Luke and Charlene are at it again. I'm telling you, that broad is trouble. It's the second fight she's started this week. The men are fed up."

Peppe was already out the door. Ray followed them to the outside area and saw the woman he had talked to earlier giving lip to a man. Both were screaming obscenities at each other.

"Is there anything I can do?" Ray asked.

Peppe stopped for a moment and turned. "Yeah, you can leave. This is private business."

Ray backed off. Obviously, this was not the time to drop a bomb on Peppe's lap. He had enough to deal with right now. "I understand. Maybe I can catch you another time."

He wasn't sure Peppe heard him.

Ray and Lou had planned to meet for lunch at La Bonne Soupe, an unpretentious bistro-type restaurant on Fifty-fifth Street Lou had discovered years ago. He was already there, standing on the sidewalk, dressed for the Arctic, while a fat man in a Santa suit rang a bell and belted out *ho ho hos*. Ray took a dollar bill from his pocket and dropped it into the Salvation Army kettle.

"Thank you, sir, and Merry Christmas to you."

"About time you got here," Lou mumbled, stomping his feet. "I'm freezing out here."

Ray opened the door and gave Lou a gentle shove. "Stop complaining and get in there."

They had to wait fifteen minutes for a table, but once they were seated, a waitress showed up right away and took their orders—vegetable soup and water for Lou, a steak, French fries and a glass of merlot for Ray.

"So, how did it go with Peppe?" Lou asked.

"He hasn't changed much. He's still the same tough, crusty guy I used to know."

"You learn anything about the others?"

"Yeah. JoJo is dead, Deano's in Florida and Manny's no longer a friend. I sensed some bad blood there."

"Stay away from him, then."

"I intend to."

"And I'd be careful about Peppe, too. The man is tied to the mob."

"That's why he can help me."

"He could also turn you in."

"He won't."

"You don't know that. You spent ten minutes with the guy."

"Ten minutes, ten hours. When you know somebody, you don't need a lot of time to decide if you can trust him or not. As it turned out, we were interrupted before I had a chance to tell him who I really was."

"Take that as an omen, Ray." A good Catholic, Lou pointed upward. "The big guy sent you a sign."

The waitress returned with their orders and Ray was spared from having to tell Lou that he was planning on a return visit to Veneti Disposal soon. "Let's forget about Peppe for now." Ray cut into his steak and pretended not to notice Lou's look of disapproval as he looked at his plate. Lou had never been a big meat eater, but the fear of mad cow disease had turned him off beef forever. "I have other news."

Lou dunked a piece of crusty bread into his soup. "About what?"

"I ran into Rick."

"Rick Vaughn?" When Ray nodded, Lou's expression turned suspicious. "There are eight million people in New York. How did you manage to *run into* Rick?"

Ray took a sip of his wine. "He spotted me following Angie and he flattened me against the wall. Nearly broke my neck. That's definitely not a man you want to piss off—"

Lou's spoon clattered into his bowl. "Jesus Christ, Ray. What were you doing following Zoe? I thought you were going to leave the P.I. work to me. You know zip about surveillance."

"I wanted to see her, okay?"

"What happened with Rick?"

"I had to tell him the truth."

Lou looked as if he was about to have a heart attack. "You didn't!"

"I had no choice. He was going to call the cops."

"I knew it." Lou pushed his bowl away. "Didn't I tell

you something like that would happen? Didn't I tell you this trip would be a complete fiasco?"

"You are the absolute voice of gloom and doom, you know that, Lou?"

"I'm the voice of common sense and it wouldn't hurt you to listen to it once in a while." To his credit, he took a calming breath and spoke quietly. "Did you at least tell him to keep quiet about your identity?"

"He's going to have to tell Zoe. Don't roll your eyes at me. She was there. She saw the whole thing. You know damn well that she's not going to let up until he's told her everything."

"I should have never let you come here," Lou muttered under his breath. "I should have tied you to the bedpost until you came to your senses."

"Everything's going to be all right. Now finish your soup or I'll force-feed you half of this steak."

Lou mumbled something unintelligible, pulled his bowl back and started eating.

Twenty-Six

Zoe sat in the back of the Greyhound bus that was taking her to Cape May, and watched the vast farmlands of New Jersey flash by her window while she reflected on the incredible news she had received last night.

Her father was alive. The sadness and yearning she had experienced years ago, as she watched her little friends interact with their fathers, were now a distant memory. At long last she, too, had someone she could call Daddy, and although she understood that they could never be a family again, the way they used to be, she thrilled at the thought of getting to know him.

But before they were reunited for the first time, Zoe needed to know much more than what Rick had told her. Above all, she wanted to know why her mother had kept the truth from her all these years. Why not tell her who her father was when she was old enough to hear it? Why keep up this complicated charade, those phony photographs and fabricated memories?

At last, the steady hum of the engine slowed, and the

bus pulled up in front of the Cape May Transportation Center on Lafayette Street. Stepping out, Zoe inhaled the crisp salt air. Gray and misty at this time of year, Cape May was still a good ten degrees warmer than New York. And snow free.

Discovered by a Dutch sea captain in the seventeenth century, the town had the distinction of being the oldest seashore resort in the country as well as the most pictur-esque. By far, Cape May's most popular attraction was the town's collection of authentic Victorian structures. Some had been converted into bed-and-breakfasts, others were still privately owned and occupied by families that had been here for generations.

The Rose Cottage was in the heart of the historic dis-trict and a short walk from the bus depot. It had been built in 1859 by a Philadelphia railroad baron with deep pock-ets and an eye for grandeur. Four years ago, the mansion was put up for sale and Catherine Foster had sold every-thing she owned, borrowed the balance and bought the property.

After months of renovation, the three-story house, which Catherine had named the Rose Cottage, had be-come one of the most attractive B&Bs in town.

It was a little after eleven, and the streets were already filled with visitors who had come to celebrate Christmas week or take part in the famous Candlelight House Tour. The Rose Cottage, painted a pale pink, looked as festive as its neighbors, with pinecone-studded wreaths hang-ing from every window and a huge Christmas tree on the front porch.

The aroma of gingerbread wafted through the door as

Zoe pushed it open. The foyer was bursting with holiday decorations—stuffed Santas, handmade Christmas pillows, glittering stockings, giant candles and other holiday items her mother had accumulated over the years. Another tree, this one laden with Victorian ornaments, stood in one corner.

"How about some service out here?" Zoe shouted.

Almost immediately, the clatter of rapid footsteps resonated on the hardwood floor. "Zoe!" Catherine Foster rushed toward her daughter. "I don't believe it. You changed your mind!"

Always elegant, even when she was helping Lulu in the kitchen, Catherine wore dark green slacks and a cranberry turtleneck. Her blond hair, still untouched by gray, was cut in a classic bob that fitted her delicate features perfectly. With those clear blue eyes and flawless complexion, she looked at least ten years younger than her fifty-four years and showed no signs of having suffered a heart attack a year ago.

After giving Zoe a warm hug, Catherine released her and held her at arm's length. "Let me look at you. No, you haven't changed. You're still the beautiful daughter I love dearly."

Zoe laughed. "Oh, Mom, it hasn't been that long."

"Almost three months."

"If you miss me so much, why don't you come to New York once in a while? You haven't been up since you helped me decorate the loft."

"Oh, you know how I hate the city. Twenty-five years was long enough." She looked around. "Where's your luggage?"

"I don't have any. I only came for the day."

"Why?"

"Because I'm behind in my work and I need to get back."

Catherine's good mood remained unruffled. "In that case, we'll make the most of those few hours. Let's start by saying hello to Lulu. We just finished baking gingerbread for our four o'clock tea. I'm sure she'll let you sample a slice."

Lulu, a stout Jamaican who had been the previous owners' cook, was delighted to see Zoe and equally eager to feed her. She and Catherine had hit it off right from the start and were more like best friends than employer/employee.

"Here's a little something that will keep you until lunch." Lulu slid a thick slice of gingerbread onto a dainty china plate and handed it to her. "It so happens that I made one of your favorites today—Southern corn chowder. I must be psychic."

"Not to mention the best baker in town," Zoe said, her mouth full. "My mother is lucky to have you."

Catherine took Zoe's arm and pulled her away. "Come on," she said with a small laugh. "Let's go upstairs before the compliment goes to Lulu's head and she asks me for a raise."

"Watch out what you say, Blondie." Lulu shook her silver spatula at her. "My voodoo doll is never far away."

"Upstairs" was the third-floor tower, with its white wicker furniture and spectacular view. From the window, Zoe could see the town trolley shuttling visitors from one event to another.

When she turned back, her mother was seated and calmly observing her. "So." She patted the cushion next to her. "Are you going to tell me what brings you down? Or shall we play Twenty Questions?"

Zoe smiled as she sat down. "Am I that transparent?"

"No, but as you reminded me just a minute ago, you are a very busy girl, which means that you wouldn't have taken an entire day from your schedule to come down unless you had something to say that couldn't be said over the phone." Then, looking suddenly concerned, she added, "You haven't been shot at again, have you?"

"No, and you'll be happy to know that my days as an amateur detective are over. The police are now officially handling the disappearance of Lola Malone."

"That *is* good news. Now." She crossed her legs and looked at Zoe expectantly. "Tell me what's on your mind."

"First, you have to promise you won't get upset," Zoe said.

"Oh, dear. I don't think I like the sound of that."

"Promise?"

"All right, I promise. And stop treating me like an invalid. I'm in better shape now than I ever was. Need I remind you that I came in third in the marathon this past spring?"

"I always said that you were an amazing woman." Zoe studied her fingernails for a moment, unsure how to start. Then, because she was always more comfortable with a direct approach, she said, "I know about Dad."

Catherine's eyes widened slightly. "What do you mean, honey?"

"I mean I know that he wasn't an insurance salesman. And that he wasn't killed in a car accident."

Catherine let out a nervous laugh. "But of course he was an insurance salesman. Where did you get the crazy idea that he wasn't?"

"Dad was a *conciglieri* for the head of a Philadelphia crime family, a man who is now serving a ninety-nine-year sentence in a federal prison. Do I need to continue?"

Catherine's cheeks drained of all color. She slowly fell back against the chair's puffy white cushion. "My God."

"It's not the end of the world, Mom. In fact—"

"Who have you been talking to?"

"That's not important."

"Of course it's important! If someone has been feeding you lies about your father—"

"Mom, stop it. They're not lies. I know the truth. All of it." She told her what she had learned, but did not tell her about Ray's reappearance into the world of the living. She was afraid the shock might be too much for her.

Catherine listened, her teeth clamped on her bottom lip.

"Why didn't you tell me?" Zoe asked when she was finished. She kept her voice gentle and free of reproach. "Why did you let me worship a man who didn't exist?"

A small resigned sigh escaped from Catherine's lips. The make-believe was over and she knew it. "I was afraid of what the truth would do to you. You were so proud of who you were, of what you had accomplished."

"I could have handled it."

"Could you really? Were you ready to hear that your

father worked for the mob? That he was gunned down by his own people? That his boss was a man who made his money selling drugs to children, prostituting women and arranging contract killings?" Her voice broke and she turned her head away.

Zoe gave her mother's hand a gentle squeeze. "I'm ready now, Mom."

Catherine stared out the window for a long time. "He was a good man," she said, echoing Rick's words. "He was kind, loving and generous. I met him after I graduated from design school in Manhattan. He was a junior associate in a law firm and making decent money. It was enough for me, but not for Tony. He had big dreams. He wanted a fancy house, a luxury car, private schools for the children we were planning to have. And he liked to shower me with gifts, gifts I repeatedly told him I didn't need."

She toyed with the crease in her pants. "Shortly after you were born, his friend Peppe Veneti introduced him to Frank Scolini, who at the time was the most powerful mobster on the East Coast. I hated him on sight. I told Tony to stay away from him. But Frank offered him a position on his legal staff at three times the salary he was earning at Berns and Jacovich.

"Tony and I argued for days. It was like talking to a brick wall. All he could see was the money and what it would do for us and for the baby. We moved to Philadelphia, and soon your father had everything he had always wanted—a beautiful house, an expensive car and all the luxuries money could buy."

"And you hated it."

"With every fiber of my being." She let out a trembling sigh. "But I stayed by his side and probably would have remained there, if it hadn't been for an incident that put the fear of God into me."

"Rocco Pugliese's execution."

She raised a brow. "You know about that?"

Zoe nodded. "Go on," she said before Catherine could question her.

"When Frank was arrested, Rocco took over. One morning, as he was about to take his little boy to pre-school, his car blew up. Both Rocco and little Robby were killed." She closed her eyes for a moment as she relived the tragedy. "We thought his wife, Gina, would lose her mind. I had never seen so much grief in my life."

"That's when I gave Tony a choice, although he called it an ultimatum. I asked him to choose between Frank and us. He fought me hard, swearing that he was safe, that Frank, even though he was in jail and awaiting trial, would never let anything happen to him, but we both knew he was lying. Everyone in the organization was either under scrutiny from the feds, or at risk of being gunned down by a rival syndicate trying to take over Frank's operation."

"So Dad let you go?"

"He didn't want to, but I held my ground. Three months after I served him with the papers, we were divorced. You and I moved to New York City. Once there, I changed our names, found a job and started a new life."

"What about my grandparents? You told me they were dead."

"Part of that is true. My parents did die in a freak accident while cruising the Caribbean. Your father's parents were alive when Tony was killed. I don't know if they still are."

"You haven't kept in touch with them?"

Her smile was bitter. "*They're* the ones who didn't keep in touch with us. When Tony went to work for Frank, they broke all ties with their son and moved to Florida. Not even the birth of their little granddaughter could turn them around."

"How did you hear that Dad had been killed?"

"I read it in the papers. A piece of me died with him that day." Tears spilled out and she wiped them off her cheeks with her hands.

Zoe wrapped her arms around her. "Don't be upset, Mom. It happened a long time ago."

"I'll never be able to forget it. Or to forgive myself."

"You have nothing to forgive yourself for. You did what you had to to keep me safe. I understand that."

"No, you don't. You see, what happened to your father, the horrible way he died, that was my fault."

"Don't say that."

Catherine pulled her hand away and took a tissue from a silver box on the wicker table beside her. "After Tony was arrested, he called me and said that the feds were offering him a deal. I told him to take it. I promised that if he cooperated with the authorities and told them what they needed to know in order to convict Frank, the three of us would get back together and start fresh. That's why he did it. If I hadn't promised to take him back, he would have never agreed to testify against Frank."

She started to cry. "I killed him, Zoe. I killed my husband. That's why I kept quiet. I didn't want to tell you that I was responsible for your father's death."

Zoe found it difficult to hold back her own tears. "Mom, stop, please."

The tears continued; pathetic, heart-wrenching sobs that rocked her fragile shoulders.

Zoe had never seen her mother in such a state. If she had known how deeply this was going to affect her, she would have never said a word.

"I did it, Zoe. I killed your father."

"Shh." Zoe wrapped her arms around her and held her. "You didn't kill him." She kept her voice just above a whisper. "Because he didn't die."

Catherine almost stopped breathing. Swollen eyes met Zoe's. "What did you say?"

"Dad didn't die. He's alive."

Catherine shook her head. "I don't understand."

"I saw him, Mom. He's in New York."

"What are you talking about? How could you have seen him? You don't know what he looks like."

She waited until Catherine had calmed down enough before she told her the rest of her story.

"Tony is alive?" Catherine looked dazed.

"Very much so." Zoe smiled. "So you see, there's nothing for you to feel guilty about anymore."

"I can't believe it." She pressed the back of her head against the cushion and sank her fingers into her carefully styled hair. "Tony is alive. He's been alive all these years." Her features tightened. "And he never let me know? He never sent me a sign?"

"He didn't want to put us at risk."

"He's putting you at risk now, isn't he? By following you around, standing outside your apartment."

"Frank is no longer watching us, Mom. Not after all this time."

"Oh, baby, you're so wrong. You don't know about the people you're dealing with. You don't know how ruthless they are, how unforgiving." She made a ball of the tissue and patted her eyes. "Don't get me wrong. I'm glad your father is alive. And I'm glad that he still cared enough to come to New York when he thought you needed help. But that's over now. You're safe, and he can go back to San Diego."

Zoe was silent.

"Zoe?" Catherine searched her daughter's face. "He *is* going back, isn't he?"

"Not until he finds out who fired those shots."

Catherine gave a violent shake of her head. "To do that, he'll have to reveal who he is and put you in danger. Talk to Rick, honey. From what you told me, he likes Tony and Tony likes him. Maybe Tony'll listen to him."

"I'm the one who asked to see Dad."

Catherine's face fell. "No! You can't."

"I'll be safe. Rick is taking care of everything."

"Rick is a fool! I was hoping he had changed, but he is just as reckless as ever. If he took time to think—"

"He tried to talk me out of it."

"Apparently he didn't try hard enough."

"I don't want to argue with you, Mom. My mind is made up. I want to see Dad." She stood up and held out her hand. "Why don't you and I go for a stroll around town. I need to work up an appetite for Lulu's corn chowder."

After a slight hesitation, Catherine dried her tears and took Zoe's hand.

Twenty-Seven

Prison gave Vince Scolini the willies. In all the years he had been visiting his brother Frank, he had never gotten used to the smell, the filthy walls and the sound, an eerie kind of shuffling the prisoners made when they were being escorted into the visiting room.

Unlike his brother and his father before that, Vince had never wanted any part of the business. Studious and hardworking, he'd had other aspirations, and he had achieved them, in spite of his father's constant pressures.

Vince liked his job as a sportswriter for the *Philadelphia Sun.* Younger than Frank by fifteen years, he was just a boy when his brother was hauled off to jail, but he remembered that morning as if it was yesterday. Mostly he remembered his mother's anguish when two federal agents had clamped the cuffs on her oldest boy's wrists. She had died ten years later. A widow by then, she had begged Vince to look after Frank, even though he was in prison. "Promise me you'll always look after your brother," his mother had pleaded from her deathbed. "Always protect him."

Vince adored his mother, and although he wasn't sure what he could do for Frank that his henchmen couldn't, he had promised to always be there for him. Surprisingly, Frank had been a model prisoner, patiently waiting to come up for parole. Already turned down twice, he remained optimistic. "The third time's the charm," he often told Vince.

Faithful to his promise, Vince had visited Frank every week, bringing him books, cigarettes, shaving cream and anything else the guards would let through. Every now and then Vince's wife would bake Frank's favorite brownies, which Frank graciously shared with his jailers. The gesture earned Frank a few perks that made life behind bars easier.

Today, Vince had come empty-handed. He had been too preoccupied with what he had found out to think about bringing a goody bag.

At last, the door opened and Frank walked in. He wore the standard orange suit and shuffled toward the plate-glass window that separated the prisoners from the visitors. Short and bald, he no longer deserved the nickname that had once fitted him so well—Frank the Whale. After losing close to a hundred and fifty pounds, he had decided to keep the weight off with a workout program he had devised himself and now taught to other inmates during the morning recess. His dedication to "bettering the system," as he put it, had earned him brownie points galore, from the prisoners as well as the administrative staff.

"Hi, Frank."

"Hi, little brother." Frank sat down. "What's up?"

"Not much."

Frank's eyes squinted to mere slits. "Really? Then how come I'm not believing you?"

Vince had never been good at keeping secrets from his brother. Or maybe Frank was too good at reading people.

Vince turned his head, just enough to see the door in his peripheral vision. The guard had left them alone. That was one of the perks Frank enjoyed and he never missed a chance to tell Vince, "They're not bad guys. You rub their backs, they rub yours, if you know what I mean."

"So what is it, bro? Did World War III break out while I wasn't looking?"

There was no point in lying. Frank had already guessed that something was up, and one way or another, he would find out, if not from Vince, then from one of his men.

Vince took a deep breath and released it. "Somebody in New York's been asking about Tony Marcino."

Frank's features seemed to freeze. "Who?"

"Guy by the name of Ray Dougherty."

"Never heard of him."

"He's from San Diego. He owns a hardware store there. Apparently, he didn't know Tony was dead."

"What's he doing in New York?"

"He says he's on vacation and is using the time to look up a couple of old buddies."

"Who has he been talking to?"

"Guiseppe Veneti."

"The trash guy?"

Vince nodded.

"How do you know all this?"

"Veneti was playing poker with your old pal Alberto Vigna. They meet about once a month, either in Philly or in New York. That same night, Alberto called me."

"Why didn't he call me?"

"He was afraid to. He heard that the phone lines are no longer secure."

"That's true. Some moron used the prison's phone to buy cocaine, can you believe it? Now the brass is monitoring all calls, incoming and outgoing. What else did Alberto tell you?"

"Just that Peppe thought the whole thing was a little bizarre. Here's this guy who claims to be a good friend of Tony's, but Peppe's never heard of him."

Frank was silent. Whenever he fell into deep thought, he did it with his eyes closed and his fingers interlaced and resting on his chest. Anyone watching him would have thought he had dozed off.

"Okay." Frank opened his eyes. "Here's what you do. Call Alberto back. Tell him to get me the goods on this Ray Dougherty. Everything he can find out, including where he's staying."

"How can he—?"

"Alberto knows how. Just give him the message."

"What are you going to do?" Vince didn't bother to hide the worry in his voice. "You're coming up for parole in less than three months. You don't want to do anything to mess that up, do you?"

Frank stood up. "Come back when you have the information, kid. And next time bring something for the guards."

Twenty-Eight

"Hi, Rick."

"Well, hello there," Rick said· after he recognized Jenny's voice on the phone. "How's everything in the Big Easy?"

"Better than I thought it would be. Rosa has been showering me with kindness."

"And the bruises?"

"Still there but getting better. In another week, I'll be as good as new."

It felt good to hear her sounding so positive. A few days ago, she had been ready to give up.

"Did you hear from Mike?" Jenny asked.

"Not personally, but I understand that the cops are giving him a hard time."

"You told them?" Alarm filled her voice.

"I had to. Brenner and I had a little tussle during which he made the mistake of threatening my ex-wife."

"He won't do anything, Rick. Mike only goes after

people who can't defend themselves. With you watching over Zoe, he won't dare lay a finger on her."

"Maybe so, but the following day, someone standing on a rooftop fired two shots at Zoe."

"Oh, no! Was she hit?"

"No. No one was, but a Detective Robinson is now in charge of the sniper's case. He and Detective O'Bryan, who is investigating Lola's disappearance, came to see me to find out if I knew of anyone who had a grudge against Zoe. I had to mention Mike and his threats."

"And I bet he's blaming me for all his woes."

"It doesn't matter. With the cops sniffing down his back, he has to remain on his best behavior. Now, are you ready for some good news?"

He heard her laugh. "Sure."

"I called a couple of nightclub owners I know in New Orleans. You got a pen and paper?"

"Wait a minute." He heard the sound of a drawer being opened, then closed. "Go ahead."

"Andy Specter. He runs a nightclub called Sunset in the French Quarter. The other is Tomas Santana, the owner of the Latin Room. Both want to talk to you, so as soon as you feel up to it, give them a call."

He gave her both numbers and waited for her to say something, but there was only silence at the end of the line. "You're not crying again, are you?"

"A little." She sniffed. "How will I ever repay you?"

"You can start by singing your heart out for my two pals. My reputation is on the line here."

"I think I can do that."

* * *

A steady rain was falling over Manhattan when Zoe's Greyhound bus pulled into New York's Port Authority at nine-thirty that night. Glad that she had packed her rain-gear, she reached into her bag, took out a hot-pink vinyl hat that matched her boots and tucked her hair into it.

Too restless to go home, she decided to stop at Blue Moon, which was only a short cab ride away. Rick should have had a chance to talk to Ray by now and she was anxious to hear her father's reaction to her request. The thought that she could have done that with a phone call made her smile. *Admit it, you want to see him.*

All right, guilty. In the last week, she had become ac-customed to seeing Rick or hearing from him almost every day, and when she didn't, she missed him. No longer having him around had been one of the most dif-ficult adjustments she'd had to make after the divorce. She had walked around the apartment for days, crying like a baby as she second-guessed her decision to leave him. It had taken her weeks to convince herself that life could go on without Rick, and that somewhere out there was a man she could love as much as she had loved her ex-husband. She had been fooling herself.

Ten minutes later, her cab stopped in front of Blue Moon. A tall man who reminded her of Lurch, The Adams Family solemn-faced butler, stood just inside the frosted door, watching the entrance.

She flashed him a smile. "Hi. Are you Stretch?"

He looked down at her but didn't return the smile. Lenny, who was at his post behind the bar, raised a hand. "It's okay, Stretch. That's Zoe Foster."

The tall man gave her a closer look. "Sorry," he said in a soft baritone. "I didn't recognize you without the hair."

She took the hat off and shook out her red curls. "Is that better?"

His face broke into a grin. "Yes, ma'am. Much."

"Hi, doll." Lenny picked up a bottle of VSOP cognac and started mixing up a Sloppy Joe. As he added grenadine to the shaker, Zoe scanned the crowded bar. It wasn't long until she spotted Rick, looking as handsome as ever in his tuxedo. He wasn't alone. Sitting beside him was a stunning brunette in a low-cut blue-beaded dress. Her head was bent toward him and they seemed to be having a great time, talking in hushed tones and laughing softly. Zoe felt a prickle of jealousy.

"Who's the bimbo?" she asked Lenny.

The bartender added a few drops of Grand Marnier to the mixture and gave it a good shake. "That's our new chanteuse."

"What happened to the other girl? Jenny?"

"Rick didn't tell you? He decided to let her go. When her boyfriend heard, he got pissed off and messed her up pretty bad."

"That's terrible. Is she all right?"

"Yeah, thanks to Rick."

Lenny poured the red drink into a frosty martini glass and placed it in front of her. At that exact time, sunny laughter erupted at the other end of the bar. "And now you have a new singer."

"Not singer. *Chanteuse.* She insists on being called that."

"What's the difference?"

He laughed. "No idea. She sounds like a singer to me."

"Rick certainly didn't waste any time getting chummy with her."

"She's a friendly sort of gal. Made herself right at home."

Zoe took a sip of her drink. "You don't say."

Rick chose that precise moment to turn around. When he saw Zoe, who barely had time to paste a civilized expression on her face, he waved. Then, holding Miss Plunging Neckline's hand, he helped her climb off her stool and together they walked over to where Zoe sat.

"I didn't know you were planning to stop by," Rick said, lightly kissing her cheek. "Everything all right?"

She gave him a sweet smile. "Peachy."

Rick drew the brunette close until they made a cozy threesome. "You're just in time to meet our new chanteuse, Chandra van Doren. Chandra, this is Zoe Foster, the creator of *Kitty Floyd, P.I.*"

Chandra gave Zoe an impersonal appraisal, her gaze drifting all the way down to the pink boots before she offered a limp hand. "I don't read the funnies," she said. "But Rick told me about your cartoon."

I bet you don't read much of anything. "Actually, it's called a comic strip." Zoe took the woman's delicate hand and gave it a hearty squeeze, smiling inwardly when she saw her wince.

When the brunette managed to extract her hand from Zoe's grip, she took Rick's wrist and glanced at his watch. "I'd better go freshen up. It's almost time for my second set." She gave Zoe a frosty smile. "Nice to have met you, Zoe."

"Same here, Sandra."

"That's *Chandra*."

"Zoe will stay for a while, won't you?" Rick asked. "Chandra needs all the support she can get."

"I'd be happy to." Zoe smiled brightly. "Do you take requests?"

Somewhere behind the bar Lenny chuckled.

Chandra's tone turned slightly condescending. "Blue Moon isn't that kind of club."

And the new *chanteuse* had no sense of humor.

Suddenly, the man on the next stool bumped into Zoe, who was propelled forward. While she managed to hold on to her glass, she wasn't as lucky with the contents. The red drink spilled onto Chandra's gown, soaking the entire front.

While Rick tapped the careless man on the shoulder and asked him to be a little more careful, the singer let out a horrified gasp. The spreading stain had turned the blue gown an ugly shade of purple.

"I am so sorry," Zoe said. "There was nothing I could do." It was the truth, but Chandra's dark look told her she didn't believe her. "Maybe some club soda—"

"Never mind," Chandra snapped. "I'll go and change."

She strode off, her back ramrod straight, although she didn't forget to sway her hips as she went, undoubtedly for Rick's benefit.

"I am truly sorry," Zoe said again.

Rick waved the apology off. "Don't worry about it. It wasn't your fault."

"I feel as though I ruined a romantic moment," she threw in.

Rick looked startled. "What romantic moment?"

She feigned an innocent look. "Between you and your girlfriend."

"Chandra is not my girlfriend."

"You could have fooled me."

Rick laughed. "If I didn't know any better, I'd swear you were jealous."

She scoffed. "Oh, please. We're not in high school. And isn't it a little vain on your part to think that your ex-wife is jealous of your relationships with other women?"

"So you didn't come here tonight to check out my new singer?"

"I didn't even know you *had* a new singer until Lenny told me."

He wouldn't give up. "You just wanted to see me?"

"Wrong again. I wanted to let you know that I went to Cape May today. I just got off the bus, in fact."

The smile faded. "You told your mother about Ray?"

"I had to. There were questions that she alone could answer."

"How did it go?"

"Not well. If I had known she would react the way she did, I would have stayed home."

"You had to know she would be shocked."

"It was more than that. She blames herself for my father's death. The memories were so painful for her, the burden of guilt so heavy, I had no choice but to tell her he was still alive. I know how you feel," she added. "You promised my father to keep the matter quiet, but the list of people who know that Tony Marcino is alive keeps growing."

"I'm sure we can trust Catherine not to tell anyone."

Lenny stopped by with the shaker. "How about a refill?"

"No, thanks, Lenny. I've done enough damage for one night." She waited until he had walked away before asking Rick, "Have you heard from my father?"

"Not yet. I left a message at the hotel where he's staying, but he hasn't gotten back to me."

"What if he doesn't?"

"He will."

"You trust him that much?"

"Never give up on a marine. That's my motto."

They were interrupted by the sound of warm applause. Zoe glanced at the stage, which had gone dark except for the spotlight in the center. Chandra stepped into it, a seductive smile on her lips.

She had changed into a strapless black-and-white gown that skimmed every curve of her body without being tight. Zoe reluctantly gave her points for style. The band struck a familiar tune and the singer took command of the room.

She had a lot of Lola's pizzazz, Zoe admitted to herself. She was also smart enough not to copy Blue Moon's former singer. Instead, she gave each song her personal touch and made it uniquely hers.

"So," Rick said after a while. "What do you think?"

"She's okay. Lola was better."

"You're prejudiced."

"Maybe." Zoe took her eyes off the brunette. "Did you hear that Rudy Goldberg was killed?"

"Detective O'Bryan told me."

"Detective O'Bryan came here?"

"And Detective Robinson. He's investigating the sniper's incident. You've made me a popular guy."

"What did they want?"

"They thought I could tell them who may have had a grudge against you."

"How would you know that? We've been divorced for six years. You don't know the people I know."

"I know of one potential enemy."

"Who?"

"Mike Brenner. He's Jenny's boyfriend—*former* boy-friend."

"What does he have to do with me? I've never even met him."

"He didn't like my butting in between him and Jenny. Before we parted company, he swore he'd get back at me by coming after you. He's lucky I didn't kill him."

Her heart melted. After all this time, he was still trying to protect her. "Well, you won't have to worry about me anymore. I've given up my little sideline as a private investigator."

"How come? Not that I'm complaining."

"All I really wanted was for the police to start investigating Lola's disappearance. Now that they have, my services are no longer needed." She let out a small chuckle. "Besides, Detective O'Bryan threatened me with jail time if I interfered in what is now official police business."

"I knew there was a reason I liked that man."

Chandra's song was coming to an end. Zoe pushed up her sleeve, exposing a large watch with a wide, hot-pink band and a drawing of Kitty Floyd on the dial. The private investigator was sitting on a stool, long legs crossed, and was blowing gently on a smoking gun.

"Is that something new?" Rick asked.

"My Kitty watch? Sort of. E.J. had it made for me and gave it to me for my birthday. I love it."

She slid off her stool. "I'd better go. Would you mind calling me a cab?"

"I'll do better than that." He took her arm. "I'll take you home myself."

Twenty-Nine

"Kleenex?" Zoe held the box out to Lizzy.

Lizzy sniffed and took a tissue. "Thanks."

Rick had dropped Zoe off at the loft moments before Lizzy called to say that she was stopping by for their annual ritual. Zoe had immediately put a bag of popcorn in the microwave, made sure there were plenty of tissues on hand and slid *It's A Wonderful Life* into the DVD player. Watching the holiday classic together at this time of year was a tradition the two friends had observed ever since Zoe had returned home from college.

As James Stewart picked up his little girl in the movie's final scene, with a radiant Donna Reed by his side, Zoe wiped away a tear. "No matter how many times I watch this movie, I always cry at the end."

"What do you mean at the end?" Lizzy blew her nose. "You turned on the waterworks half an hour ago."

"I didn't want you to cry alone."

"Want to watch it again?"

"You're not tired?"

"Nope."

"In that case, instead of the movie, why don't we watch something shorter. Like Detective O'Bryan's six o'clock news conference. I taped it. No tissues required."

"That's right, you weren't here today."

"What makes you say that?"

"I tried to call you and couldn't get you. Even your cell phone was turned off." Lizzy took another handful of popcorn from the fresh bowl Zoe had brought out moments ago. "Where were you?"

Zoe wasn't ready to tell her about Ray, so she did the first thing she could think of, she pretended not to have heard the question. "There he is," she said as the detective appeared on the screen.

As O'Bryan introduced himself to the media, Zoe couldn't help admiring his poise and diplomacy in handling the reporters who crowded the sidewalk. With a possible connection between Lola's disappearance, Rudy's murder and the sniper incident, public pressure was increasing and the press demanded answers. The sniper in particular was on everyone's mind.

"What are you doing to find him?" a man in the front row asked. "How can you reassure a city of eight million people that they will be safe during this holiday season?"

"Believe me, we all share your concerns," O'Bryan replied. "We are talking to witnesses, questioning business owners and searching all five boroughs. Unfortunately, the sniper could be hundreds of miles away by now."

A woman raised her hand. "Can you guarantee that there won't be another shooting?"

"I'd rather let Detective Robinson of the First Precinct answer questions regarding the sniper. In the meantime, we're asking the public to be vigilant and to report any suspicious activities."

Dissatisfied with that answer, the assembled crowd grew restless. A reporter Zoe recognized from one of the local stations spoke loudly. "What about Ms. Malone? "What are the chances that she'll be found alive?"

Others immediately chimed in.

"Were there signs of foul play in her apartment?"

"Did she leave a note?"

"Whose fingerprints did you find?"

At the rapid-fire questioning, O'Bryan put up his hand. "Ms. Malone's apartment was clean. By that I mean that we found no sign of a struggle and no blood evidence. We are still in the process of checking with the various airlines and other modes of transportation, but so far we have found nothing to support our earlier theory that she may have left town. As for the fingerprints, those were inconclusive."

"Do you regret not having started your investigation when Zoe Foster reported the crime more than a week ago?"

Lizzy nudged Zoe. "You're famous, girlfriend."

"The *alleged* crime," O'Bryan corrected. "We still don't have any proof that a murder was committed." Before he could be pressed to answer the question, he said a brief thank-you and was gone.

"He's a pretty straight shooter," Lizzy commented. "What do you have against him?"

"I don't have anything against him, other than he

makes me beg for every morsel of information." In the kitchen, the clock bonged twice.

Lizzy put her empty popcorn bowl on the table and stood up. "I'd better let you get some sleep. Hey, you want to go Christmas shopping tomorrow?"

"I'd love to. I still have a few gifts to get."

"Let's meet at noon at the Roc Café. We'll have lunch first, then we'll hit every store between Rockefeller Plaza and Central Park. How's that?"

Zoe wrapped an arm around Lizzy's shoulders and walked her to the door. "*Every* store? You don't even celebrate Christmas."

"Not the way you do." Her eyes shimmered with glee. "But we all like presents."

Vince wished that Alberto had given him better news. Anything but what he had told him. As Gus, one of the guards Vince knew well, escorted him to the visiting room, he kept toying with the idea of not telling Frank what he had found out. Maybe he could fabricate something that made sense, something Frank would believe. Because once he knew the truth, all hell would break loose and Vince would be responsible for the bloodbath that was sure to follow.

He hated to see people hurt. Vince was a pacifist. At the paper they called him "The Mediator" because he was always trying to find a workable solution to other people's problems.

This was different. This was no nickel-and-dime gripe, or a fight for a better parking space. This was a matter of life and death and Vince held fate in his hands.

"Promise me you'll always look after your brother, always protect him."

By keeping the truth from Frank, Vince would be protecting him. He would be fulfilling his mother's wish. He would walk out of this stinking prison with a clean conscience.

There was only one problem. Alberto. How long would it be until he started spreading the news? And how long until Frank heard it?

Once Frank knew that Tony Marcino was alive, his brother's former *conciglieri* wouldn't be the first casualty. Vince would be, for if there was one thing Frank hated more than a snitch, it was to be lied to. The fact that they were brothers wouldn't make any difference. Frank had his own set of values, and betrayal by a family member ranked at the top of the list.

"Here we are." The guard let him into the visiting room where another cubicle was already occupied by a teary young woman on one side of the plate glass and a punk with a shaved head and an attitude on the other.

"Thanks for the cheesecake," Gus said. "The guys are gonna love it. You're one lucky fellow to have a wife who bakes like that. The last time my old lady tried to make a cake, she set fire to the kitchen."

Vince laughed, but only halfheartedly. His mind was on the decision he had to make—tell Frank the truth and watch the carnage, or lie and suffer the consequences. He was chewing his fingernails when they brought Frank in.

"Hey, Frank." He walked over to the chair and sat down.

Frank was watching him. The guy had eyes like radar. They saw right through you.

"Well? The cat got your tongue or what?"

Vince licked his lips. Time was running out. "I was just thinking."

"That's my job. Yours is to bring me the information I asked for."

Forgive me, Ma. "Tony Marcino's alive."

Frank closed his eyes and kept them closed for a good twenty seconds. When he opened them again, his expression was blank. No anger, no emotion, nothing but an empty look. "Are you sure?"

"Alberto found out where Ray Dougherty was staying and bugged his hotel room. He thought he'd learn what the guy's connection to Tony was. Instead, he found out that Dougherty and Marcino are one and the same."

"So the son of a bitch didn't die after all." Frank's jaw tightened. "Not only did he betray me, but he made a fool out of me. When this comes out, I'll be a laughingstock from here to Seattle."

"You're making way too much of this."

Frank pushed his face against the smudged glass. "I'm making too much of this? Look at me. Look where I'm sitting. Look what I'm wearing. It was Marcino's testimony that put me in here. Thirty stinking years I've been rotting in this place. Are you forgetting that?"

"No."

Frank calmed down. "What's he doing in New York?"

"From what Alberto heard, someone is trying to kill Marcino's daughter and he's come all the way from San Diego to find out who's behind it."

"Why would someone want to kill Angie?"

"She discovered the body of a woman last week. But by the time the cops arrived, the body was gone and no one believed her. So she started her own investigation. She may have gotten a little too close to the truth."

"Who's the dead broad?"

"No one is sure she's dead. Right now, she's just missing. Her name is Lola Malone. She's a singer. It's been in all the papers. I thought you would have seen it by now."

"I don't have time to read."

"She used to sing at Blue Moon, a nightclub owned by Rick Vaughn, Angie's ex-husband."

Frank pursed his lips. After nearly a minute of silence, he spoke again, in that calm, even voice that had always scared the daylights out of Vince.

"Call Alberto again and tell him to put a bug in Angie's place. And her mother's. Their last name is Foster now— Catherine and Zoe Foster. It's been years since I've had them watched, so they've probably moved, but they should be easy enough to find. And while he's at it, tell him to do the same with that Rick Vaughn character. You got all that?"

"What are you going to do?"

"Don't you worry your pretty head about it. You did good, kid. But from now on, what happens is between me and Alberto. *Capisce?*"

"Frank, listen to me. It's been thirty years."

"Enough with the math, already."

"What I'm trying to say—"

But Frank was already walking away.

* * *

"Are you doing this just to annoy me?" Lou asked. "Because if you are, you'll be happy to know that it's working."

They were standing at the window of Ray's hotel room, watching the Friday-afternoon rush-hour traffic come to a grinding halt. The sidewalks were no better. There were only eight days left before Christmas and New Yorkers were in a shopping frenzy that made an outsider dizzy just looking at them rushing from store to store in search of holiday bargains.

"I just want to see my daughter. Is that a crime?"

"Ever since I met you you've wanted to see your daughter. But you were smart then. You knew it was dangerous. You've changed since arriving in New York. Maybe all the pollution is screwing up your brain."

"She wants to see me, too."

"And I'll say it again, it's too dangerous. If you don't believe me, call that new contact you have at the FBI. He'll set you straight."

"I'm not calling anybody." He pointed a finger at Lou. "And don't you dare do anything behind my back. You cross me, and you and I are finished."

"Ray—"

"It's going to be okay. Rick is in charge of the arrangements. Believe me, he's taking every precaution imaginable. He's worse than you."

"What kind of precautions?"

"I don't know yet. I'm supposed to call him tomorrow for the details."

But Lou was relentless. "What happened to your intentions of finding the sniper? I thought that's why you came to New York in the first place."

"It is. As soon as I've met with Angie, I'm going back to Queens to talk to Peppe."

"What good will that do? You told me yourself he practically kicked you out of his office."

"It'll be different when I tell him who I am."

Lou slapped his forehead. *"Dio è testardo."*

"If you're going to insult me, do it in English."

"I called you stubborn. You deserve worse."

"Come on, Lou. You're a smart guy. Think. How am I going to find out anything if I keep pretending to be Ray Dougherty? The reason Peppe gave me the boot is because he thought I was some nosy outsider. It'll be different when he knows the truth."

"If you say so." But the look on Lou's face remained doubtful.

Thirty

"Why not requisition Mona's phone records?"

Zoe held up one of the e-mails she had received today. That particular letter had caught her attention because it was a clue she should have thought of herself. Requisitioning a victim's phone records was one of the first steps in a criminal investigation.

Had Detective O'Bryan already thought of it? It wouldn't hurt to find out. Who knew, she might even find him in a good mood and willing to share information for a change. Feeling hopeful, she picked up the phone on the side table and dialed his number.

"Detective, this is Zoe Foster."

"Good morning, Miss Foster." His tone was almost friendly. "To what do I owe this pleasure?"

"I caught your news conference last night. I thought you did an excellent job."

"I'm glad you approve."

"Detective, I was wondering. Did you, by any chance, requisition Lola's phone records?"

He took a moment to answer. When he finally did, she couldn't tell if he was amused or annoyed. "Are you trying to tell me how to do my job, Miss Foster?"

"No, not at all. I don't know if you're aware of this, but I've asked my readers to send me daily clues for my new strip."

"I remember reading something to that effect."

"One of today's clues was about the phone records and I thought—"

"Well, think no more. I did requisition Lola's phone records, and not by any chance. It's standard procedure."

She tried not to feel too foolish at her poor choice of words. "Did you find anything?"

"Look, Miss Foster, I'm grateful for all the help you've provided so far regarding this case, but the fact remains that I can't discuss the investigation with you. I stuck my neck out a little more than I normally would because you're a friend of Joe Santos, but there are limits to how much I'll do. So why don't we make a pact right here and now. You let me do my job, and by that I mean you stop calling me every day, and if I need to talk to you for any reason, I'll contact you. Do we have a deal?"

"Do I have a choice?"

"Not really. Now, if we're finished, I need to go back to work. Two homicides popped up during the night, and as always we have a shortage of detectives."

"Does that mean you won't have time to investigate Lola's disappearance?"

"No. It means that I have to schedule my time even more carefully than I did last week. Have a good day, Miss Foster."

"You, too."

She clicked off her phone. Although she had hoped for a little more cooperation on his part, she wasn't surprised at the polite but firm way he had handled her request. Joe had warned her that O'Bryan was a cop who went strictly by the book.

Still holding the clue, she walked over to the drawing board and gazed at the four frames she had completed the previous day. In a corner of the page, she had jotted down the names of all the suspects in the disappearance of Mona Gray.

The one at the top of the list was still Mona's ex-husband, who stood to inherit Mona's vast fortune in the event of her death. Next was the understudy, who aspired to being a star. A close third was an actor on the show, a former heartthrob who no longer had any interesting story lines. Zoe hadn't modeled him after anyone. He had popped out of her head and she had added him to the mix because he made an interesting character. She had named him Alan Ralston. Alan hated the growing popularity of the two main characters—Mona and her on- and off-screen lover. Without Mona in the starring role, Alan stood a strong chance of having his story line jazzed up and brought back into the limelight.

And finally, there was the show's handsome director himself. Several readers had alluded to the possibility that Nicholas had had an affair with Mona before she broke it off. One reader in particular, Lonesome Me, was rather adamant about Nicholas's guilt and kept asking Zoe why she wasn't taking his clues and investigating Nicholas's *darker side,* as he put it.

Zoe didn't know what to make of Lonesome Me. He continued to write daily, but his attitude was changing. He had begun to sound as though the strip was real to him and he wanted to control the characters through Zoe.

She reread his latest message, which definitely showed a side of him she hadn't seen before. Who was he? She kept referring to him as a he, but he could just as easily be a woman, although the more she read the letters, the more she was convinced they were written by a man. The style and the words he used indicated that he was male—and angry.

Why are you being so stubborn, he wrote. *You keep going in a dozen directions when the culprit is right in front of your nose. Nicholas is the killer. Stop treating him with kid gloves and have Kitty investigate him.*

She crumpled the note into a ball and dropped it into the wastebasket with the others. She was tempted to tell Maureen not to forward any correspondence signed Lonesome Me, but didn't. The man intrigued her, and occasionally, his long tirades helped her look at the mystery under a different light.

Spurred by a sudden burst of inspiration, she worked furiously. In this strip, a frustrated Kitty was trying to get information from a reluctant cop and getting about as far as Zoe had with Detective O'Bryan. Luckily, Kitty had friends in all the right places and she wasn't shy about calling on them whenever she needed to. One of those friends was a recurring character who worked for the phone company. He was more than a friend, actually. He was a former flame who still carried a torch for Kitty and would walk through fire for her. Just as Joe would do for Zoe. To give him a Hispanic name would have been too obvious, so she named him Clark. As a compromise, she gave him thick, curly hair and Joe's broad shoulders. Tomorrow's strip would reveal whether or not Clark was willing to risk his job to help Kitty.

After one last stroke of her pen, Zoe finally stopped and went to get ready for her date with Lizzy.

"Lizzy, look." Zoe grabbed her friend's arm and pulled her back in front of the Radio Shack window. "This cell phone would be perfect for your brother. He loves gadgets."

After lunch at the Roc Café, Zoe and Lizzy had headed up Fifth Avenue for a shopping extravaganza that threatened to go on long after four o'clock, the time Lizzy had to be back at the restaurant. They were slowly heading toward Rockefeller Plaza, their earlier departure point.

"Jimmy already has a cell phone," Lizzy said.

"Not like this one. It's a video camera, too."

Once inside, she grabbed an eager salesman, got him to take the phone out of the display case and explain all its features.

"You're right." Lizzy was getting excited. "Jimmy would love this."

Zoe had picked up the instrument. She particularly liked the text-messaging option. Unlike phone calls that could be easily traced, text messages could not.

If her father had one of those, she could activate the text-message option on her own phone, and they could communicate with each other as often as they liked, with no fear of anyone finding out. It would be completely safe.

"I'll take one, too," she told the salesman.

Lizzy nodded her approval. "Joe will love it."

"It's not for Joe." She bit her lip the moment the words were out.

Lizzy's mouth fell open. "Zoe, you sneaky little thing. What have you been keeping from me? The phone is for Rick, isn't it?"

"No." She gave her a gentle shove toward the cash register. "Now, shut up and pay the man. You may also show a little gratitude."

"For what?"

"For helping you pick a gift Jimmy will *not* return this year."

"You're changing the subject."

Once their purchases were completed, Zoe and Lizzy walked out and were once again swallowed by a sea of shoppers.

But Lizzy, who, like Zoe, had a one-track mind, would not let her off the hook. "What's going on between you and Rick? Are you seeing him?"

"I told you, the phone isn't for him."

Lizzy tapped a finger to her bottom lip. "Let's see, the phone is not for Joe, or for Rick. E.J., then?"

"No." Christmas music could be heard coming from the ice rink at Rockefeller Plaza. Zoe grabbed Lizzy's hand. "Come on. Let's go watch the skaters."

Lizzy yanked her back. "Not until you've told me what's going on."

"Maybe this is something I don't want to talk about."

Her friend looked hurt. "I don't get it. You and I have always told each other everything. What's changed? Don't you trust me anymore?"

Zoe let out a sigh. Lizzy, like the rest of her family, had a fragile ego and their friendship was too precious to risk damaging it. "You know I trust you."

"Then tell me what's going on. Why are you being so secretive?"

Zoe looked around her, saw the Dean & DeLuca sandwich shop at the corner and dragged Lizzy inside.

"Two coffees, please," she told the girl behind the counter. Then, mugs in hand, both made their way toward an empty table in the back.

Zoe put her packages on the floor. "You can't repeat what I'm about to tell you to anyone, not even your family."

"Now you're scaring me."

"Good, because a single indiscretion could have deadly consequences."

"All right, you've made your point. Does all this involve Rick?"

"No. Well, yes, but not in the way you think." She looked around her. Satisfied no one was close enough to eavesdrop, she said, "The phone is for my father."

Because the statement was so unbelievable, considering that Lizzy had known Zoe for over fifteen years, her friend laughed. "And I suppose you'll be going all the way into the afterlife to give it to him?"

"You want to hear this? Or you want to crack jokes?"

Lizzy sobered up instantly. "You're serious."

Zoe nodded.

"But your father—"

"Died. Well, that's just it. He didn't die. He's very much alive."

She tried to give her an abridged version, but this was Lizzy, the queen of details. By the time she had asked all her questions, an entire hour had passed.

"Wow, honey. My head is spinning." Fond of intrigue, she added in a whisper, "You're the daughter of a mobster. How cool is that?"

"I'm glad you find this exciting, but please don't refer to my father as a mobster. He is a respectable, law-abiding citizen. He was also brave enough to risk his life so the authorities could put a scumbag like Frank Scolini behind bars."

Lizzy reached over to touch Zoe's hand. "I'm sorry. I didn't mean any disrespect. The truth is, I'm thrilled for you. I can't remember the last time I saw such a glow on your face." She winked. "Well, actually, I do, but you don't want to talk about *him*."

When Zoe pointedly ignored that comment, Lizzy hurried on. "What concerns me, though, is you and your safety. I understand why you would want to spend time with your father, but what if something goes wrong?"

"Nothing will go wrong. Rick will see to that."

"You're not even a little bit worried?"

"I'm worried how this meeting with my father will go. What if I'm not what he expects? What if I say or do something stupid?"

A gentle squeeze restored her confidence. "He's going to love you, Zoe, I guarantee it."

Thirty-One

Rick was behind the bar, pouring himself a club soda, when Zoe arrived at Blue Moon shortly after five that afternoon. Except for him and a maintenance man changing lightbulbs, the place was empty.

At the sound of her footsteps, Rick turned around. Taking one look at the half-dozen shopping bags in her hands, he asked, "What did you do? Buy out Manhattan?"

"Just about. Remind me to never take Lizzy shopping again. That woman has the stamina of a long-distance runner. Once she gets started, nothing can stop her. I'm exhausted."

Rick set his glass down and came around the bar. "Here, let me put these in my office. We can talk in there."

Grateful for the opportunity to finally get off her feet, Zoe handed him her bags and followed him down the hall. She barely waited for Rick to close the door before she asked, "Did you talk to my father? What did he say?"

Rick set the bags by the door. "He wasn't an easy sell."

"Why? I thought he wanted to see me as much as I wanted to see him."

"He does. But his primary concern is your safety."

"He can't possibly be worried about Frank."

"He knows him too well not to be worried. I had to do some serious convincing before he finally said yes."

"Oh, Rick!" She threw herself in his arms and planted a loud kiss on his cheek. "You're wonderful. Thank you."

Rick held her tightly for a few seconds before releasing her. "You're welcome. Do you want to hear the plan?"

"I'm all ears." She sat down and listened earnestly.

"A friend of mine has a summerhouse in Spring Lake, New Jersey. You've met him—Gary Lewis. The builder?"

"I remember Gary. I don't remember a house in Spring Lake."

"He built it about five years ago. It's a real showplace."

"Doesn't he close it for the winter?"

"Many of the residents do, but Gary likes to go there year-round. A caretaker keeps an eye on the place when he's not there, and handles a number of chores. He goes twice a week in the summer, less often in the winter."

She was starting to see where he was going. "My father will be the caretaker?"

"It's the perfect setup. I've met Larry. He and your father are about the same age and build. Ray will be there when we arrive, working in the yard, doing whatever needs to be done."

"Do we have a reason for being there?"

"We do, but it will involve a little acting on your part."

She remembered what he had said a couple of days ago about being realistic. "What kind of acting?"

That little spark she knew so well returned to his eyes. "We'll have to pretend that you and I are…well, an item again, or on the verge of becoming one."

"Is that necessary?"

"If, and I agree that it's a big if, Frank Scolini has someone watching you, they'll wonder what we're doing there together, after being divorced for six years. Appearing to be in love again will put an end to speculation."

"What exactly does 'appearing to be in love' entail?"

"Oh, I don't know. We'll play it by ear. A little smooching will be required." He was trying to keep a straight face but was having a hard time. "Can you handle it?"

"You're enjoying this, aren't you?"

"You will, too. I'll make sure of that."

Just as long as her emotions and feelings didn't get all tangled up, the way they had the other night, when she'd been a breath away from kissing him. "What happens after we arrive?"

He was serious again. "We'll stop to talk to 'Larry' for a couple of minutes, then I'll get him to come inside, supposedly to repair a leaky faucet, and make myself scarce."

Alone with her dad. It still didn't seem possible. "Will he stay the entire weekend?"

"He wanted to come back on Sunday, but there isn't

that much to do. It could have looked suspicious. Instead, we'll try to arrange another meeting at a later date."

She felt her excitement grow. "When do we leave?"

"Tomorrow morning. I'll pick you up at about nine. It shouldn't take us more than an hour to get there."

Ray checked himself in the mirror, pleased with what he saw. Earlier today, he had made a list of what a caretaker might be wearing on a cold, drizzly morning and then he had gone shopping. Back at the hotel, he had changed into dark-blue jeans two sizes too big, a gray sweatshirt and a lumberman jacket. A floppy hat covered his hair. Not only did he not look like Tony Marcino, those who knew him as Ray Dougherty would never recognize him, either. Even Lou, on whom he had tested his disguise earlier, had taken a step back.

Ray was more nervous now than he had been on the day Angie was born. All he had wished for at that time was a healthy baby. He had a lot more to worry about today. Would she like him? Would she be resentful of the choices he had made?

Would she suddenly decide she didn't want to see him after all?

He turned his head around, changing the angle on the hat. All those precautions were probably unnecessary. He had been in New York for four days now and nothing had happened. Always careful not to take anything for granted, he had checked with the hotel clerk twice a day every day to make sure no one had asked for him.

So far, no one had. At least, that's what the clerk had told him. In New York City, as anywhere else, money ruled. He had thought of buying the clerk's loyalty with a handsome tip, but he had decided against it, concerned the gesture would attract undue attention.

He shrugged the negative thoughts aside. Today was a special day, a day he had thought would never come, and he wasn't about to spoil it by worrying himself to death. That was Lou's job.

Ready, he took the gardening gloves from the dresser and put them in his pocket. A pickup truck that belonged to Rick's bouncer was waiting at Kramer's Parking Lot on Columbus Avenue. It held everything a gardener could need. All he had to do was get behind the wheel and follow Rick's directions to Gary Lewis's house in Spring Lake.

In a great mood, he tilted his hat at a rakish angle, grinned in the mirror and left.

Always punctual, Rick picked Zoe up at nine on Saturday morning. As per his instructions, she had packed an overnight bag that contained a change of clothes and some toiletries, all she needed for a weekend at the shore.

"All set?" Rick waited until she had buckled her seat belt before brushing her lips with his. "To make it realistic, remember?"

"Hmm."

"Oh, come on, you can do better than that. What if someone is watching?"

"No one is watching, Rick. This is just a silly ruse on your part to…"

"To what?"

"To make me feel stupid." And excited. More excited than she had been in years.

"Is that how kissing me makes you feel? Stupid? I'm hurt."

She laughed. "All right, you win." She pressed her lips to his. "That's as realistic as I'm going to get at nine o'clock in the morning. Now drive."

Grinning, he pulled away from the curb. "That's more like it."

Within moments, they had left the city behind and were headed south toward the Garden State Parkway. In spite of Rick's chatter, her anxieties grew as they got closer to their destination. She wished she could remember the dad she had known as a little girl, but her only memories were those her mother had kept alive for a while. Even Ray's face, which she had glimpsed the other night, kept being overshadowed by the face of the man whose photograph still sat on her bedside table.

Rick, on the other hand, was the picture of calm and serenity. Why shouldn't he be? He had no emotional ties to Ray. He was just the middleman in a rather unusual drama, the connecting link between line A and line B.

He seemed to sense her mood. "You're okay?"

"A little nervous."

"That's understandable."

"What if I don't know what to say?"

Rick chuckled. "That will be the day."

"Stop it. I'm serious."

He took her hand and brought it to his lap, another gesture from the past. "I know. Try to relax, and look at the view. We're almost there. Are you familiar with the Spring Lake area?"

"Never been there."

"It was named for the fountains of crystal-clear water that flow out of a number of underground springs. It's the quintessential, turn-of-the-century small town with wide, tree-lined streets, quaint shops, summer concerts at the gazebo and a shady park."

"Do you come here often?"

"Every chance I get, which is not nearly enough. Here we are." Rick turned on Essex Avenue and pulled the Audi along the curb of the quiet side street.

He hadn't exaggerated. The house was a spectacular, three-story Victorian with peaked roofs, dormer windows and a wraparound porch, all painted pale yellow. In the huge backyard, a gazebo, painted the same color as the house, held center stage.

Then she saw him.

She held her breath as a man in a plaid jacket, worker's pants and a tan hat threw debris into a wheelbarrow.

Rick wrapped an arm around her waist. "Remember," he whispered in her ear. "He's just the caretaker."

Zoe gave a light nod, took Rick's hand and let him lead her through the gate.

Thirty-Two

"Larry!" Rick raised his hand. "How's everything?"

The man turned around and went still for a moment. Then he, too, raised his hand in greeting. "Hello, Mr. Vaughn." He looked at Zoe and touched his hat. "Miss."

"This is my friend, Zoe Foster." Rick kept his arm around Zoe's waist. "Gary told you we were coming down?"

"Yes, sir, he did. I stocked some fresh supplies in the house, food and stuff, and I'll bring some firewood in a minute. In the meantime, if there's anything I forgot, you just let me know."

"I'm sure everything is fine, Larry. Except maybe that faucet Gary told me about?"

"Larry" nodded. "That's right. I'll come in and take a look at it."

Zoe's heart pounded as she followed the interaction between the two men. The father she hadn't seen in thirty years stood less than twenty feet from her and it took every ounce of willpower she had to appear unaffected. Inside, her emotions were on a roller coaster.

Rick touched her arm. "Shall we?" He waited until they were inside before saying, "You need to get a grip, Red. You're white as a ghost."

"I'll be okay. Is he coming in?"

"Momentarily."

As if to confirm his statement, there was a discreet knock at the door. Rick went to answer it and Ray walked in, carrying a bag of firewood in one hand, a toolbox in the other.

"That should do you for a while," he said. Then, as he started to walk toward the floor-to-ceiling fireplace, Rick took the wood from him. "Go say hello to your daughter, Ray. I'll be upstairs."

Ray took his hat off and held it in front of him as though waiting for instructions. Then, suddenly aware that he no longer needed to pretend, he opened his arms. "Angie." His voice was filled with emotion. "My little Angie."

In an instant, Zoe was in his arms, crying and laughing at the same time. There was so much she wanted to say but the words got stuck in her throat.

After a fierce embrace, Ray let her go. His eyes had gone misty, but his smile was radiant. "You don't know how long I've been waiting for this moment."

"I think I do."

He took her hand in his. "Come on, let's find a place to sit. Away from the window." He scanned the room, found a table and two chairs in a quiet corner and led her there. "Sit down, princess." He gave her a sheepish smile. "I guess you don't want to be called that anymore."

"As a matter of fact, I do."

"Good." When they were both seated, he gave a slow shake of his head. "You are so beautiful. I could look at you all day."

She let out a nervous laugh. "We don't have all day."

"I know." He hitched his chair closer. "Tell me all about yourself. Everything."

She smiled. "I thought you already knew everything."

"Not the little details that make you the person you are."

They spoke for the better part of an hour, Zoe first and then Ray as he filled in some of the details her mother had left out. He had taken a small notebook and a pencil from his jacket pocket and had started to draw while they talked.

She took advantage of a slight lull in the conversation to ask, "Why didn't you ask the FBI to put all three of us in the witness protection program?" As she had with her mother, she made sure not to sound accusing. "If it worked for one, couldn't it have worked for three?"

He nodded as though he had been expecting the question and stopped drawing. "Your mother had already left Philadelphia and settled in New York City. If, after my so-called death, the two of you had suddenly left New York and vanished, Frank would have known he had been duped. And no matter how well the FBI disguised our identity, his hounds would have found us. We would have spent the rest of our lives looking over our shoulders."

"Isn't that what you've been doing? Looking over your shoulder?"

"Pretty much, but I only have myself to worry about. It's different when your wife and kid are involved." He was silent for a moment. "How's your mother?"

"She's doing well. She runs a B&B in Cape May." She hesitated. "I had to tell her." At the question in his eyes, she added, "I hadn't planned to. I went down to Cape May to find out why she hadn't told me the truth when I was old enough to hear it, but…"

"What happened?"

"She became distraught, blaming herself for your death, saying over and over that she had killed you."

"I never blamed her for anything. You have to tell her that."

"I did. She's glad you're alive. She…wishes you well," she improvised.

He looked sad for a moment and she wondered if he had hoped for more. Or was her romantic side wishing for things that could never be?

"What would Frank do if he found out that you were still alive?" she asked.

Ray's voice went flat. "He'd send his goons after me."

"Does he still have that kind of power?"

"Just because Frank Scolini is behind bars doesn't mean he's lost control. Frank is, and will always be, a powerful figure. His organization didn't dissolve when he went to prison. It's still being run by people he's handpicked, men he trusts."

"But why come after you now?"

"Because he has no choice. If he flinched now, if he passed up an opportunity to have me executed, he would lose face. And to Frank, face is everything."

"Then maybe you should consider returning to San Diego."

"Not until I find out who fired those shots at you, little girl."

"Rick said you have a friend who might be able to help you?"

"Peppe. His real name is Guiseppe Veneti. He owns a trash-disposal business in Queens." He stopped drawing again. "If anything should happen to me before I have a chance to talk to him again, that's the person you should contact. You'll remember that? Guiseppe Veneti. In Queens."

"Nothing is going to happen to you."

He smiled and glanced toward the staircase. "That's quite a guy, your Rick."

She felt herself blush. "He's not my Rick."

"He should be." After a few more strokes of his pencil, he turned the paper around so she could see it.

"That's me!" she exclaimed.

"I didn't do you justice."

"Yes, you did! It's an amazing likeness." She looked at him in awe. "Rick told me you were an artist, too."

"Oh, I wouldn't call myself an artist. I did caricatures of people when I was a college student. It wasn't high art but it helped pay my tuition."

"You're very talented." She looked at the drawing again. He had captured it all, the thick, curly hair, the wide eyes, the narrow nose and full lips. Even the little hair clip in the shape of a butterfly was there, at a cocky angle. "May I keep this?"

"Of course."

"Oh, I almost forgot. I bought you something. An early Christmas present."

"You shouldn't have."

"You don't mean that. People always say that but never mean it. What they really want to say is, 'Hurry up and give it to me.'"

Ray laughed, the first happy, relaxed laugh she'd heard in the last hour. For an instant, she thought she remembered that laugh. She even had a brief vision of a little girl sitting on her father's shoulders, shouting, "Faster, horsey, faster." Then the vision was gone. It was probably one of those memories her mother had made up for her.

She walked over to her overnight bag, which Rick had set in the foyer, and retrieved the brightly wrapped package with its pert little red bow. "Here," she said, handing it to him.

Looking as excited as a child on Christmas morning, Ray tore open the paper. "A cell phone," he said, taking it out of the box.

"Ah, but not just any old cell phone." She took out the instruction booklet that came with it. She had earmarked the text-messaging page. "With this feature, which you'll have to activate when you get back to San Diego, you and I can text message each other as much as we want and no one will be the wiser."

"Are you sure?"

"Very sure. My friend Joe, the detective, told me. Text messages are untraceable. I had to do some research a few months ago for one of my Kitty adventures. That's how I found out."

"Thank you, Ang—I mean, Zoe. It's a wonderful gift. You'll have to give me your number."

She tapped the booklet where she had jotted it down. "Already did."

He looked at her as though she was the smartest, most resourceful person in the world. It was a look fathers all over the world had perfected, just for their daughters. After a moment, he reached in his jacket pocket and took out a small, black velvet pouch. "It so happens that I brought you something, too. I hope you like it."

Zoe watched him as he carefully opened the pouch. She let out a small gasp as he pulled out an exquisite double-strand pearl necklace.

"It belonged to my mother," he said. "It's one of the few things the FBI agreed to let me take out of my house before I went into the witness protection program. I dreamed of the day I could give them to you, even though I knew that day would never come. Before I left San Diego, I slipped them in my pocket, just in case."

Zoe couldn't take her eyes off the lustrous gems. "They're beautiful."

He stood up. "May I?"

She lifted her hair so he could clasp the necklace around her neck.

He walked back to face her. "They look as though they were made for you."

"Thank you...Dad. I love them." The word, said a little timidly, had come out on its own.

Rick suddenly reappeared. "I hate to be a killjoy, but you probably should go," he told Ray.

Ray nodded. "I'll take the pickup back to Stretch."

"You have the directions to his house in Brooklyn?"

Ray tapped his jacket pocket. "Right here."

"We'll walk down with you. I want to take Zoe downtown for a look at the Christmas decorations."

Ray turned to Zoe and opened his arms. "I'll be in touch, princess. Take good care of yourself." He pressed his mouth to her ear. "Tell your mother I love her."

Zoe felt her throat close. "I will."

The three of them walked out together. An early fog was creeping in from the ocean, turning the area a misty gray.

"That faucet should be working just fine now, Mr. Vaughn," Ray said at the door. "Sorry it took so long." He shook hands with Rick and gave a nod to Zoe. "Merry Christmas to you both."

As Zoe and Rick walked down the path behind him, the sixth sense Zoe often relied on made her cast a casual glance around her.

She wasn't sure what she noticed first—the slow-moving SUV with black windows all around, or the horrified look on her father's face as he, too, spotted the vehicle.

And then she saw it—the barrel of an automatic weapon sticking out from one of the SUV's rear windows.

It was aimed straight at her.

Thirty-Three

"Angie, down!"

Her father ran as though he had been given wings, but Rick was closer and already reacting. He lunged, knocking Zoe to the ground and rolling with her into a row of winter shrubbery.

The *rat-tat-tat* of an automatic weapon shattered the quiet as a spray of bullets hit her father in the back. His arms flew out. His knees buckled. He hit the gravel face-down and lay motionless as the SUV tore out of the street.

"Dad!" Zoe struggled out of Rick's grip and scrambled to her feet. She fell at her father's side, hands above him, afraid to touch him. The back of his jacket was punctured with half a dozen holes. Beneath him, a pool of blood turned the gravel crimson.

A handful of people were coming out of their houses. She was aware of someone shouting, "My God, there's been a shooting. Call 911!"

Zoe bent over the inert figure, her hair brushing Ray's face. "Dad, please, talk to me." His head was turned to the side. His eyes were wide open. Those eyes that had looked at her with such pride and joy a few moments ago now stared at her blankly.

Rick crouched beside her. "Zoe."

"Do something, dammit!" she cried. "Don't let him lie there."

"It's too late, baby. He's gone."

"No!" She turned back to look at the still face, refusing to believe that he was dead. Then, with an anguished sob, she fell on him and didn't stop crying until two strong arms pulled her up.

Tears of grief and rage stung her eyes. "They killed him, Rick. Those bastards killed him."

"I'm sorry, baby."

"How could this happen? We were so careful."

She tried to break free again, but he wouldn't release his grip. In the distance, the wail of a siren grew louder. Neighbors had ventured into the yard, eager to take a glimpse at what would most likely be labeled by the press as "a mob killing."

"He died trying to save me."

Before Rick could answer, an ambulance and two police cars came to a screeching halt in front of the house. Men and women in uniforms spilled out while two men in blue scrubs ran over, pushing a stretcher. They knelt beside Ray and quickly realized that it was too late for any kind of medical attention.

After they had placed him into a body bag, a woman in a police uniform approached Zoe and Rick. "I'm Officer Lorraine Shamong." She looked from one to the other. "Are you two related to the victim?"

There was no longer any need to conceal the truth. "I'm his daughter," Zoe said. "This is Rick Vaughn. My ex-husband."

"Did you both witness what happened here?"

They nodded.

Officer Shamong lay a gentle hand on Zoe's arm. "I'm going to have to ask you a few questions. Is it all right if we go inside?"

Instead of answering, Zoe's gaze followed the stretcher the two attendants were wheeling toward the rear of the ambulance. "Where are they taking him?"

"The Monmouth Borough morgue, ma'am."

"Come on," Rick said softly. "Let's go inside."

As Zoe obediently followed him, she looked down at her hands.

She hadn't realized that she still held her father's drawing.

A homicide detective had been dispatched from the Spring Lake Detective Bureau to take over for Officer Shamong. The questioning had been repetitive and emotionally exhausting, but Detective Wiley, who was young and meticulous, had insisted on hearing every little detail, even those Zoe didn't feel were important enough to mention. In order to corroborate her story, Wiley had contacted the FBI. An agent by the name of Gordon Sully had declined to make any comment over the phone, but was flying in from San Diego.

An autopsy would be performed, after which Ray's body would be released to his next of kin.

His body. In spite of what she had witnessed, Zoe still

found it difficult to think of her father as a body. He had
been so alive, so full of joy and excitement. They had
made plans, had just begun to learn how to be father and
daughter again. How could he have gone, in such a short
time, from all that to being a body?

Rick took her home, not to her loft, but to his apartment on Central Park West. A uniformed doorman with
gold braids on his shoulders quickly opened the door.
"Can I help you with anything, Mr. Vaughn?"

"Not at the moment, Carl. Thank you."

The elevator doors hissed shut and then they were
moving up, all the way to the twenty-ninth floor.

"Sit down, Zoe." Handling her as though she were a
paper doll, Rick helped her onto a maroon sofa with a
mountain of pillows piled up along its curved shape. "I
need to make a call."

While he talked to Lenny, Zoe let her gaze roam over
the room. She had often wondered where Rick had
moved after their divorce. On a mutual agreement, she
had kept the studio on Greene Street and he had bought
something closer to the club. Gallant to the end, he had
offered to pay off her mortgage, pointing out that on her
salary as a children's-book illustrator, she might not be
able to meet the payments. Instead of simply saying,
"No, thank you, I'll manage," she had been very mature
about the whole thing and told him to mind his own
beeswax. He had been right, though. Six months after the
divorce, she had realized that she couldn't carry the mortgage. She had sold the studio and signed a lease on an
apartment in Chelsea.

He hadn't done too badly. The Rosenthal was among

the city's first grand-luxe apartment buildings. Besides twenty-four-hour security, a health club and a cinema room, the building offered an uninterrupted view of Central Park from every apartment.

The furnishings were understated and tasteful—a sectional sofa and matching chairs, Oriental rugs over bare wood floors and accent lamps placed in strategic places. Artwork by William Wegman, for whom Rick's brother had had a fondness, hung on a wall. From where she sat, she had a glimpse of a dining-room table and six chairs.

Did he entertain often? she wondered. Beautiful, eligible women, perhaps? He had always enjoyed tinkering around the kitchen, cooking up exotic food he had discovered during his travels as a marine.

At last, Rick hung up. He didn't look happy. "Lenny found a bug in my office. That's why the call took so long. I wanted him to take a look."

"A bug? Someone put a listening device in your office? Why?"

"Because whoever ordered the job, and my bets are on Frank Scolini, knew that you and I were working together. That's why I called Lenny from Spring Lake and asked him to do a sweep. Chances are your loft is bugged, as well. I'd like Lenny to check it out in the morning, if it's all right with you."

"Yes, of course." She remembered that Lenny had worked in intelligence when he was in the Marine Corps. "How did they become suspicious?" she asked. "We were so careful. *Ray* was so careful."

"There must have been a leak. Someone your father thought he could trust and shouldn't have."

"Lou?"

He shook his head. "No, not Lou. Not the way your father talked about him."

"We'll have to tell him. God, I don't know how."

"There's no hurry. Lou wasn't expecting to see Ray until Sunday, and it will be several hours until the news of the shooting breaks out." He sat down beside her. "We'll go see him in the morning. Right now, you need to sleep."

She thought of the images that would start haunting her the moment she closed her eyes. "I'm not sleepy."

"I'll whip up something to eat, then." He pulled her to her feet. "Come on. You used to like my cooking, remember?"

She wasn't hungry, either, but she followed him into a gleaming, all-white kitchen and watched him open the refrigerator.

"If you're planning on making one of your Thai or Turkish creations, I have to warn you, my stomach is not up to it."

"Just a plain cheese omelet from the good old U.S. of A." He took out a carton of eggs, butter, chives and a package of shredded cheese, and started cracking eggs with an expert hand. "Why don't you try to relax. I know it's a lot to ask, but we've done all we can for the time being."

"I can't get that scene in Spring Lake out of my head."

"No one expects you to. I'm having a hard time processing it myself."

"That gun was pointed at me, Rick. They were going to kill me."

"That was the plan all along. To kill you first while Ray watched, then kill him."

"He could have saved himself. The shed was only steps away from him. Instead, he ran to save me."

"Did you expect him to do anything less?"

"No. Not after I realized how much he loved me. An hour wasn't very long, but it was enough. I felt as though I had known him all my life."

"I'm sure he felt the same way."

She heard the sizzle of eggs hitting hot butter. Using a whisk, Rick stirred the mixture until it started to set. Then he added a generous amount of grated cheese, a sprinkle of chopped chives, salt and pepper. He rolled one half of the omelet over the other and waited a few more seconds before transferring the finished dish onto a plate.

"Here." He handed her a fork.

"That's way too much."

"No problem." He took another fork from a drawer. "We'll share."

Sharing food reminded her of old times, when they used to come home after a late night at the club. Too hyper to go to bed right away, Rick would drag her into the kitchen of their little studio apartment, and "whip up something."

She took a forkful of the omelet, which was very good. "I haven't had a chance to thank you."

"For what?"

"For taking over with the police when I was so incoherent, for comforting me, for being there. I don't know what I would have done without you."

"You'll never have to go through a crisis alone, Zoe, not as long as I'm alive. I told you that when we separated, maybe not in so many words, but you knew that, didn't you?"

"That I could always count on you?" She nodded. "Yes, I knew."

"Good. Now finish your eggs. Then I'll show you to your room."

"You want me to sleep here?"

"Can you think of a safer place?"

"I'm no longer in danger. Didn't we agree that the only reason Scolini wanted to kill me was to get back at my father?"

"Still, I'll feel better if you stay here for a few days. Tomorrow, I'll make arrangements to have your clothes and your drawing board brought here. Don't worry," he added when she opened her mouth to protest. "You'll have all the privacy you need. I usually leave the apartment at ten and don't return until after midnight. You won't even know I'm here."

He gave her that same charming grin she had always found impossible to resist. "So you see, you have no reason to say no."

Well, one thing that hadn't changed about Rick was his take-charge ways. Not that she had ever complained about that. Despite the fact that she considered herself the decisive type, she didn't mind a man taking the reins every now and then.

She carried her plate to the sink. "In that case, show me the way."

The guest room was small but attractive, with contemporary furniture and a big brass bed covered with a thick yellow comforter. A television set sat on the dresser, along with a DVD player and a large selection of movies.

He set her overnight bag on the floor. "The bathroom is over there," he said, pointing. "Sleep as late as you want."

At the door, he turned. "Call if you need anything. My room is just down the hall."

Thirty-Four

Zoe tried every sleep-inducing trick she knew. She watched a movie, took a warm bath and counted sheep. She even went in the kitchen to heat up some milk, which she sipped standing at her bedroom window, watching the lights of Manhattan shine brightly in the night.

It was no use. Her mind was like a movie reel spinning out of control. At 2:00 a.m., physically exhausted and still unable to sleep, she got out of bed and went in search of Rick's room. She found it by following his scent—that citrus aftershave she knew so well.

She stood in the open doorway, listening to the sound of his deep, even breathing. She shouldn't be here. He needed his rest, too.

She was about to leave, when he suddenly sat up.

"Zoe?"

"I couldn't sleep," she murmured.

He turned on the light, blinking as his eyes adjusted to the sudden brightness. "Come on over, then." He threw the covers aside and patted the empty space next to him.

"No. I shouldn't—"

"Yes, you should." He gave the mattress another pat. "Jump in. If you don't, neither of us will get any sleep tonight. So come on. I promise I'll be on my best behavior."

A laugh, or maybe a sob, caught in Zoe's throat. Then, glad not to have to go back to her lonely room, she hurried to Rick's bed and slid under the covers.

As if it was the most natural thing in the world, he wrapped his arm around her shoulders and brought her close. "Comfy?"

"Yes." Oh, yes. Very.

He reached for the light switch, and darkness surrounded her again. But this time she didn't mind. This time she wasn't alone.

His fingers gently stroked her hair, the way they used to. "You want to talk?" he asked.

She was starting to feel groggy. "Maybe…later?"

He kissed the top of her head. "Good night, Red."

Zoe woke slowly, lazily, arms and legs tangled into the cozy softness of a puffy comforter. Feeling achy without knowing why, she started to stretch.

Then it hit her. The shooting in Spring Lake.

Feeling calmer but immensely sad, she let yesterday's events unroll slowly in her head. She thought of the father she had lost a second time, and the future they would never have. She thought of his face, which she had committed to memory, the hard lines softened by the gentlest of smiles. She thought of the way he had held her, of the look of pure joy when he had taken his mother's pearls out of the black velvet pouch. Her fingers went to her neck. The pearls were still there.

The images went away on their own, without her forcing them out. As Zoe sat up and realized that she wasn't in her room, other thoughts slowly came into focus. She had needed comfort and kindness last night and had known exactly where to find it. She couldn't remember much of anything else, except snuggling into Rick's arms, closing her eyes and falling into a blissful sleep.

The clock on the bedside table read 9:00 a.m. Kicking off the covers, she saw the note lying on the pillow beside her. It was written in Rick's hasty handwriting:

Hope you still like chocolate croissants. Just help yourself. If you need anything, call the doorman on the intercom by the front door and he'll have it sent up. I took the liberty of going through your purse for the keys to your loft so Lenny and I could bring back whatever you'll need for your stay.

She got out of bed and, passing a mirror, took a look at herself. There were some superficial scratches on her cheeks and across her forehead where her face had dug into the gravel, but she could barely feel them. As for the achiness she had felt earlier, its source was no longer a mystery. She had hit the ground hard and had bruised a few areas.

Barefoot, she walked into the living room. Tucked in a sunny corner was her drawing board with all its accessories, her laptop and a suitcase. She opened the latter and smiled. Rick had made some good choices, right down to the shoes.

In the kitchen she found a basket of fresh chocolate croissants along with a pot of coffee, which smelled heavenly. Sipping and munching on the flaky pastry, she wandered back into the living room. From the wide window she could see Central Park as it stretched from Fifty-ninth Street all the way to Harlem. Almost eight hundred and fifty acres of green meadows, lakes and winding paths. The park had been one of her and Rick's favorite places, their little oasis, where they had biked and jogged in the summer and ice-skated in the winter. The trees were bare now, the bikers and Rollerbladers gone, but the park was still alive with strollers out for their daily dose of fresh air.

Once she felt sufficiently revived, thanks to Rick's excellent coffee, she called him, using the phone on a side table.

"Thanks for bringing my things," she said when he answered.

"You're welcome. Did you sleep well?"

"I must have. I didn't wake up until a few minutes ago. Any news?"

"Detective Wiley just called. He was on his way to Ambrose State Penitentiary in Philadelphia, where Scolini is serving his sentence. He's not very optimistic. Although the hit has Scolini written all over it, the man is going to deny any involvement in the shooting. And whoever was hired to do the job is not about to talk."

"So he's going to get away with my father's murder?"

"Not necessarily. Until now, there was a very strong chance that Scolini would be granted parole. But if Wiley can cast enough of a dark shadow on him, the parole board, which is due to meet in less than three months, might be influenced to turn down Scolini's request. For extra weight, Wiley is taking Agent Sully along. Both will be stopping by my apartment tomorrow, by the way. Sully wants to talk to you."

"All right." She paused, already dreading the task. "What are we going to do about Lou? He needs to be told."

"That's why I called. If you're up to it, we can go right now."

She gulped the rest of her coffee. "Give me twenty minutes."

Rick waited for her to slide into the passenger seat before handing her back the loft keys. After she dropped them into her purse, he set a brown paper bag on her lap.

"What's that?"

"Take a look."

She peeked into the bag where she saw several small items. She took one out, the size of a credit card. "What's this?"

"A UHF transmitter equipped with a highly sensitive microphone. It only transmits when it receives audio. All you need at the other end is a receiver and you'll hear everything going on within a hundred-foot radius."

"Where did you find it?"

"In your loft, taped under your sofa. I left the apartment early this morning so Lenny and I could check your place. I had an identical one in my office." He stopped for a red light, looked into the bag and pulled out another gadget. That one was much smaller, the size of a quarter. "This baby here was found inside your phone and will transmit *both* sides of the conversation. It's powered by the current in the phone line and simply tunes in to any standard FM radio receiver at a preset frequency."

Zoe looked at him, openmouthed. "How do you know all that stuff? Were you a spy in another life or something?"

"Lenny gave me a quick course."

The light turned green and they were moving through the thick midtown traffic again. "We found all those listening devices with his bug detector. They're all fairly common, by the way, and because they're so readily available, tracing them back to the buyer is practically impossible. Scolini's men probably get them on the black market."

The next item Zoe pulled out of the bag was something that she recognized immediately. "What's my power strip doing in here?"

"That's not your original power strip but one made to look just like it. Lenny's detector picked up a signal."

"That's the one I was using on my PC?"

Rick nodded. "It's fully operational. Unfortunately, Lenny doesn't know anything about this type of device, and we didn't want to take the power strip apart. We'll let Agent Sully and Detective Wiley take a look at it."

"Why so much equipment? Wouldn't one bug and the phone tap be enough?"

"You would think."

He had pulled under the canopy of the Select Hotel on Forty-sixth Street. After locking the bag in the trunk, Rick turned his keys over to the attendant with a twenty-dollar bill. "We'll be about an hour. Do me a favor, will you, and keep it right here in front of the hotel?"

The young attendant nodded as he pocketed the tip. "Sure thing, sir."

Lou Agnelli was an impeccably dressed, nondescript man in his early sixties. From the relaxed expression on his face when he opened his hotel door, it was clear that he hadn't yet heard about the shooting in Spring Lake. However, after the first look of recognition, his face drained of all color.

"Mr. Agnelli?" Rick asked.

The man had to hold on to the door for support.

Zoe gently touched his arm. "May we come in?"

Shoulders hunched, Lou let go of the door and led them into the room. He barely made it to the bed, where he sat down heavily. He looked from Zoe to Rick. His eyes had already filled with tears. "They got him, didn't they?"

"I'm sorry," Rick said.

Lou closed his eyes and waited a beat before adding, "How did they find out?"

"My loft was bugged," Zoe explained. "So was Rick's office. And probably Ray's room here at the hotel, as well."

Lou ran an unsteady hand across his gray hair. "What did they do to him?"

Zoe didn't feel up to going over the events at Spring Lake again, so she looked at Rick, who took over. He was as specific as possible without being too graphic. When he was finished, Lou was silent for a long time. His head hung down, as if the string that had held it up all this time had suddenly broken. A tear rolled off his cheek.

"I shouldn't have let him go," he said at last. "Like a dummy, I let him convince me that everything would be all right when I knew all the time that it wouldn't be."

Feeling close to tears herself, Zoe sat down beside him. "What happened is not your fault. If you insist on taking the blame, then I should, too. I'm the one who wanted to see him."

Lou shook his head. "He would have suggested it if you hadn't. He wanted to see you more than he had ever wanted anything in the thirty years I've known him. He was just waiting for the right moment." He took a trembling breath. "It's that scum Scolini who's to blame. The man may be rotting in a Philadelphia prison, but if he wants something done, all he has to do is snap his fingers and it's done."

"Do you have any idea who did the actual shooting?" Rick asked.

Lou shook his head. "Frank runs a large organization. The guy in charge now is a man by the name of Gino Medina, but I'm not sure Frank would confide in him about something that could keep him in prison for the rest of his life. Frank doesn't trust too many people. He trusted Tony and look what happened."

"Anyone else?"

"Maybe Peppe would know. Ray felt he could trust

him." Another shake of his head. "Me? I'm like Frank. I don't trust anybody."

Zoe remembered her father's words. *"If anything happens to me, go to Peppe."*

"Agent Sully and Detective Wiley will be in town sometime tomorrow," Rick said. "They want to talk to you as well as Zoe."

"I'll be here. I'll tell them everything now."

Zoe's gaze swept over the tidy room. It would be lonely here, now that he no longer had Ray to talk to. "You're welcome to stay at my loft," she said on impulse. "It'll be much more comfortable than a hotel room." When he looked undecided, she added, "I'm staying at Rick's apartment for a few days. You'll have the place all to yourself."

Sensing that he needed more convincing, she took her keys out of her purse and handed them to him. "Ray thought of you as family. I'd like to do the same."

His mouth tightened as he fought tears, but he took the keys. "Thank you."

Thirty-Five

It was midafternoon when Zoe and Rick returned to the apartment on Central Park West. While Rick took the brown bag into his room, Zoe sank into a chair, gathered her hair behind her neck and tied it loosely. Oddly enough, the visit to Lou Agnelli hadn't left her as drained as she had expected. Although his grief had opened fresh wounds, the comfort she had given him had been therapeutic for both.

On the way back, she had asked Rick to make a stop at the *Herald*, where she had assured everyone that she was fine. E.J. had fussed over her like a mother hen and told her to take all the time she needed. Her fans would understand.

Much remained to be done. Besides working on the strip and reading her mail, Zoe had a funeral to plan. She would also have to meet with Agent Sully and Ray's attorney, who was flying in from San Diego to read Ray's will. Catherine would be arriving momentarily. She had planned on staying at the loft, but after hearing that it was occupied, she had accepted Rick's offer to stay at his apartment.

"Will you be all right by yourself?" Rick asked. "I can stay if you want."

"Don't you have to meet with a representative of the Liquor Control Board?"

"I can reschedule."

"Don't. I'll be fine. I have a stack of readers' mail to keep me company."

"I thought E.J. told you to wait on that."

"I don't like to be idle."

"All right, then. I'll be home early." He kissed her lightly on the lips, which he had started to do in Spring Lake as part of their playacting, before all the madness had started. "Call if you need anything. Or if you just want to talk."

"Thanks, Rick."

Once she was alone, she sat on the sofa and started to sort through her e-mail. She was halfway done when the intercom buzzed.

She went to answer it. "Yes, Carl?"

"You have a visitor, Miss Foster. A Detective Santos from NYPD."

Joe. She had turned her phone off before going to see Lou and had forgotten to turn it back on. "Thank you, Carl. Please ask him to come right up."

"Yes, Miss Foster."

She was waiting for him at the door when he stepped out of the elevator.

He took her in his arms and held her fiercely. "Thank God you're all right," he murmured, burying his face in her hair.

She patted his back. "I'm sorry I worried you."

He released her. "Worry me? I was frantic. I finally called Rick and he told me you were here. Why didn't you call me from Spring Lake? You know I would have wanted to be with you."

She closed the door and led him into the living room. "I wasn't thinking clearly." They both sat down on the sofa, side by side. "I take it you've heard?"

"About your father having worked for the mob and not being dead?" He nodded. "The story hasn't made the national papers yet, but one television network just got wind of the shooting and is having a field day with it. This place will be crawling with reporters before long."

"No one knows I'm here. And Carl has orders not to let any unauthorized person through."

"Still, you'd be safer at my house. And you know how my mother would love to have you." He looked around. "Of course, it's not as luxurious as these digs, but—"

"I don't care about that. The only reason I agreed to stay here was because it seemed convenient at the time."

His trained eyes picked up the drawing board. "You're planning to stay a while?"

"A few days."

"Is that what you want? To be locked up here, alone, unable to go out? If you moved into my house, I could take some time off, keep the press at bay, stay with you until this mess is all clear—"

"For God's sake, Joe, this isn't a contest! Please don't turn it into one."

One look at the hurt expression in his eyes and she

immediately regretted the outburst. "I'm sorry. I guess I'm still on edge."

His next question took the wind out of her. "Are you falling for your ex-husband?"

How could she answer that, when her feelings were in such turmoil? "No." Then, because she thought too much of Joe not to be completely honest with him, she added, "I don't know."

The strong jaw tightened. "Did you sleep with him?"

"Joe—"

"Did you sleep with him?" He enunciated each word slowly.

"No! And I resent this kind of questioning."

"You can't deny that you've been spending a lot of time with Rick lately. And now you've moved in with him? How am I supposed to feel?"

"Why can't you be happy that I'm safe and well cared for? Why does my stay here have to be such a problem for you?"

"What about us? And don't tell me that there is no us," he added as she started to protest. "Not after the way you kissed me back the other night. You felt something, Zoe. I didn't imagine it."

She looked away, knowing that what she needed to say next would hurt him deeply. "I shouldn't have let that kiss happen. I was too vulnerable that night."

"You were vulnerable last night, too. The difference is that Rick took advantage of the moment and I didn't. I'm too much of a gentleman to ever put you under that kind of pressure."

"Rick didn't take advantage of me! Nothing happened! And I can't believe that we're fighting at a time when what I need most from you is support and understanding."

The words had the desired effect. His cheeks flushed with embarrassment while his expression went from angry to contrite in a flash. "I'm sorry. I don't know what came over me."

"I do. You worry, maybe a little more intensely than most."

"Tell me what I can do."

She was trying to think of something, when she remembered the brown bag in Rick's bedroom. "Since you asked…" She stood up. "I'll be right back."

Once in Rick's room, she looked around, hoping he hadn't locked the bag in a drawer. When she spotted it on his dresser, she took it back into the living room and emptied the contents on the sofa.

"Well, well," Joe said, picking up the credit card–size bug. "What have we here?"

"Rick and Lenny found it in my loft, taped under my sofa."

"Lenny the bartender?"

"He was an intelligence officer in the Marine Corps. His detector found the bug. That's how Frank Scolini knew about my father," she added after a short pause. "He bugged my apartment. And Rick's office."

Joe was no longer listening. He had picked up the seven-outlet power strip. "Is this yours?"

"No. Someone replaced mine with this one. Lenny picked up a signal, but he didn't want to take it apart. We're waiting for Agent Sully. What are you doing?" she asked when he took a Swiss Army knife out of his pocket.

"Checking to see what kind of device is inside."

"Shouldn't you let the authorities do that?"

He looked up. "What am I? Chopped liver?" Using a miniature screwdriver, he opened the strip and gently tapped a device no larger than an aspirin tablet. "Son of a gun."

"What?" Zoe said excitedly.

"This baby, which by the way is built into the wiring system, is the latest in digital audio-recording technology. They're made exclusively for government agencies such as the FBI and the CIA. Anyone else interested in buying one would need preauthorized approval."

"Are you saying that the CIA bugged my loft?"

"Or someone else."

"But you said that this device is not available to the general public."

"There's always the black market." Joe screwed the power strip back together. "What I don't understand is why Scolini would go to all that trouble and install two different devices when one would have sufficed."

The frown on his face was one Zoe knew well. "What are you thinking?"

"That Scolini is not the only person interested in your activities." Before she could reply, he asked, "Where is your cell phone?"

"In my purse. Why?"

"May I see it?"

She walked over to where she had left her purse, took out the phone and handed it to him.

He opened it as expertly as he had the power strip and reached inside. "This," he said, holding up a button-shaped object, "is of the same quality as that UHF transmitter Rick found under your sofa and not nearly as sophisticated or sensitive as what's in the power strip." He looked at her. "Any idea how anyone could have had access to your cell phone?"

"That's easy. I'm always leaving it somewhere. It's a wonder I haven't lost it yet." She watched him put the phone back together. "So if Scolini didn't plant the hi-tech device, who did?"

"I have no idea. Maybe Agent Sully will be able to trace it back to its owner."

Zoe shivered as she folded her arms around her. The thought that people, *strangers,* had come into her loft, touched her things and spied on her, gave her the creeps. "What's going to keep them from planting other devices?" she asked.

Joe started putting everything back into the bag. "I doubt if Scolini will, now that he got even with your father."

As he stood up, she lay a hand on his arm. "Are we okay? You and I?"

The side of his mouth lifted into a little smile. "Yeah, we're okay." He pointed a finger at her nose. "But don't think I'm giving up on you."

Thirty-Six

The next few days passed in a flurry of activity. Agent Gordon Sully, a tall, lanky man with sharp eyes and a quiet way about him, had stopped by as promised and put Zoe through another round of questioning.

As predicted, the agent hadn't gotten anywhere with Frank Scolini. After acting shocked to hear that Tony Marcino was still alive, the mobster had categorically denied having anything to do with his death. During their two-day visit to Philadelphia, Sully and Detective Wiley had questioned more than a dozen people from Scolini's organization, including his brother Vince. All swore not to have known about Marcino's death until they heard it on the news.

But while Agent Sully's talk with Scolini had been inconclusive, his visit with the parole board had not. Thanks to the agent's detailed account of the Marcino/Dougherty case, it was now highly unlikely that the mob boss's request for parole would be granted.

As for the sniper's incident and Rudy Goldberg's

murder, there was still no progress on that front. The police had retrieved all three bullets. The two fired by the sniper were found embedded in the wall of the electronics shop and had come from a .30-caliber rifle. The third, taken from Rudy's chest during the autopsy, was a standard .38 caliber, like those fired from most handguns.

Zoe's mother arrived on Tuesday, looking strong and ready to tend to Zoe's every need, while Lizzy made sure that everyone was properly fed. E.J. was a lifesaver. To satisfy the hundreds of queries that were coming in regarding Zoe, he had written a short editorial, stating that Zoe was doing well and Kitty Floyd's adventures would resume shortly.

Rick and Joe, undeclared enemies but enemies just the same, became unexpected allies bonded by the same goal—to keep Zoe safe.

Ray's attorney, a stout man with the improbable name of Woody Bark and a briefcase he wheeled around like carry-on luggage, had agreed to read Ray's will in Rick's office. The document was ten years old and fairly simple. Having no family he could afford to acknowledge, Ray had left his condo and bank account to a charitable organization that fostered orphaned children. The hardware store was bequeathed to his dear friend, Lou Agnelli.

Loyal to the end, Lou had offered to stay in New York until Zoe was out of danger. After a lengthy discussion, she had finally convinced him to go back to San Diego after the funeral and reopen the store. As an added incentive, she had promised to call him every day and keep him informed of the smallest developments.

The inability of the media to reach Zoe hadn't kept reporters from milking the story for all its worth. Every day a new headline popped up on the front page of every newspaper in the country: Mobster Gunned Down in Front of Daughter's Eyes. Mobster's Daughter Watches in Horror as Father is Gunned Down. Popular Cartoonist Was Mobster's Daughter. And on and on.

Following the release of Ray's body, a quiet graveside funeral was held at Skyview Lawns on Staten Island, the only cemetery where Zoe could schedule a burial on such short notice.

Standing on the damp grass between Rick and her mother, Zoe looked at the small group that was assembled. Joe, Lizzy and their respective families had come to offer their support. So had E.J. and more than two dozen people from the *Herald.* Across from Zoe, a man she didn't know had arrived late and stayed in the background behind Joe's mother. He was short but powerfully built and never took his eyes off Ray's casket until Reverend Harris finished his sermon.

"That's Peppe, in case you were wondering," Catherine whispered to Zoe. "I'd recognize him anywhere."

"Did he recognize you?"

"Why don't we go find out?"

Excusing herself to her friends, Zoe followed her mother. When the man who had once been her father's best friend saw them approach, he took off his hat and walked over to meet them.

"Stephanie," he said, gripping her arms and kissing her cheek. "I am so very sorry."

"Thank you for coming. How's Elena?" Catherine's

tone wasn't friendly as Zoe had expected, but rather cool.

"She wanted to come, but she hasn't been well lately."

"I'm sorry to hear that." She drew Zoe close to her. "I don't believe you've met my daughter, Zoe."

Peppe gave her a warm hug. "You have your mother's beauty and your father's hair."

Zoe studied him for a minute before deciding to take her father's advice and ask for his help. "Peppe? May I call you Peppe?"

"Of course."

"Before my father died, he told me that if something happened to him and I had questions, I should come to you."

He looked suddenly uneasy. "He said that?"

"You were best friends, weren't you?"

"We were like brothers, but I'm not sure how I can help you now."

"Are you aware of the sniper incident that took place downtown a few days ago?"

"I heard about it, but I didn't realize you were the intended victim until I saw you on TV."

"That sniper is what brought my father to New York. He thought you might be able to help him find out his identity."

Peppe dug his hands in his raincoat pockets and shook his head. "Maybe twenty years ago I could have helped him, but not anymore." He looked at Catherine. "I lead a pretty dull life these days—I work, I go home and I play with my grandkids on weekends. That's about it."

Zoe started to say something, but her mother's gentle hand on her arm stopped her. "What about all those contacts you used to have?" she asked quietly. "If I recall, you were one of the best-connected men in the city."

"That was then, Stephanie."

"You didn't keep in touch with Gino and Sonny, or the rest of the clan?"

He seemed to grow more and more uncomfortable. "No."

"You do know that the authorities believe that Frank ordered Tony's slaying, don't you?"

"The poor guy is in a maximum-security prison, Stephanie. He can't hurt anyone."

She gave him a thin smile. "You and I know that that's not true. What puzzles me most, though, is not so much who killed Tony—I already know that—but how Frank found out that Tony was in New York in the first place." She cocked her head to the side. "I wonder if you could help me with that."

"Like I said—"

"I know what you said, Peppe," Catherine snapped. "I'm just having difficulty believing you."

"Why, for God's sake?"

"Because Tony was killed so soon after he came to see you. You do remember his visit, don't you?"

Peppe seemed to have regained his composure. "I sense some hostility in your voice, Stephanie. Do you blame me for Tony's death?"

"Should I?"

Zoe watched her mother with new interest. She had never seen her be so assertive. Apparently, Ray's death had affected her more than she wanted to admit and she was out for blood. But why Peppe? A man Ray had trusted so implicitly?

"I've done nothing wrong," Peppe protested. "I didn't even know who Ray Dougherty was until that fed walked into my office yesterday—the fed that *you* sent, Stephanie," he added accusingly.

"Don't worry. From what I heard, you came out smelling like a rose. Frank should be pleased."

Peppe looked hurt. "You're wrong about me, Stephanie. I don't dance to anyone's tune. I—"

"Lead a dull life, I know." She smoothed down her black leather gloves, one finger at a time. "You have my sympathy." She turned to Zoe. "Come on, honey. The stench here has become unbearable."

"What was that all about?" Zoe whispered as they walked away. "You sounded as if you hated that man."

"*Hate* is a strong word. Let's just say that your father and I never saw eye to eye when it came to Peppe. I didn't like the fact that he had mob connections, and regardless of what he is saying now, I don't believe he severed those ties. He knows who ordered your father's murder and who the executioners were. Just as I know that *he* is the one who alerted Frank that your father was in New York. He's just too gutless to admit it."

"After what happened to Dad, do you blame him?"

"He could have found a way to help the authorities, quietly, without Frank knowing. It's been done before."

Zoe was aware that her friends, who hadn't moved even though the minister was long gone, had watched the interaction with great interest. She stopped walking so what she had to say would only be heard by her mother.

"You'll never cease to amaze me, Mom. Just when I think I know you, you go and do something that completely floors me."

Catherine let out a short chuckle. "You should have heard me in the old days. One of your father's colleagues in Philadelphia nicknamed me 'Typhoid Mary.' It's a wonder Frank didn't put out a contract on *me*."

"I'm glad he didn't."

Catherine's gloved hand touched Zoe's cheek. "Will you be okay, baby? I'll stay another day if you want me to."

"Absolutely not. I need to get back to work and so do you." She kissed her. "See you next week?"

"I can't wait." Catherine glanced over at the group. "Since Joe can't come for Christmas dinner, why don't you—" she cleared her throat "—bring Rick?"

"Why, Mom, are you starting to change your mind about him?"

"He's a different man. He seems more grounded, more protective of you, more attentive. And it was sweet of him to invite me to stay at his apartment."

Zoe grinned. "I'm sure he'll be very happy to join us for Christmas dinner." She wrapped an arm around her mother's waist. "Come on, you'll want to say goodbye to everyone." She lowered her voice. "Just don't mention inviting Rick in front of Joe."

Thirty-Seven

After a post-funeral catered lunch at Blue Moon, Catherine and the rest of the mourners left, with the exception of Joe.

"What are you doing for the next two hours?" he asked Zoe when she returned from seeing her mother off.

"Try to catch up with my work. Why?"

"I need help buying Christmas presents for my sisters. If you could take a couple of hours off, I'll be forever in your debt."

"You say that every year at this time. Don't you know by now what young women like?"

"Not when they keep changing their minds every three weeks."

Their little spat forgotten, Zoe laughed. "I know what you mean. Lizzy's nieces are the same way. Yes, I'll be glad to help you." She glanced at her Kitty Floyd watch. "Give me a minute to say goodbye to Rick and I'll be right with you."

She turned in time to catch her ex-husband watching them while giving instructions to the cleanup crew.

"What's up?" he asked, walking across the room to meet her.

"Joe needs my help shopping for his sisters' Christmas presents."

"Really." Rick glanced at Joe, who smiled and waved. "What if I told you that *I* need help finishing my Christmas shopping?"

She laughed. "I'd call you a liar. You order from catalogs."

"Just kidding. How long will you be?"

"No more than a couple of hours. In the meantime, thanks for the luncheon. It was very thoughtful of you to go to all that trouble. My mother was touched." She lowered her voice. "She wants you to join us at the Rose Cottage for Christmas dinner."

"Why are you whispering?"

"I don't want Joe to hear."

"The golden boy wasn't invited?"

"He *was* invited. He can't come. He's having Christmas with his family."

"And he would resent me going? Even though the two of you are not romantically involved?"

"I just don't want to rub his nose in it. Is that so difficult to understand?"

"No, and I'm sorry. I won't mention it to him."

"Thanks. I should be home around six."

She and Joe were heading for the door when Rick called out her name. Zoe turned around.

"Tell your mother I'd love to have Christmas dinner at the Rose Cottage. What can I bring?"

She threw him a murderous look, grabbed Joe's arm and walked out.

"Rick is having Christmas dinner with you and your mother?" Joe asked as soon as they were out.

She could strangle Rick for that stunt. And he had the nerve to call *her* jealous. "My mother found out that his parents were on a cruise and he wouldn't be flying to Florida as he does every year. That's the only reason she invited him."

"Poor little rich boy," Joe said sarcastically. "All that dough and nowhere to spend it."

She gave his arm a slap. "Don't be that way."

"He started it, shouting his RSVP for the whole world to hear. He couldn't have waited?"

"Yes, he could have and don't think I won't give him hell for being so insensitive. Now, can we please forget about Rick and concentrate on the shopping? I'd like to show you what *I* want for Christmas."

They spent the next two hours going from store to store, gawking in front of Macy's windows like two kids, sharing a bag of roasted chestnuts Joe bought from a vendor and taking a break at Rockefeller Plaza to watch the skaters glide over the ice.

She was glad that their friendship was back on solid ground, in spite of Rick's efforts to derail it. Although, if she wanted to be completely honest, she enjoyed having two gorgeous guys fighting over her.

She and Joe had reached the Greenwich Village area

and were standing outside a jewelry-shop window, debating whether Joe's youngest sister would prefer a gold cross necklace over a gold bangle bracelet, when Zoe stopped in midsentence.

A man sat huddled in a doorway, watching her with bloodshot eyes. He wore layers of clothes several sizes too big for him, wool gloves with the tips cut off and a dirty wool hat. Held tightly against his chest was a green trash bag she assumed contained all his belongings.

He kept watching her with a strange kind of intensity, almost as if he knew her, which was entirely possible. Although she had done her best to avoid all publicity, she hadn't been able to keep the media from showing her face on television every two minutes. Even a homeless man with no TV was bound to have caught a glimpse of a newscast somewhere.

Her heart went out to him. Life in the city was difficult for the thousands of homeless people who called the streets home, but the holiday season had to be particularly hard. Quickly, she reached into her purse and took out a handful of one-dollar bills. Then, smiling at him, she approached, holding the money so he could see it.

The man sprang to his feet and bolted.

"Don't run! I only wanted—"

Joe turned around. "What's wrong? Who are you talking to?"

Zoe felt as if the sky had suddenly come crashing down on her. *"Oh my God!"*

"What? What is it?"

"That homeless man over there." She pointed in the direction of the fleeing figure. "I know who he is!"

"Who?"

"He's the man who sold the cupid charm to Rudy Goldberg, the pawnbroker. You've got to catch him, Joe."

"Are you sure it's him?"

"Well, not *sure* sure, but…almost sure. Hurry, Joe, please. I need to talk to him." She gave him a shove. "Don't let him get away."

"Zoe, are you insane? I can't go after him. There are laws against that kind of harassment."

"I just want to find out if my hunch is right. And if it is, I want to talk to him." When Joe still didn't budge, she handed him her packages. "Will you take those, please?"

"Why?"

"Because if you aren't going to go after him, *I* will."

Joe rolled his eyes. "The foolish things I do for you."

He took off at full speed, arms and legs pumping. She ran too, though slower. The pursued man was moving just as fast, turning around from time to time and looking terrified.

As a last resort, Joe shouted, "Stop! Police!"

Zoe watched in dismay as Joe zigzagged between panicked pedestrians and collided with a woman, sending her packages flying into the air.

"I'll take care of it," Zoe said, crouching down beside the angry woman and gathering the packages. "You catch that man."

But by the time Joe was back on the chase, the homeless man had disappeared and Joe stood helpless, scanning the crowd.

Out of breath, Zoe came to stand by him. "Where did he go?"

Hands on his hips, Joe turned right, then left. "I don't know." He, too, was breathing hard. "That bastard could run."

Although disappointed, Zoe knew the chase had ended. She put a hand on Joe's arm. "You tried. Come on. Let's go check out that cross for Donna."

Zoe was a nervous wreck the following morning as she waited for Rick to leave the apartment. She must have been painfully obvious, because at one point he looked up from his morning newspaper and asked if something was wrong. She had blamed her restlessness on the events of the last couple of days.

"Why don't you stop by Lotus and have lunch with Lizzy?" he suggested. "She always lifts your mood."

"Maybe I'll do that."

She hated lying to him, but if she told him what she was up to, she would have one hell of a fight on her hands.

At last, Rick left. Zoe grabbed her purse, threw on a coat and ran out of the apartment. Fortunately, living in a fancy building had its perks. There was no waiting for a cab, no fear of getting drenched or being run over. One whistle from Carl, the doorman, and a shiny Yellow Cab slid to the curb.

She gave the driver the address of the jewelry shop in Greenwich Village where Joe had bought the little cross, and from there she started walking, heading south, as she had the previous day. Before leaving the apartment, she had drawn a sketch of the homeless man. Hopefully it would help identify her elusive witness.

She walked the streets of Greenwich Village for almost two hours, talking to vendors, store owners and other homeless people she met on the way. No one recognized the man in the sketch, or if they did, they weren't saying.

A light snow had begun to fall. With only one hope left, she ventured into a shelter, deserted at that time of day. The director was a man by the name of Barry Tuney.

When he saw the sketch, he smiled. "Why, I believe that's Archie. But I haven't seen him for a while."

"Can you tell me anything about him? Where I could find him if not here?"

"No, I'm sorry. Archie doesn't say much."

Zoe left him her card and asked him to call if Archie showed up.

Thirty-Eight

Chandra had just finished the ten-o'clock show when Rick's phone rang. It was Dr. Keefer at Sagemore.

"You're working late, Doctor."

"It comes with the job. Mr. Vaughn, I was out of town for a few days and just now heard that Lola Malone was missing. Why wasn't I informed?"

"Because I wasn't sure that she was missing until the police started investigating. Is Frieda all right?"

"That's why I called. She's asking for Ms. Foster."

Rick didn't hide his surprise. "After what happened last week?"

"She has no recollection of that incident. She says that I chased her niece away and she wants me to bring her back."

"She thinks Zoe is Lola?"

"Apparently. And since she's been rather agitated lately, I thought a visit from Ms. Foster might calm her down. I was a little rough on her the other day, so if she turns me down, I'll understand."

Rick was thoughtful for a moment. Now that the police had taken over Lola's case, and Zoe had promised not to get involved, he had no qualms about taking her to Sagemore.

"I'm sure Zoe will be happy to see Frieda again, Doctor. She felt badly about upsetting her last week. Maybe another visit will be good for both of them."

Frieda barely glanced at Zoe when she and Rick arrived a little after eleven-thirty on Thursday morning. Zoe put a box of Godiva chocolates on the window ledge, where Frieda could see it, and sat down.

The older woman looked at the festive box with its red velvet ribbon and frosted berries, while Zoe held her breath, waiting for the shouts of accusation to begin. Frieda remained quiet.

"Hello, Frieda," Zoe said gently. "Remember me?"

"No." Her tone was indifferent. "I'm waiting for Lola."

"Lola couldn't come. I'm her friend, Zoe."

"Why didn't she come?" She looked from Zoe to Rick. "Isn't she feeling well?" She cast a furtive glance toward the door as if she expected someone to eavesdrop, then leaned closer to Zoe. "Is she still having morning sickness?" she asked in a whisper.

Zoe and Rick exchanged a startled glance. "Morning sickness?" Zoe repeated.

Frieda's expression turned suspicious. "What kind of friend are you if you don't know that she's pregnant?"

Lola had been pregnant.

That bombshell left Zoe speechless. A pregnancy

opened a whole new set of problems, especially if the father was a married man. She thought about the clue she had received from Lonesome Me not too long ago. *Maybe Mona was blackmailing someone. A former lover?*

A pregnancy also meant that a doctor may have entered the picture. There would be a medical file, blood work. Maybe even the identity of the father.

"She didn't tell me," Zoe said at last.

"It's a secret." Frieda had lowered her voice again. "She doesn't want anyone to know."

"Frieda." Zoe assumed the same secretive expression as the old woman. "Did Lola tell you the name of the baby's father?"

But Frieda was no longer paying attention to Zoe. She was observing Rick with a keen eye. "What did you do to your hair?" she asked.

Rick ran a hand through his light brown hair. "Nothing. Why?"

"It's different."

"Different how?" Zoe prompted.

Frieda ignored the question. "Maybe the baby will look like you," she said, her eyes still on Rick. "I would like that. Did I tell you that before? Or maybe I told Lola. I'd like the baby to look like you if it's a boy and like Lola if it's a girl."

Zoe was having difficulty processing all she had heard. Could there be some truth to what Frieda had said? Or was it just the rambling of a demented woman? She was about to question Frieda again, but Lola's aunt had returned her attention to the white expanse of snow outside her window, a sure sign that she was no longer connected to them. When Zoe said her name, there was no response.

A hand touched Zoe's shoulder. She turned to see Dr. Keefer standing behind her. He was much more amiable than he had been on her previous visit. "I heard about your father's death, Ms. Foster. You have my deepest sympathy."

"Thank you." She glanced at Frieda. "I'm afraid I didn't accomplish much."

"Oh, I don't know. She's calmer than I've seen her in days."

"I could come back," Zoe offered.

"That would be very kind of you. Why don't I give you a call if there is any change. Do we have your number?"

Rick stood up to leave. "You have mine."

Zoe and Rick had barely passed through the double doors before Zoe turned to Rick. "Did you have any idea that Lola was pregnant?"

"How could I? I'm her friend not her confidant." He opened the door on the passenger side to let her in. "And anyway, how much stock can you put in anything Frieda says? Look at the comment she made about my hair. She's seen me dozens of times and has never said anything."

"Yes. Why exactly did she make that comment?"

"Isn't it obvious? She mistook me for someone else— an orderly, or any of the four other male doctors on staff at Sagemore."

"Or Lola's mysterious boyfriend."

"I'm not sure Lola would bring her boyfriend here."

"But she could have." She held Rick's arm. "You're pretty friendly with Nurse Mendoza at the front desk, aren't you? I believe you called her by her first name?"

"Penny."

"Let's go talk to Penny." She was already walking back toward the building, Rick behind her. "Maybe she, or another nurse, can tell us if Lola brought anyone else here besides you and Annie."

Nurse Mendoza looked up in surprise when she saw them approach her desk. "Forget something?" she asked.

"Not exactly." Rick rested his arms on the blue counter. "Did Lola ever come here with someone other than Annie and myself?"

The nurse searched her memory, then shook her head. "Nope. I work on weekends occasionally, and I've never seen Lola with anyone else other than you and Annie. Why do you ask?"

"Frieda made a remark about my hair being different. I think she may have been talking about another man."

"Like I said, I don't recall ever seeing anyone else with her, but I can tell you this. About a month ago, I heard what I thought was crying coming from Frieda's room. I rushed there and realized that Frieda wasn't crying. She was laughing, which is not something you often hear coming from her room. Lola was there. She had her wallet out and was showing Frieda what looked like the photograph of a man. When I walked in, Lola snapped her wallet shut. I made sure that Frieda was all right, and then I left."

"Can you tell us anything about the photograph?" Zoe asked.

"If you mean can I describe the man—" Penny shook her head "—I'm afraid not. Lola made it clear that it was none of my business. And that's all right with me. Frieda was having a happy moment and that's all that mattered."

Once in the car, Zoe fell back against her seat. "This is so frustrating. That's the second time in twenty-four hours that I came this close to getting a break." She held two fingers together.

Rick began the slow, winding descent from the nursing home. "What do you mean, two days in a row?"

She told him how she and Joe had chased the homeless man and then lost him.

"How can you be so sure it's the same man who sold Rudy the charm?"

"It's the way he was looking at me, as if he wanted to talk to me."

"If he wanted to talk to you, why did he run?"

"I don't know. A lot of homeless people have cause to be suspicious. Maybe I did something to frighten him."

"Maybe you'll run into him again."

She shook her head. "That's what I was hoping when I went looking for him yesterday, but—"

Rick almost drove off the road. "You went looking for him?"

"I had to."

"Zoe! You said you weren't going to meddle in police work anymore."

"I wasn't meddling. And I was completely safe. Unfortunately, I didn't find out much except that his name is Archie."

Rick drove in silence for a while. "I might be able to find that homeless man for you," he said after a short silence.

"You?" She sounded skeptical. "How?"

"You remember Clarence?"

"Preacher Man?"

"The one and only."

Although he was not a preacher, residents in and around Broome Street where Clarence ran his food cart had named him Preacher Man because of the short sermons he liked to give to his customers. Zoe had met him when she had first moved into Rick's studio. For some reason, Clarence had taken a liking to her and she never went by his cart without stopping for a hot dog and a chat. Kind and generous, Clarence made it his mission to know everyone in the neighborhood. "How else am I going to rid them of their sins?" he liked to say.

"He might have seen Archie around," Rick said. "I'll ask him."

"That's a great idea, Rick. Thank you. And since you're in such a generous mood, how would you like to do something else for me?"

He frowned. "Does it involve meddling?"

"Not unless you consider searching Lola's apartment meddling. I don't, because the police have already been there."

To her surprise, Rick laughed. "I was wondering when you'd get around to asking me that."

"Does that mean you'll do it?"

"You realize that any photographs, her appointment book or other personal items have already been taken as evidence. In other words, anything vital to the investigation is gone."

"I'd still like to take a walk-through."

"In that case, I'll need to stop at Annie's for the key." He took out his phone and started dialing.

Thirty-Nine

Zoe and Rick had stopped at Annie's apartment after returning from Sagemore, and although Lola's friend had been happy to lend them the key, she had been shocked to learn that Lola may have been pregnant.

"Lola was certainly a stickler for privacy, wasn't she?" Zoe said when she and Rick were back in the Audi.

Rick pointed the car toward Third Avenue. "She learned that from her aunt, who was hounded by paparazzi all her adult life and hated it. Lola told me some very funny stories about the little games Frieda often improvised to throw off reporters."

"But to not tell your best friend that you're expecting a baby? Isn't that a little extreme?"

"*If* she is expecting a baby."

"True."

Rather than circling Lola's building in search of a parking space, Rick drove the car into an underground garage near the Guggenheim Museum. "The Belvedere is only three blocks away," he said.

"That's fine. I like walking."

Martha, the manicurist, was nowhere in sight, and the concierge was not the same one Zoe had talked to a few days ago. This one was younger, friendlier and quick to recognize Rick.

"Good afternoon, Mr. Vaughn." Then, looking concerned, he added, "Any news on Miss Malone?"

"Not yet, Al. Don't lose hope, okay?"

"I won't. She's got to come back real soon. The place's just not the same without her."

Rick held up the key Annie had given him. "I thought I'd take a look at her apartment and see if I could find anything the police missed."

The concierge bobbed his head. "You go right ahead, Mr. Vaughn. Let me know if I can help."

"Al is a lot more congenial than the other concierge," Zoe said as the elevator doors hissed shut.

"Philip is all right. He takes his job, and himself, a little more seriously, that's all."

The elevator stopped at the seventh floor, and a moment later, Zoe stood in Lola's living room.

"Stunning." Her gaze swept over the immaculate white carpet, the white suede sofas and chairs and champagne drapes. "Lola Malone didn't just look like a Golden Era vamp," she remarked. "She lived the part."

"Her aunt had the apartment redone after Lola moved in."

Zoe walked over to the wall-to-wall bookcase crammed with books. "Which of the two loved to read?"

"Lola. She was a bookworm." Rick picked up a copy of *Rebecca* from the coffee table and flipped through it.

"She spent a lot of her spare time browsing through used bookstores in search of old classics. Sometimes, when she couldn't get Annie to go, she'd drag me out of my office, telling me I needed more culture in my life."

Zoe smiled, remembering that Rick's taste in literature had been limited to the Travis McGee series by John D. MacDonald. He wouldn't have touched *Rebecca* with a ten-foot pole. "Am I supposed to believe that you've become a fan of Daphne du Maurier?"

"For your information, I've read this book." He put *Rebecca* back on the table. "What do you say to that, Miss Know-It-All?"

"I say congratulations." She opened a desk drawer, but except for a few paper clips, it was empty. "A well-read man is a man to be treasured."

"I'll remember you said that."

Zoe continued to search the room. "You liked her a lot, didn't you?"

"She and I have a lot in common. She had a tough childhood, lost her parents at an early age, then her aunt took her in and made her feel as if she could do anything."

"You seem to have a lot in common with most of the women you hire."

"Are you referring to Jenny?"

"I am. How is she doing?"

"Settling into her new life, which is improving every day now that she no longer has to put up with that jerk of a boyfriend."

"I'm glad for her."

With Rick in tow, she strolled into the bedroom,

where the Hollywood glamour continued. Together, they searched Lola's closets but found nothing of interest, no baby booties, no prenatal vitamins, no telltale sign that an expectant mother had occupied the premises. And no photograph of any man. The only photo Zoe was fairly certain existed was the one Lola carried in her wallet.

Disappointed to have struck out, Zoe closed the last drawer. "I'm beginning to think that this pregnancy existed only in Frieda's imagination."

"That's possible. In her confused state, the past and the present intermingle constantly."

"Did Frieda have any children?"

"No. She had two pregnancies, though, and miscarried both times."

"That would explain her attachment to Lola. She was the child she could never have."

Small bottles of perfume were neatly arranged on a mirrored tray—Mitsouko, Chanel No. 19, Opium, Joy. Zoe opened the bottle of Joy and inhaled deeply. "The lady has good taste." She put the bottle back beside the others. "A woman so fond of perfume wouldn't go anywhere without her scents."

"Just as you wouldn't go anywhere without your shoes?"

"It's a woman thing. I wouldn't expect you to understand." She looked around the room one more time, knowing she had inspected every nook and cranny, yet she couldn't leave.

"I feel her here, Rick," she said quietly, not expecting him to understand that, either.

"It's normal, isn't it? You're in her apartment."

"It's more than that. I know it sounds silly, but it's almost as if…she wants me to be here. She wants me to find something."

"You're psychic now?"

"Aren't we all? Just a little?"

Not expecting an answer, she wandered into the kitchen, with its stainless-steel appliances and dark granite counters. She opened a cabinet. Dishes and glasses in various shades of blue were stacked on all three shelves. Canned goods occupied another cabinet.

"We liked the same tea," Zoe observed, touching a tin. "Twining's Earl Grey."

"If this is bumming you out, maybe we should leave."

"What are those?" She pointed at several plastic bags filled with small, foil-wrapped squares.

"Bite-size nougat from France. Lola was addicted to them. She couldn't find them in any store, so she ordered them online and filled up individual bags that she took everywhere."

Zoe let the door of the last cabinet swing shut and let out a disappointed sigh. They were done. As much as she hated to leave empty-handed, there was no point in searching any further.

Unless some miracle happened, the identity of Lola's lover would remain a mystery.

Clarence, whose last name was unknown, was as much a landmark in the NYU area as the famous university a block away. According to one of Rick's old neighbors, Preacher Man had claimed the busy corner more than a decade ago and had turned the lowly hot dog into a culinary experience no New Yorker dared to miss. While he always stocked up on traditional accompaniments such as sauerkraut and chili, he also liked to improvise, creating exotic concoctions he reserved for those he felt "appreciated the unexpected."

Rumor had it that Clarence was a millionaire, and worked just for the fun of it. If that was true, then the man had earned his fortune. He opened his cart at ten every morning and worked straight through until eight, seven days a week, rain or shine. And he never failed to serve his customers with a smile. Rick couldn't remember ever seeing him in a bad mood.

A few feet from the cart, Rick stopped to watch a young man with a backpack and a ponytail order a hot dog.

"Here you are, young man," Clarence said in his booming voice. "Enjoy. And as you savor this piece of fine cuisine, you might want to remember the less fortunate. Give generously this holiday season, my friend, and you will be given back."

But the student was already out of earshot. Clarence shook his head and mumbled under his breath, "Might as well talk to a brick wall."

"Or you can talk to me."

Clarence's mahogany face split into a huge grin. "Rick, my man! What brings you to this part of town?"

The two men shook hands. "The energy, Clarence, what else? I miss it."

"Serves you right for leaving us. When you goin' to come to your senses and move back where you belong?"

"One of these days, Clarence. One of these days."

Clarence opened a steaming bin. "So, what are you in the mood for, brother? The tame? Or the wild?"

That was a challenge if Rick had ever heard one. He laughed. "Surprise me."

"Now, *that's* what I like to hear." Clarence went to work, and moments later he handed Rick a hot dog buried under a mountain of black beans, Monterey Jack, chopped romaine and a few chipotle peppers poking through the mix.

The first bite nearly took Rick's head off. He blinked once, chewed bravely as he fought the tears, and finally swallowed the fiery combination. "That's a winner," he said, trying not to choke.

"Thank you. I'm thinking of calling it Friendly Fire, and making it a daily special." He popped two orange sodas open and handed one to Rick, who took a long gulp.

"I see your lady from time to time, but she don't see me. She's always in a hurry, rushing from here to there."

"She's not my lady anymore." Rick took a second bite, bracing himself for another assault of his senses, but his mouth seemed to have gone numb.

"And a damn shame, too," Clarence commented. "Man has to be a fool to let a fine woman like that get away." He dragged out the word *fine* for extra emphasis.

"I won't deny that, Clarence." Using his left hand, Rick pulled Zoe's sketch from his pocket, gave it a snap and handed it to the vendor. "Does this man look familiar?"

Clarence chuckled. "You bet he does. That's Archie."

Zoe's Archie. That was a good sign. "You know him?"

"I keep his belly full whenever he's around but that's about it. I tried to talk to him once or twice but the poor man is scared of his own shadow. All I got out of him was his first name."

"What is he scared of?"

Clarence shrugged. "Don't know. I think he's paranoid."

Meaning he was probably unreliable.

"What's he done?" Clarence wanted to know.

"Nothing bad. He may have some information I need. I'd be willing to pay."

"You'd have to track him down first. Archie never stays in one place long."

"Doesn't he come around every day, knowing he can get a good meal?"

"He gets that at the shelter, along with a bunk."

"When was the last time you saw him?"

Clarence thought for a moment. "Maybe a week. He was flush for a change, and insisted on paying for his hot dog."

A week. That would make it about the time he had sold the charm to Rudy.

Clarence took Rick's empty soda can and tossed it in a bag behind the counter. "Want me to let you know when he shows up again?" Shrewd eyes watched him. "Maybe keep him busy until you show up?"

"Would you?" Rick handed him his business card. "I'll owe you big-time, Preacher Man."

Clarence pointed his index finger at him. "And don't you think that I won't hold you to it. Clarence never forgets a favor taken or a favor given."

Forty

After a four-day hiatus, Kitty Floyd was back to her old tricks, zipping around town in her miniskirts and leather boots, following clues and driving NYPD detectives crazy with her constant phone calls.

Zoe was astonished to see how quickly she had immersed herself back into her work, finding new leads for Kitty to explore and new names to add to her growing list of suspects. It felt good to be working, to see the story develop under her fingers. Her only regret, now that she no longer had an active part in the investigation, was that she felt as if she was letting Lola down. On the other hand, not having to stick to the facts allowed her to be more creative. She could now use her imagination and put Kitty in situations where she might not have been before.

She had just started to draw the private investigator climbing over the balcony of an Upper East Side apartment, when her phone rang. It was Martha, Lola's manicurist.

"I can tell you the name of that florist now," Martha said excitedly. "I just saw the delivery truck drive by. The shop is called Blooms. The address is East Eighty-third Street."

At last, a break. "Thank you, Martha. You're a life-saver."

"Glad I could help. I read what happened to you in New Jersey. I'm sorry about your dad, but I was happy to hear that you were all right."

"Thank you."

After hanging up, Zoe immediately called Detective O'Bryan. A colleague by the name of Reynolds an-swered.

"Detective O'Bryan is out on a case. Do you want to leave a message?"

"No. What time did you say he'd be back?"

"I didn't."

"Then perhaps you could give me his cell-phone num-ber?"

"Sorry, Miss Foster. That's not for public informa-tion."

"I'm a little more than the 'public,' Detective," Zoe replied pointedly. "I assure you that Detective O'Bryan will want to hear what I have to say. It's about the Lola Malone case."

"I'm sure it is." His tone was mildly sarcastic, as if he was humoring her. After all the calls she had made to the department over the last week, she had no trouble imagining what the men in the squad room had been say-ing.

"I tell you what," he said, sounding as though he

was doing her a huge favor. "I'll let him know you called. If he wants to talk to you, he'll call you back. How's that?"

"Fine." As she hung up, she muttered, "Don't say I didn't try."

Blooms was an upscale shop discreetly tucked between a clothing boutique with price tags in the four digits and a skin-care clinic. The window was a work of art, featuring pink and white poinsettias, bejeweled wreaths and bunches of holly, all set against a snowy background.

A tan delivery truck with Blooms scrawled in dark green letters was parked at the curb, and a young man, barely out of his teens, was loading the back with holiday arrangements of every size and shape.

Certain that no one inside would give her the kind of information she was after, Zoe opted to take her chances with the delivery boy. She waited until he came back out before approaching him. "Hi," she said cheerfully.

The young man looked her up and down. He grinned. "Hi, there. Do I know you?"

"No, but I was wondering if you could help me with something."

Another long look. "Anything for a hot babe like you."

Zoe took the compliment with a smile. "Have you been working at Blooms for more than four months?"

He raised a brow. That was probably not a line he was accustomed to. "It'll be a year in March. Why?"

She held a small piece of paper where she had typed Lola's name and address. "During the months of June,

July and August of this year, you delivered a dozen roses to that address every Monday morning. Do you remember that?"

The friendly smile disappeared. The young man was now looking at her as if she had suddenly come up with an infectious disease. "What of it?"

"I was hoping you could give me the name of the sender."

This time, he gave a vehement shake of his head. "Sorry, ma'am. I can't do that." In an instant she had gone from a babe to a ma'am.

"There's a twenty in it for you."

He didn't even blink. In this part of town, a twenty was probably something you wiped your shoe on.

"Fifty?"

He may be young but he wasn't stupid. He could tell how badly she wanted the information. He scratched the back of his head. "I could get in a lot of trouble. I could even lose my job."

"A hundred, and that's my last offer. I have to work for a living, too."

This time, the response was swift. "Okay."

Without saying another word, Zoe took five twenties out of her bag and folded them.

He looked around him before pocketing the money. "I don't always remember the names of our customers, but I remember that one because Mrs. Ledoyenne— that's my boss—told me the guy had tacked on a weekly twenty-dollar tip for me. That's more than I make in tips in a month. I was sorry when the order was canceled."

Zoe smiled patiently. "I would remember him, too." She cocked her head to the side. "The name?"

"E. J. Greenfield."

Forty-One

Zoe cut through the throng of holiday shoppers, barely aware of the jostling. E.J. had lied to her, not once but twice. And he had done it so convincingly there hadn't been a single doubt in her mind that he was telling her the truth.

Didn't he think she would find out? Probably not. What were the odds that she would track down a florist located clear across town?

E.J. and Lola Malone.

No matter how much she tried, she couldn't picture them together. He was a short, chubby, middle-aged man with grown children, an affinity for Cuban cigars and a wife who sang in the church choir. She was a young, beautiful, sexy vixen who wouldn't give a man like E.J. the time of day.

So what was he doing sending her a dozen red roses and paying a kid twenty bucks a pop to make sure they were delivered at the same time every Monday morning? Sure, he could have been an appreciative fan with nothing more in mind than expressing his admiration for a talented artist, but Zoe didn't buy it. Men didn't throw away that kind of money without expecting something in return. And if E.J.'s motives were so innocent, why hadn't he told her the truth when he had the chance?

Which brought up another disturbing question. What else had he lied about?

E.J. sensed something was wrong the moment Zoe entered his office, unannounced and unsmiling. "Zoe." He stood up and came forward to greet her. "Everything all right?"

"Can we sit down?"

"Of course." He started to take her arm to lead her to one of the chairs facing his desk, but she involuntarily pulled back.

Concerned eyes studied her face. "What is it, Zoe?"

The question came out before she could formulate it in her mind. "Did you kill Lola?"

Panic flashed across his eyes. "What?"

"I know about the roses."

Walking back to his desk, he let out a long, loud whoosh, as though he had been holding his breath forever and was finally releasing it. Then, bracing his hands on the leather ink blotter, he sat down slowly and closed his eyes.

Zoe's heart started to beat like a drum. She had so hoped to be wrong. Out of fondness for E.J., who had been like a father to her, she had prayed for some miraculous explanation, one of those strange coincidences that in the end would make perfect sense.

The man slumped in the chair across from her blew all those hopes away. "Did you kill her?" Her voice cracked as she repeated the question.

She waited for an emphatic denial. All he gave her was a weak shake of his head.

"I don't believe you."

"I don't expect you to." He pressed the palms of his hands against his eyes for a second or two. "I should have told you everything the other day, when you confronted me."

"Why didn't you?"

"I was afraid I'd become the prime suspect."

"Because you and Lola were lovers?" Even now, the concept was impossible to fathom.

"Sounds crazy, doesn't it? A girl like her, an old man like me." He took a shallow breath. "Lola and I had the kind of relationship not too many people would understand."

"Try me."

He took a moment to collect his thoughts. "I had been at Blue Moon, three, maybe four times. Then one night, instead of going home after Lola's last set, I decided to approach her, maybe ask her out for a cup of coffee."

"Right there? In Blue Moon? In front of all those people?"

"No, of course not. I waited for her to come out the back door. I was like a teenager waiting for his first date to show up at the top of the staircase. I kept rehearsing what I wanted to say to her, not giving a damn that I sounded like a bumbling idiot. To my surprise, she agreed to go out for coffee. We talked until three in the morning."

"Did you tell her you were married?"

"No." He looked down at his ink blotter and started to play with one of the corners. "The following day, I took her to the aquarium at Baltimore Harbor. We were like a couple of kids. She made me feel so alive, so young. I think that's where I fell in love with her—in Baltimore."

A sad smile crossed his lips. "Oh, don't get me wrong, I was no fool. I knew what I was getting into, just as I knew that it couldn't last. I was content that someone as beautiful as Lola, someone who could have any man she wanted, would spend time with me. When I told her that, she laughed and called me a fool for having such a low opinion of myself. She said she loved being with me because I was kind and considerate, a true gentleman. With me, she felt free to shed her 'femme fatale' persona, as she called it, and be herself. She admitted having terrible taste in men and said I was a refreshing change. She seemed tough on the outside, but inside she was gentle and vulnerable, two traits that, unfortunately, attracted the wrong types of men."

"Did she talk about those men?"

"Never. She was very discreet about that. That's why I felt safe with her. As selfish as this may sound, I didn't want to lose my wife."

"Who broke up with whom?"

"I did. Not because I wanted to, but because I had to."

"What does that mean?"

"Lola had fallen in love."

The mysterious married man Annie had told her about? "With whom?"

"She wouldn't tell me. She wouldn't even admit it at first, but I eventually got it out of her."

"You must have been upset." Upset enough to kill her?

"I won't deny that, but my mind was made up. I didn't want her if I couldn't make her happy."

"And she was happy? With that new man?"

"I don't know. I never saw her again after that." He leaned forward, meeting Zoe's gaze for the first time. "I didn't kill her, Zoe. I think you know me well enough to believe that I could never harm anyone, especially a person I cared for."

She did believe him, partly because she desperately wanted to and partly because his story rang true. "Did you give her the cupid charm?"

"No. I never saw it before your sketch."

Zoe let a moment pass before she heaved a small sigh. "E.J.…."

But he was way ahead of her. "I know. I have to go to the police."

"I wish there was another way."

"Don't apologize. I've been battling with my conscience long enough. It's time to put this matter to rest."

"I'll come with you. I know the detective in charge of Lola's case. He might be able to keep your statement confidential. Detective O'Bryan can be understanding when he puts his mind to it."

Forty-Two

In spite of her optimism regarding Detective O'Bryan, Zoe had her doubts about the extent of his understanding. And judging from E.J.'s tense demeanor as they walked into the busy precinct, he felt the same way.

To her surprise, and relief, O'Bryan was much more sympathetic to E.J.'s situation than she had expected. He listened quietly as the publisher talked about his relationship with the nightclub singer. Every now and then, one of his thick brows would go up, but for the most part, he remained his unemotional self.

He didn't speak until E.J. was finished. By that time, the publisher was much more comfortable and able to answer the detective's probing questions with aplomb and credibility.

"We keep all witnesses' statements confidential," he said as he shut off the tape recorder he had placed on the table. "And since, at this point, you are not considered a suspect, you can relax."

E.J. looked nervous again. "What do you mean, at this point?"

"I'm still waiting to hear whose fingerprints were found in Ms. Malone's apartment."

"But I told you I was never there."

"In that case, you have nothing to worry about." He stood. "And you won't mind if we fingerprint you?"

"Not at all."

Ten minutes later, Zoe and E.J. walked out of the police station. "Didn't I tell you it would be painless?" Zoe asked.

E.J.'s limousine was waiting for them at the curb. He gave one last wipe at his ink-stained fingers, then opened the back door to let Zoe in. "Nothing about being interrogated by the police is painless, Zoe, but I appreciate your optimism. Detective O'Bryan's fondness for you didn't hurt, either."

Zoe scoffed as he sat beside her. "Fondness? He thinks I'm a pain in the butt. If Houdini came back from the grave and made me disappear, O'Bryan would be the first to cheer."

"I got that, but it doesn't change the fact that he likes you and respects you, now more than ever. The way you tracked down that flower shop and bribed the delivery boy into giving you the information impressed him more than you realize. I know, because I was impressed, too."

"Where to, sir?" the driver asked.

E.J. looked at Zoe.

"Rick's apartment on Central Park West."

"You heard the lady, James." He reached into a small side compartment. "I know it's early, but I need a drink. What about you?"

She peered over his shoulder. "What have you got?"

"Vodka, scotch, rum."

"Vodka. Straight up." What the hell, she wasn't driving.

E.J. took a bottle of ice-cold Absolut from the small refrigerator, filled two column-shaped glasses and handed her one. *"Skoal."* He touched her glass with his. "To the truth. Hopefully now I'll sleep."

Zoe took a long sip, letting the eighty-proof liquor slide down her throat like hot silk. E.J. also sipped in silence for a while, then, unexpectedly, he started to talk about Lola and her dream of someday becoming a stage actress, like her aunt.

"I wonder why she was so unsuccessful in landing a role," Zoe said.

"I know why." He let out a sad little chuckle. "She was awful."

Zoe turned around in her seat. "You don't mean that."

"Sadly, I do. I loved the girl and encouraged her as much as I could, but when she rehearsed for her auditions in front of me, I wanted to run."

"How could she be so good at Blue Moon and so bad on a theater stage?"

"Two different beasts. All she needed to be appreciated as a singer was that golden voice of hers and her sensual looks. With acting, you have to know how to reach deep into yourself and project what is there in a way that will make the audience laugh or cry with you. Lola couldn't do that. She was stiff and dull. God bless her, though, she kept trying. That was one of her most endearing qualities, the faith she had that, in spite of all those rejections, tomorrow was filled with promises."

"I wonder if her aunt was aware of her shortcomings as an actress."

"I don't know how she could not have been. Frieda probably loved her too much to tell her the truth. Just as I did."

He studied his glass, as if trying to decide whether or not to have another drink, then he put it down. "So, who am I going to be?"

"I beg your pardon?"

"In your strip. Who am I going to be?"

"No one. You don't exist. I'm not putting you in the strip."

He looked surprised. "You don't find me interesting enough?"

She laughed. "Do you *want* to be in the strip?"

"God, no." He held up the bottle of vodka, but Zoe shook her head. One of those was about all she could handle on an empty stomach.

He reached for a bulging manila envelope on the seat across from them. "Here. A new batch of e-mails. Maureen says you're setting daily records. You might want to make those readers' clues a permanent thing."

She took the envelope from him and opened it. "I'm considering it."

She sifted through the thick stack, glancing at the clues, smiling at some, shaking her head at others.

Then one stopped her cold. It was from Lonesome Me. He sounded much more hostile than he had previously. Once again, through his words, she sensed this need to control her actions.

"Something wrong?" E.J. was watching her.

"This letter."

"What about it?"

"It's from a reader, a man who signs his e-mails Lonesome Me."

"I remember him. He sent you your first clue."

"He's been sending me others and getting a little more angry each time because I'm not using them."

"What is he saying?"

"'Dear Ms. Foster,'" she read out loud. "'Instead of working as a private investigator, Kitty Floyd should be doing nothing more challenging to her lame brain than cleaning toilets.'"

E.J. took the letter from her. "Who is this bozo?" He finished the rest of the letter. "'I have given you more than a dozen clues in the last week, all good, but except for the first one, you aren't using them. Why is Kitty so determined to ignore the obvious? Is she just plain stupid? Or is the creator behind the character the one who lacks imagination? It's time to bring this dreadful story to a satisfying conclusion and move on. Yours truly, Lonesome Me.'"

E.J. handed the letter back. "I hope you haven't been answering him."

"No, but that doesn't seem to stop him."

"And now he's attacking you on a personal level. I don't like it, Zoe. Maybe you should show this to the police."

"And tell them what? He hasn't done anything illegal."

"They could find out who he is and keep an eye on him."

"On what grounds?"

"On the grounds that he is an obsessed fan and could be dangerous."

"You don't think I've given NYPD cops enough aggravation as it is? Three precincts have been monopolized because of me."

"That's an exaggeration."

"Maybe, but I'm not going to involve the police."

"We need to know who this guy is."

"I may be able to do that without going to the authorities." She knocked on the partition separating the back of the limo from the driver. "James, I changed my mind. Could you please drop me at Lotus Restaurant instead? It's in Chinatown, on Baxter Street."

Sitting in the back of Lotus's busy kitchen with Zoe, Lizzy slowly lowered the note. "Why didn't you tell me about this nut before?"

"Because there was nothing to tell. He sounded a little eccentric, a little controlling perhaps, but other than that I didn't see him as a threat."

Lizzy glanced at her brother, who was trying to settle a mild argument between two of his assistants, before returning her attention to Zoe. She seemed uncharacteristically worried. "A thought just occurred to me."

"You're in one of those philosophical moods, aren't you? I can tell."

"I'm serious. What if he's the killer?"

"The thought crossed my mind. And E.J.'s, although he didn't come right out and say it. But if Lonesome Me was the killer, he wouldn't be sending me antagonistic letters. He'd want to stay in the background as much as possible."

"Not necessarily. While many killers take great pains in concealing what they've done, others like to brag about what they consider 'the perfect crime.' Maybe that's what this reader is doing. You've given him a forum, Zoe, a place to show his superiority." She read the letter again. "He sounds like a man who craves attention."

"Which I haven't been giving him."

"And he doesn't like that. He doesn't like to be ignored." She dropped the letter on the table. "I'm worried about what he might do next if you continue to snub him."

"Are you suggesting that I take one of his clues?"

"No, I'm suggesting that you listen to E.J. and let the police find out who this guy is."

"I was hoping *you* could do that."

"Me?"

"You know your way around the Internet better than anyone I know."

"Just because I designed my own Web site doesn't make me an expert. Anyone can do that. On the other hand, NYPD has a number of computer-crimes wizards. Joe should know."

"Joe should know what?"

Zoe turned to see Joe standing beside a tray of cut-up vegetables. He selected a green-pepper strip before approaching the two women.

"How did you know I was here?" Zoe asked.

"E.J. called me. The man is worried sick about you. He said something about a threatening letter?"

"E.J. is being melodramatic."

"Don't let her fool you, Joe," Lizzy interjected. "There's definitely cause for concern." She gave Zoe's hand a sisterly tap. "Let Joe read the letter and see what he has to say. I bet you a bowl of wonton soup he'll agree with me."

Suddenly, the kitchen, which until now had been relatively calm, erupted like an active volcano. One of the two cooks Jimmy had been trying to pacify was pointing at a pot on the stove and talking in rapid Chinese, while another banged a bok choy cabbage on the counter to emphasize his point.

Lizzy sprang out of her chair and dived into the chaos. Joe took this opportunity to grab Zoe's hand. "Come on, let's get out of here before we become fatalities."

They sat in Roma's Pizza, where the crust was crisp, the tomato sauce fresh and the slices generous. The letter from Lonesome Me sat on the table. Joe glanced at it from time to time as he ate and questioned Zoe.

"Does he always use the same e-mail address? 2nats@worldcap.com?"

"Yes. That should make him fairly easy to locate, right?"

"Not if he doesn't want to be found. The Internet is a haven for all types of criminals who want to remain anonymous—con men, identity thieves, pedophiles. All you need is a little know-how."

"How can they remain anonymous? I'm not anonymous."

"There are ways. Giving a phony name and address is only one."

"How can you give a phony name if you have to pay your provider with a credit card?"

"A lot of providers now offer free e-mail." Joe took out his cell phone.

"Who are you calling?"

"Art Burgess in Computer Crimes. He used to be a hacker before the department wised up and hired him. He's one of the best. Art," he said when his friend answered. "Joe Santos. How are you, buddy?" Joe laughed. "I'll give you a rematch anytime you want. Hell, I'll even give you a ten-point lead."

Another laugh and then he turned serious. "Art, I need your help with something." He told him as much as he knew, listened, then thanked him and hung up. "It'll be about an hour," he told Zoe. Pointing at her empty plate, he added, "Want another slice?"

"Don't you have to go to work?"

"I had a couple of days off coming to me." He grinned. "I'm all yours."

"In that case, why don't we go back to the Village, where we were the other day? With a little luck, we might run into that homeless man again."

Joe finished his soda, left a generous tip for the waitress and followed Zoe out the door.

An hour later, the heavy dark clouds that had threatened Manhattan all morning finally broke loose and they had to seek shelter from the deluge inside Joe's Crown Vic, parked on a side street. Zoe was spinning the radio dial in search of a jazz station, when Joe's cell phone rang. He listened attentively, nodded a few times while making grumbling sounds Zoe didn't think were encouraging.

"It's not good news, is it?" she said after he hung up. "Your friend struck out."

"Yes and no. Your Lonesome Me is registered with Worldserve under the name Douglas Brooks. He lives at 1710 Northwest Boulevard in Springside, Wisconsin." Zoe waited for the bad news she knew was coming. "However, Douglas Brooks doesn't exist and 1710 Northwest Boulevard is the address of a parking lot."

"Can't the e-mail itself be traced?"

"Art is working on that, but he's not optimistic. If Douglas Brooks, for lack of another name, went to the trouble of establishing a phony account, then chances are he sent you this e-mail using someone's Wi-Fi connection."

"What's Wi-Fi?"

"It's a fairly new technology that stands for wireless fidelity. It works on a high-frequency, wireless network and allows several people in different places to use the same Internet connection. However, more and more people are discovering that you can use a subscriber's connection without anyone's being the wiser. All you have to do is place yourself within a certain radius of a facility that has Wi-Fi, such as a library, an airport, a campus or a warehouse, and you're in business."

"And there is no way to find the culprit?"

"None whatsoever. The information in the e-mail itself will reveal a general geographical location of where the message originated, but not the exact location. And it won't give a single clue about the unauthorized user. He might as well be invisible."

"So a murderer could admit to a crime, in writing, and there's nothing anyone can do?"

"Welcome to the twenty-first century."

Zoe started to search through her bag. "I need to write all this down."

"Why don't you wait until after we've talked to Art. He wants to take a look at that e-mail. We can go right now."

"That's fine, but I still need to write this down before I forget it. I may want to use it in my strip. Do you have a pen?"

Joe patted his pockets. "Look in the glove compartment."

She opened the small box in front of her and ran her hand through it. "How do you find anything in there?" She took out a pair of sunglasses, an old Johnny Cash cassette, a set of handcuffs, a pack of Kleenex. And something else.

"There's a pen way in the back," Joe said.

But Zoe was no longer listening. Every muscle in her body had gone rigid as she stared at the last item she had taken from the glove compartment—a small plastic bag containing five gold, foil-wrapped squares with the name *Nougat de Montélimar* written on the labels.

Forty-Three

"Where did you get these?"

Joe glanced at the bag while pulling out of the parking space. "Some supermarket. Help yourself if—"

"Stop the car, Joe."

He turned to look at her. "What?"

"Stop the car."

The commanding sound of her voice had an immediate effect. Joe jammed on his brakes. Too intuitive not to realize that whatever was happening had something to do with the bag in her hand, he locked eyes with hers and said nothing.

"Those confections aren't sold in supermarkets," Zoe said. "In fact, they're only available from a Web site that imports them from France."

His face had turned as gray as the sky above them, but he offered no explanation.

"They're called nougat," Zoe continued. Her heart was pounding so wildly she wondered if he could hear it. "Not everybody's cup of tea. In fact, I know of only one person who loved them enough to carry them with her wherever she went."

Joe's pronounced Adam's apple moved up and down. He had yet to say a single word to dispel the insane thought that had found its way into her head.

"My God." Instinctively, she pulled away from him. "It's you. It was you all along."

Although he looked like the same old Joe, something about him changed. The look of panic in his eyes was unmistakable. She had caught him off guard, forcing him to think on his feet. The meticulous planner in him didn't like that.

"You are Lola's mysterious lover."

At last he spoke, but he had to clear the emotion from his voice twice before he could get the words out. "Give me a chance to explain."

He wasn't denying it. Like she had with E.J., she was waiting for a disclaimer that wouldn't be coming.

"Don't look so frightened," he said softly. "I'm not going to hurt you."

That was a lie. He would do what he had to do to survive. "Did you kill Lola? No bullshit, Joe. Just a yes or a no."

So much was happening in those dark eyes, she couldn't keep up. Panic gave way to fear, then regret and finally, sorrow. "Yes."

Lola was dead. She felt a deep pain, as if she had just lost a close friend. Joe was still watching her. For the first time in her life, Zoe was truly afraid. She was in the presence of a murderer.

"Will you listen to me now?" he asked.

She didn't want to listen. She wanted to be as far away from him as possible.

Without taking her eyes off his face, she reached behind her, searching for the door handle.

The click of all four doors locking made her jump. She was trapped. In unmarked police vehicles, as in patrol cars, the locking mechanism was on the driver's side, inaccessible to any of the passengers.

"I just want to talk," he said quietly.

She looked around her. Although it was still daylight, the downpour was keeping people away. The few pedestrians she saw rushing up and down the narrow street kept their heads down, paying no attention to the car parked askew. Would they hear her if she screamed and banged on the window?

She looked back at Joe. "Did you know that Lola was pregnant?"

"Oh, yes." His tone had turned bitter. "She rammed it down my throat often enough."

"So you killed her."

"That's not why I killed her, and don't look at me like that. You have no idea what she put me through. She became pregnant so I'd marry her. All the time, I thought she was on the Pill and she was setting me up. *That,* Zoe, is the woman you've grown so fond of, the woman whose death you so fiercely want to avenge. You have this high opinion of Lola Malone and she was nothing but a conniving, unscrupulous, back-stabbing tramp."

"What about you? Pretending to be in love with me while carrying on with another woman. How scrupulous is that?"

"I do love you! I've never loved anyone but you. Everything I did, I did for you, for us."

She laughed. "You screwed Lola Malone for us? That's good, Joe. Almost as good as 'the devil made me do it.'"

"Sleeping with Lola was the only way I could find out what Rick Vaughn was all about."

She gave him a stunned look. "What does Rick have to do with Lola's murder?"

"Everything. Rick was the wall between us, Zoe. That's right. You're still hung up on the guy. You always were. Lola's disappearance may have brought you back together, but the feelings you had for him never went away. That's why you turned down my proposal. And why you won't sleep with me."

He reached for a strand of her hair, but she jerked her head to the side, leaving him empty-handed.

He pretended not to notice. "So I decided to find out for myself what made Rick so special," he continued. "I went to Blue Moon to observe him, and to listen. You'd be amazed at how much you learn when you hang around a bar. I always stayed in the background, away from the lights and away from him."

"You told me you had never been to Blue Moon."

"I'm sorry that I had to lie to you. I'm sorry about a lot of things, but I was determined to make you fall in love with me, even if that meant becoming a copy of your ex-husband, in every way but physically."

"That's sick."

"Don't say that."

"It is! You sought out, then seduced, an innocent, unsuspecting woman so you could win another woman? You find that normal?"

"I didn't seek her out. She's the one who came after me. She spotted me in the back of the club one night and when I left, she followed me to my car, told me I looked like I could use some company."

His gaze drifted briefly toward the bag of candy in Zoe's hand. "She was so easy, a sucker for a pretty boy with a badge."

"How did you keep her from talking about you to Annie and Rick?"

"I told her that I was married to a very suspicious woman. She agreed to meet me at out-of-town motels, to never take any pictures of me, and to always wait for my calls."

So Lola's married lover wasn't married after all, Zoe thought. She could have investigated every married man in the city until she ran out of suspects, and she wouldn't have found the killer. "Why all the secrecy?"

"I didn't want to run the risk of you or anyone finding out. It's a small world. I learned that lesson a long time ago. And Lola didn't mind. She understood why I had to be careful."

"But you didn't count on her falling head over heels in love with you. Annie told me," she added, when he raised a questioning brow.

"No, I hadn't counted on that. Just as I hadn't counted on her getting pregnant. That's the reason I told her I was married, so she wouldn't get any big ideas."

"And you hated the idea of being a dad so much that

you killed the mother? And her unborn child?" Zoe was finding it difficult to keep the revulsion from her voice.

"I told you, that's not why I killed her." He ran a shaky hand through his hair. He wasn't handling the stress well. Whether his anxieties would work in her favor or not was another story.

"Then why did you?"

"She started bugging me about getting married. I would try to appease her with little gifts. One of them was that charm you've been hunting for. Those little baubles helped for a while, then the circus would start all over again. We fought about everything—the abortion she refused to have, her fixation on marriage, the way she clung to me, smothering me with attention I didn't want. She had her little scenario all figured out, chapter by chapter. I would ask my wife for a divorce, and then I would marry her. She was going to leave her job at Blue Moon and focus on raising a family. She wanted two children—one boy and one girl. She even showed me brochures of places where we would go on our honeymoon—Tahiti, Fiji, New Zealand. She was driving me crazy, talking about all the things I wanted to do with you. One day, it got too far and I spilled the beans. I told her I didn't love her, that I loved only one woman and that was you."

The revelation hit Zoe like a kick in the gut. "You told her my name?"

"It was stupid, I know. I hadn't meant to do it that way, but she pushed me too far and I lost control, unaware of the weapon I had just handed her."

"She threatened to tell me."

He nodded. "I don't know how she found out about the *Herald*'s Christmas party, but she did. The day of the party, she looked at me, very smug, and said, 'Zoe didn't answer any of my calls, so I think I'll crash that little bash tonight.'"

"I saw all my hopes for you and me melt away. I knew that once you found out about Lola and the baby, you'd never have anything to do with me. I got scared, Zoe." His eyes were pleading. "Can't you understand that? I didn't want to lose you."

"You never had me!"

"I had you the other night, when I kissed you. You wanted me that night, every bit as much as I wanted you."

There was no point in arguing about something he so strongly believed. "And all the wonderful things you did, introducing me to Detective O'Bryan, intervening with Rick, explaining about the various types of listening devices. That was all for show?"

"It was a way of detracting attention from me."

"You must have felt very sure of yourself."

"I had an advantage. I know how to cover a crime scene and I know about listening devices and where to get them. By bugging your loft and your cell phone, I was able to keep track of your whereabouts. I knew who you were going to see, where and when at all times."

"Like poor Rudy."

"Rudy should have kept his mouth shut."

"And what about me? You could have killed me when you fired those two shots."

"I'm too good a marksman for that to happen."

Of course. His marksmanship was something he had always been proud of. "When I called you from the electronics shop and you told me you were circling my building, that wasn't true. You knew where I was the whole time."

"That was a little tricky, coming down that fire escape with all those people looking up and yelling, then getting back to my car in the middle of all the commotion."

"You had everything planned."

"Not everything. You popped a few surprises on me."

"Archie."

He nodded.

"You never intended to catch him, did you?"

"I knew Archie from when I was a rookie cop. I had no idea he was in the alley that night, but when I saw him run away after he saw me, I realized that he was the one who had found Lola's charm, and that he had witnessed the killing. I couldn't let you talk to him."

"What if he comes forward on his own?"

"He won't. He's too scared of cops, me in particular."

"Why? What have you done to him?"

"The man is crazy, Zoe. I was just trying to get him off the streets, for his own good."

"Are you going to kill him, too?"

"I've got my hands full at the moment, trying to decide what to do with you."

"I can't believe what I'm hearing. I don't understand any of it. How could you go from being this wonderful, kind, honorable man everyone loves to a cold-blooded killer?"

"I told you once that I would do anything for you. I proved it."

"Don't you dare put the blame for your actions on me. You did this all by yourself. *You* created that beast inside of you."

He continued to look at her, in silence now. What was he thinking? What was he going to do? What *could* he do?

She glanced down at the bag of nougat she still held. "Amazing, isn't it? How something as harmless as a little bag of candy could give you away."

"I forgot I had them, or I would have removed the candy the moment you found them in Lola's apartment."

Her head snapped up. "How did you know that I found them? You could no longer eavesdrop. All the bugs had been removed."

"Not all." His gaze drifted down to her left wrist.

"My watch?"

All thought of remaining calm and rational flew out the window. "You son of a bitch!" She unstrapped the watch and threw it at him. "How could you do this to me? You're a monster! A sick, twisted monster and I hate you! Let me out of here, do you hear?"

"Oh, Zoe." His eyes filled with regret. "You know I can't do that."

At that moment, an old man carrying a grocery bag with a stalk of celery peeking over the top appeared at the end of the street. The wind had picked up and he was struggling to hold his umbrella from being blown away.

She had to catch his attention.

"Help!" Before Joe could stop her, she started bang-

ing on the windshield as hard as she could while screaming, *"Help! Sir! Help me!"*

Joe's fist caught her on the cheekbone. Pain exploded
in her head, then she felt nothing at all.

Forty-Four

The call from Clarence came as Rick was signing bonus checks for his employees.

"Rick, my man," the familiar voice said. "You may want to mosey on down to my gourmet hut pronto, if you know what I mean."

"Archie showed up?"

"He's sitting not five feet from me, munching on one of my delicacies."

"Please keep him there, Clarence."

"I will do my best."

Rick was thankful that some gut instinct had told him to drive to work today. He normally didn't, preferring to use his car for out-of-town trips. The traffic was brutal, but he tried not to break any laws. Getting stopped by the cops now wouldn't help his situation.

When he neared his destination, he spotted a space and took it, even though it was two long blocks from Clarence's cart. He ran all the way, stopping only when he started drawing strange looks from passersby.

Clarence was at his post, delivering one of his sermons to two construction workers who looked as if they had heard it all before but didn't mind hearing it again. Across from them, sitting on a stoop and sipping one of Clarence's sodas, was a man wearing several layers of gray clothing. His hands were wrapped around the can and his eyes were watchful as they observed the activity around him.

Hoping he looked completely unthreatening, Rick went to sit beside him. "Hi. My name is Rick."

The man gave him a frightened look and started to stand, but Rick stopped him. "Please don't go."

"You the cops?"

"No, I'm a friend of Clarence."

Right on cue, Clarence, whose audience had just left, raised his hand. "That's okay, Archie. Rick's cool."

Rick gave the man what he hoped was a trustworthy smile.

Archie did not return it. "What do you want with me?"

Rick's cell phone chose that exact moment to ring. He took it out of his pocket, glanced at the caller ID display and answered the call. "Lizzy, is something wrong?"

"I'm worried about Zoe. I just received an e-mail from her, telling me she had a lead on Lola and had to follow it. She'll be gone for a few days."

"*What? Gone where?*"

"I don't know. I've been trying to reach her, at your place, the loft, on her cell phone. She isn't answering. I'm afraid she found out who Lonesome Me is and went after him."

"Who the hell is Lonesome Me?"

"She didn't tell you?"

"Apparently not."

"He's the reader who gave her the first clue for her strip a couple of weeks ago. He's been writing her every day and acting a little strange."

"How strange?"

"He's angry that she's not taking any more of his clues. Today's e-mail was particularly vicious. It shook her a little, and me."

"What did it say?"

"I don't remember the exact words, but he was insulting, and this time, he made it personal." She paused. "I'm afraid he might be the killer, Rick. E.J. thinks so, too. He was concerned enough to call Joe, who came right away."

The little twist in Rick's gut was now a familiar one. He felt it every time Joe Santos's name was mentioned. "Did Joe take her to the precinct so she could file a complaint?"

"I don't know. He may have. All hell broke loose in my kitchen when I was talking to them and they skipped out on me. Not that I blame them—it sounded like a war zone in here for a while. Then about half an hour ago, Joe called. He talked to my mother and said that he had dropped Zoe at your place and she seemed fine. I didn't worry anymore until I received the e-mail I mentioned."

"Are you sure it's from her?"

There was a slight pause. "Yes, of course it's from her. Who else would send it?"

"Could you check it?"

"Wait a sec. Let me log on." A minute later, she spoke again. "I'm checking it now." He heard her gasp. "Rick, it's not her e-mail address. It's almost the same. I guess that's why I didn't notice. To tell you the truth, I hardly look at it anymore. All I need to see is Kitty and I know it's from her. This e-mail did not come from *Kittyf@search.com,* which is Zoe's e-mail address. It came from *Kitty@alta.com.* It's one of those free e-mail providers."

"Then Zoe didn't send it."

"Oh, Rick." He heard the fear in her voice. "What happened to her? Where is she?"

"Lizzy, could you do me a favor?"

"Yes, anything."

"Go to my apartment and see if she's left a note or any kind of clue. And check her laptop, if it's still there." He glanced at Archie, who was watching him with a great deal of interest. "I'd do it myself but I'm tied up at the moment."

"How do I get into your apartment?"

"I'll call the doorman. His name is Carl. He'll let you in. Do you have the address?"

"The Rosenthal on Central Park West."

"That's it. Call me on my cell as soon as you know something."

He made the call to Carl, then snapped his phone shut and turned his attention back to Archie. The sooner he found out what the man knew, the better he could help Zoe. "Archie, I'm going to be honest with you. A woman I care about very much is in trouble."

"You knocked her up?"

Rick smiled. "Not that kind of trouble."

"What then?"

"It's complicated. You may have seen her. She's been on TV a lot lately."

"I watch TV sometimes, at the shelter. What she look like, your girlfriend?"

"She's not…" Rick cut his sentence short. Why confuse the poor man when there was no need? "She's very pretty, with long, curly red hair."

Looking scared, Archie shook his head. "I ain't got nothin' to say."

"I think you do, Archie. I know you're the person who sold that cupid charm to Rudy Goldberg."

"I didn't steal it!"

"I know you didn't. But it would help me a lot, and help my lady friend, if you told me exactly how it came to be in your possession."

"I found it."

"Where?"

Archie pulled out a large plastic bag that he had pushed behind him, and wrapped both arms around it, holding it tight against his chest. He looked up and down the street, looking like a scared rabbit. "I don't have it no more."

"I know. You sold it to Rudy."

"And Rudy's dead."

What did he say to that? How could he promise this frightened, helpless man that the same fate wouldn't happen to him when people were dying right and left? "I know you're afraid, Archie, but what would you say if I promised to keep you safe?"

"How?"

By the time this mess was over, Rick thought, he'd owe his two best friends a ton of favors. "I have a friend, an ex-marine, who can put you up until all danger has passed."

"A marine?"

"A good man, Archie. He's been my friend for fifteen years."

He seemed to mull the idea over for a moment. "Okay."

Rick let out a small sigh of relief. "Where did you find the charm?"

A bony finger pointed south. "Over there, in an alley, next to…"

"Next to what?" Rick tried to keep the urgency from his voice.

"Next to her. The blonde. The *dead* blonde."

Rick took a long silent breath. All this time, he had held on to the hope that Lola was still alive. That hope had vanished with Archie's last three words. "Did you see what happened, Archie? Did you see who killed her?"

Archie gave a couple of slow nods.

"Will you tell me what you saw?"

"She was runnin'. And she was scared. I could tell."

"Where were you?"

"Inside a Dumpster, looking for stuff."

"And where was she? The blonde?"

"Runnin'. He was runnin', too, tryin' to catch her."

"And he did?"

Another nod. "I look up over the Dumpster, and there he was, holdin' her. She couldn't move or nothin'."

"And then what happened?"

"They talked. I couldn't hear what they was sayin', then she started to cry. I wanted to help, but I was scared." His voice became a hushed whisper. "He strangled her, with his bare hands. When she couldn't stand no more, she fell down, like a rag doll. She was dead. It was too late. I couldn't do nothin'."

"What happened next?"

"That cute redhead came runnin' and limpin'."

"Limping?" That didn't sound like Zoe, but how many cute redheads could there have been?

Archie nodded. "She went down on her knees and tried to help the blonde, but she couldn't, so she ran back to get help."

"Where was the killer while this was happening?"

"Hidin' inside a doorway, watchin' her."

"What did he do after the redhead left?"

"He ran back to the dead woman, picked her up and carried her off, like a sack of potatoes."

"Did you see a car? A license plate you may have memorized?"

Archie shook his head. "I was too busy gettin' out of the Dumpster. That's when I found the little charm."

It must have fallen off in the struggle. "You didn't wait for the police to get there?"

His eyes widened and he shook his head again. "No, sir. I don't like cops. Cops always threaten to throw me in jail. I don't like jail. Jail's a bad place. Friend of mine died there. Cops beat him up till he died."

"I'm sorry."

"I don't want to go to jail."

"You won't go to jail, Archie, but you're going to have to trust me, because what I'm going to ask you next requires a lot of trust."

"You want to know who killed the blonde."

Smart man. "All I need is a description."

"I know him."

Rick frowned. Another homeless man? That didn't make sense. A homeless man wouldn't have access to a sniper's rifle. Or a computer. "Who is he?" Rick prompted.

The man's face closed up. Frightened eyes darted right and left again, but pedestrians kept walking by, paying no attention to the two men on the stoop.

"Are you afraid of him?"

A nod was all he could get out of the man.

"Why? Did he do something to you to make you afraid?"

"He calls me names, tells me I'm dirty and no damn good. Once he told me that if I didn't stay off the streets, he'd throw me in jail."

Rick went still. "How can he throw you in jail?"

"'Cause he's a cop!" He leaned toward Rick and gave him a whiff of his body odor. "The cop that was with your redhead."

Forty-Five

Zoe felt something cold and wet stroke her face, her temples, her forehead. She opened her eyes, and for a moment, her mind was a total blank. Then she saw Joe bending over her, a washcloth in his hand and a concerned expression in his eyes.

She slapped his hand away. She was in a savage mood. "Don't touch me."

"Come on, Zoe, don't be difficult."

"Don't be difficult?" She touched her cheek where the blow had landed. It was swollen and sore. She was lucky not to have any broken bones. "You hit me hard enough to knock me out, you kidnapped me and you have the nerve to call me difficult?"

"I didn't want to hit you. You gave me no choice."

"I was trying to get away from a killer."

The word made him wince.

"Where am I? Where did you take me?"

"To a quiet place, where we can talk without being interrupted."

Zoe looked around her, at the log walls, the shiny hardwood floor, the stone fireplace where a cheery fire crackled, the rustic furniture. A Christmas tree filled with old-fashioned wooden ornaments, garlands and tinsel stood between the sofa where she lay and an easy chair. It was an all-purpose room, with a kitchen and living/dining room all in one. An open staircase led to a loft.

Through a window, she could see a thick cluster of evergreens. She guessed they were somewhere in the mountains. The Catskills? Or maybe the Poconos in Pennsylvania? Wherever he had brought her, electricity was apparently nonexistent, because the only light in the room came from three oil lamps.

Her inventory taken, Zoe sat up, noticing for the first time the gun in Joe's hand. It wasn't pointed at her, but it was there, resting on his lap. "What is this place?" she asked, trying not to look at the weapon.

"You like it?"

"No. I want to go home."

Joe tossed the washcloth on the coffee table. "That's not possible, Zoe."

"You can't keep me here indefinitely. People know I'm with you—Lizzy, for one."

"I took care of that."

"How?"

He walked over to the fireplace, picked up the wrought-iron poker and jabbed at the logs. "I told her I had dropped you off at Rick's apartment and that you were fine."

"She'll try to call me. You don't know Lizzy. She won't give up. What happens when I don't answer?"

"She'll understand when she gets your e-mail."

"What e-mail?"

He nodded toward the open laptop on the desk. "The one where you explained how you just received a lead on Lola's case and you'll be gone for a few days."

"I won't do it! I will not write that e-mail and you can't make me."

"I won't have to. I wrote it myself and made it look as if *you* sent it."

She remembered the quick lesson he had given her earlier today. "You're Lonesome Me." It wasn't a question. "You've known about phony registrations and wireless fidelity long before you talked to your friend in Computer Crimes."

"I guess you could call me something of an expert in Wi-Fi technology."

"It never occurred to me to doubt you. You were the last person on earth I would have suspected of any kind of wrongdoing. I trusted you with my life."

"You can still trust me."

She laughed. "Yeah, right."

"Why do you think I brought you here?"

"To bury me?"

"To give myself some time to think. I didn't plan this. Now I have to figure out what to do next."

If he meant it, if he wasn't planning on killing her, then she had a chance to get out of here.

To keep her mind off her predicament, she let her gaze sweep slowly across the room once more, this time taking in details she hadn't noticed before. Two citations that praised Joe's valor and courage hung on a wall. Between them was a photograph of Joe, in uniform, standing beside former mayor Rudy Giuliani. On a low table in front of that same wall, newspapers were neatly stacked. There must have been more than a dozen copies. She could see the top one, with another picture of Joe, again in uniform, being awarded a medal. Underneath, the caption read: "A hero among us."

"He's a man who craves attention," Lizzy had told her, talking about Lonesome Me. *"He doesn't like to be ignored."* Looking at all those awards and accolades, Zoe realized how well that remark described Joe.

"Is this house yours?"

"Are you surprised?"

"You never told me about it."

"It's my little secret retreat, a place where I can get away from the rat race and truly unwind. It was nothing more than a shack when I bought it. I've been working on it for the last eighteen months."

He had calmed down, so she let him talk. "I did everything myself," he continued, looking proud. "I put in new floors, refinished the walls, rebuilt the fireplace. It's getting dark now, but wait until you step outside. The cabin sits on a hill and the view is breathtaking."

He talked as if they were newlyweds moving into their first home.

"There's even a lake nearby where you can skate in the winter and fish in the summer, just like you used to do with Rick. In fact, don't you think the cabin looks a lot like his house in Connecticut?"

Was that why he bought it? Because it reminded him of Rick's country house? A shiver ran through her. This was just too spooky. "Couldn't you have bought something that had electricity?"

"The power is out. It should be back in another hour or so."

"Does anyone know about this place?" Probably not, or he wouldn't have brought her here.

"No. Not even my mother."

"Why the big secret?"

"If my family knew that the cabin existed, they'd all be here, every weekend, every holiday, turning the place into a henhouse."

"Speaking of your mother, have you thought what this will do to her? Can you see the look on her face when she finds out that her son, the son she's so proud of, is a murderer and a kidnapper?"

He looked away.

She needed to reason with him, appeal to his compassionate side, which right now was in a state of confusion. "I know you don't want to hurt her, Joe. You just feel trapped right now. You haven't had a chance to—"

"Shut up!" He jumped up and for a moment she thought he was going to hit her again. "Stop all this talking. This isn't a Dr. Phil moment, Zoe. I didn't bring you here to psychoanalyze me."

"I was just trying to help."

"I don't need you to tell me what I'm all about, okay?" He sat down again. "Why did you have to turn into Nancy Drew? Why couldn't you just leave it alone? You ruined everything. Maybe I *should* kill you and bury you, right next to your precious Lola."

"Lola's buried here?"

He didn't answer. Gun in hand, he started pacing, like a caged animal who knows there's no way out.

"Maybe you could run," she suggested, out of ideas herself. "You could tie me down, jump on a plane and disappear."

The look of distaste in his eyes told her that running wasn't an option. He was a hero, a man who had stared death in the face. A man who had stood on a podium with the mayor of New York City while thousands of people cheered. He *had* to go back.

Zoe felt her insides clench. In order for him to go back to his job, his family, his life, he would have to kill her.

Forty-Six

As Rick walked down Sixth Avenue with Archie by his side, he called Lenny and asked him to meet him at the Ninth Precinct. "I'll explain everything when I see you," he said before hanging up.

Next, he called Detective O'Bryan. "You'll want to sit tight," he told the detective. "I'm bringing you the only eyewitness to Lola Malone's murder." He hung up when O'Bryan started shouting questions in his ear.

Every now and then Archie, looking a little befuddled, stopped walking. Rick stayed with him, talking softly and telling him he was doing the right thing. After a while, the homeless man would start walking again.

When Rick stopped in front of the Audi, Archie made no move to get in. "You sure they won't throw me in jail?"

Rick opened the passenger door and tried not to think about the stink that would linger for days. "Very sure. They should give you a medal for what you're about to do."

"What about the bad cop?"

"With your help, the police will catch him and put *him* in jail. What do you think of that?" Only then did Archie step into the car.

Rick walked around to the driver's side. *Joe Santos.* It felt strange to hear NYPD's golden boy being referred to as "the bad cop." And to think Rick had actually liked the guy, for a while anyway. The thought that he might have Zoe gave him chills. Where the hell had he taken her?

Archie was watching him. "What'd she do?" he asked suddenly.

Rick shot him a quick glance before pulling into traffic. "I beg your pardon?"

"The cute little redhead. What'd she do to get herself in trouble?"

"She was a little too nosy, Archie. She found out some things she wasn't supposed to know. Now the bad cop has her and I don't know where he took her."

The possibility that he might not find her was inconceivable. Although the past six years without Zoe hadn't been all that bad, they hadn't been all that good, either. Waking up alone was particularly tough. He hadn't fully realized that until the other morning when he had awakened with Zoe in his arms. She had curled up against him during the night, all soft and warm and smelling of honeysuckle. He had just lain there, aching to make love to her while reminding himself that what Zoe needed during those difficult few days was comfort and tenderness, not an ex-husband with raging hormones. Muttering under his breath, he had kicked off the covers and gone in the bathroom to take a cold shower.

He wasn't sure what exactly he was feeling for her, besides affection and desire. All he knew was that since she had reentered his life two weeks ago, he found himself thinking of her, of the woman she had become, far too often. Yes, she was still as stubborn as ever, to the point of being exasperating at times. On the other hand, the qualities he had always admired— loyalty, tenacity, strength—far outweighed her flaws. How many women he knew would have risked so much for someone they had never met? Not many. Actually, none.

"Hang in there, baby." He hadn't realized he had spoken out loud until he heard Archie chuckle into his bag. "What's so funny?"

"You. You got it bad for that girl."

"You think so?"

"I do, yes, sir." Archie kept laughing.

Rick gave a little nod. "You know something, Archie, I think you're right. I didn't want to admit it to myself, but hearing you say it made me realize that there's no shame in admitting that you love a woman." There—he had said it. The *L* word. And it felt damn good.

Rick slowed before pulling up in front of the Ninth Precinct. "Here we are."

Archie's happy mood seemed to dissolve as he looked up at the building. Before he could change his mind and run off, Rick hurried to let him out. "The name of the person we're going to talk to is Detective O'Bryan," he said. "He's going to ask you a lot of questions. He might even try to trick you."

"Why?"

"To see if you're telling the truth."

"I don't lie!"

"You tell him that, Archie. He'll believe you. Just as *I* believed you."

Lenny was already waiting for them when they stepped into the lobby. Looking puzzled, the ex-marine stood up and watched the odd pair enter, but refrained from asking any questions until Rick took him aside.

"What's up?" Lenny asked, glancing at Archie above Rick's shoulder. "Who's your friend?"

"His name is Archie. He's the homeless man who found Lola's charm and sold it to the pawnbroker."

"What is he doing with you?"

"He was in the alley when Lola was murdered. He saw the whole thing."

Lenny's expression turned grave. "So she's dead? There's no doubt about that?"

"Not anymore."

"Who did it?"

"Joe Santos."

He was as shocked as Rick had been earlier. "The NYPD poster boy? You've got to be kidding."

"Not only am I not kidding, but Joe now has Zoe and I have no idea where he took her."

"Shit." Lenny scratched his head. "What can I do?"

"I need you to take Archie home with you while I look for Zoe. Let him take a shower, give him clean clothes, some food."

"*My* home?"

"I told him I'd keep him safe."

"Why don't you leave him here, then? What could be safer than a police station?"

"He doesn't trust cops. But he'll stay with you."

"He doesn't know me."

Rick managed a grin. "I gave you a great buildup."

"Gee, thanks."

"He's scared, Lenny, but he came anyway. I can't let him down. And I can't let him go back on the street with Santos on the loose."

Lenny still looked skeptical.

"If you'd rather take him to my apartment, that's all right with me."

"And suffer the indignity of your doorman's scorn as we walk in? No, thanks." He let out a resigned sigh. "I'll take him to my place." He inspected Archie from head to toe. "What's in that bag he's holding?"

"His belongings. He won't go anywhere without them."

Lenny's nose twitched. "You'll owe me big-time after this, boss. I'm thinking of an all-expenses-paid trip to Paris, at the very least."

Rick gave him a friendly tap on the shoulder. "You've got yourself a deal."

After asking Lenny to wait for them, Rick and Archie walked over to the desk sergeant. Rick gave him their names and said that Detective O'Bryan was expecting them.

The sergeant, who had probably seen worse, gave them both a neutral look, made them sign a register and pointed down the hall. "The squad room's that way."

O'Bryan rose from behind his desk and shook Rick's hand, but he only nodded at Archie, who probably wouldn't have wanted to shake hands with a cop anyway. "So, Mr. Vaughn," he said with only a small trace of sarcasm. "You like to play detective, too?"

"This sort of fell in my lap," Rick offered as an apology.

"Where's the other half of the dynamic duo?"

"I'll tell you in a minute. Right now, I'd like you to listen to Archie's story. And please keep an open mind."

"That's not a good start, Vaughn." Then, focusing his attention on Archie, he asked, "What is your name, sir?"

At the "sir," Archie's chest seemed to grow two sizes bigger. "Archibald Newton III."

O'Bryan stopped writing and looked at Rick, who just shrugged.

"Like the fig newton," Archie added.

"Very well." O'Bryan started writing again.

"But you can call me Archie."

"Thank you, Archie."

Rick waited patiently while O'Bryan went through the formality of establishing Archie's identity and asking him questions such as where he resided and the name of his next of kin. *For God's sake,* he wanted to scream. If the guy had a residence and a next of kin, he wouldn't be sleeping on the streets.

Oddly enough, though, the questioning seemed to put Archie at ease. As his confidence grew, he became less skittish and was able to express himself remarkably well.

As he told O'Bryan what he had witnessed in the alley, Rick watched the detective, whose expression didn't change. A recorder on his desk was taking down every word and he had brought out several mug-shot books for Archie to look at. When Archie was finished, he dropped one on the desk.

"Archie, I'm going to show you some mug shots—"

"That won't be necessary," Rick interrupted.

O'Bryan looked annoyed. "And why not?"

"Because I know who killed Lola. Archie identified him for me."

"Don't keep me in suspense. Who is it?"

"Detective Joe Santos."

After a stunned couple of seconds, the detective threw his head back and let out a laugh loud enough to attract the attention of two other detectives. When he felt he'd had sufficient fun, he gave Rick a hard look. "You're lucky no one else heard you say that, or your life wouldn't be worth a plugged nickel right now."

"Will you let me explain?"

O'Bryan spread out his hands as if to say, "Go ahead, be my guest."

"Joe Santos and Zoe were in the Village, doing some last-minute Christmas shopping, when they ran into Archie. Thinking that he might be the person who'd sold Lola's charm to Rudy Goldberg, Zoe tried to approach him, but Archie got scared and ran.

"At Zoe's request, Joe ran after him, but Archie was too fast and he lost him. Or so Joe claims. Personally, I think he let him get away. Who was going to contest it? Zoe was too far behind to see much of anything. All she witnessed was Joe's effort to catch Archie."

The detective glanced at Archie. "Is all that true?"

"Yes, sir."

"May I ask why you ran?"

Archie tightened his hold around his bag, as if he feared that someone would take it from him. "You tell him, Rick."

Rick nodded. "Archie's had some run-ins with Santos before. But this time, he had an even greater reason to be afraid. He recognized Santos as Lola Malone's killer."

O'Bryan shook his head. "That's absurd. Joe is a friend of mine, and I assure you he's no killer. He's a hero, for God's sake!"

"You'll have to put that aside for the moment and look at the facts. You asked me earlier where Zoe was. I believe Joe has her."

"You have any proof of that?"

"Zoe's friend, Lizzy Min, called me earlier. Zoe had started to receive some disturbing e-mails and Lizzy was worried that the man who signed his letters Lonesome Me was the killer. The last time Lizzy saw Zoe was when she left Lizzy's restaurant with Joe Santos. Shortly after, Joe called the restaurant and told Lizzie's mother that he had dropped Zoe at my place and she was fine.

"Moments later," he continued, "Lizzy received an e-mail, supposedly from Zoe."

"What do you mean, supposedly?"

Rick repeated what Lizzy had told him. "She's on her way to my apartment to see if Zoe left a note. I should hear from her any—"

Rick's cell phone rang. His hand dived into his pocket. "Hello?"

"Rick, it's Lizzy, again." She sounded much more concerned than she had earlier. "I'm at your apartment."

"Lizzy, hold it. I'm with Detective O'Bryan. I'm going to put you on speakerphone." He pressed a button. "Go ahead."

"She didn't leave a note, Rick. And I looked at her computer. There's no record of that e-mail she sent me." Her voice, calm until now, filled with sudden panic. "She would never disappear this way after all that's happened. Besides, all the clothes you brought from her loft are still here. And her shoes. Can you imagine her going away for a few days without taking at least four pairs of shoes with her?"

Rick felt the hard fist of fear lodge itself in his gut as he drew the parallel with Lola's disappearance. He could tell from the grim expression on O'Bryan's face that the detective had drawn the same conclusion.

"We'll find her, Lizzy. Try not to worry, okay? I'll call you as soon as I know something."

O'Bryan was already on the phone. He waited several seconds before hanging up and dialing another number. "Joe's not answering his car phone or his cell," he said as he hung up.

"He won't," Rick said. "Because he's got Zoe."

Forty-Seven

Finding Joe would have been easier if he had been driving a regular patrol car. Unfortunately, the unmarked vehicles assigned to detectives were not equipped with GIS, the geographic information system that approximately twenty patrol cars in all five boroughs now had on their dash. Integrated with GPS, Global Positioning System, and primarily used to handle road emergencies, the network allowed the command post to know exactly where each car was at any time.

O'Bryan had questioned two of Joe's closest friends, Nash Riley and Wayne Pembrose. Both worked at the same precinct, but had no idea where Joe might be. All they knew was that he had taken a couple of days off before starting back on the day shift.

An all-points bulletin for him and Zoe was issued, along with a description and license plate of the Crown Victoria. "Joe still lives with his mother and two younger sisters," O'Bryan told Rick as he looked up Mrs. Santos's address and jotted it down. "She might be able to help us."

In the waiting room, Rick turned Archie over to Lenny, and quickly waved aside O'Bryan's suggestion to stand by the phone and wait for his call. "I'm going to be sticking to you like glue, Detective. You might as well get used to it."

It was dark by the time the threesome arrived in Queens—Detective O'Bryan and a uniformed officer in an unmarked car, and Rick behind them in the Audi.

Mrs. Santos was a petite, attractive woman about thirty pounds overweight, with big brown eyes that grew fearful when she saw the uniformed officer. She pressed her hands to her chest. "*Madre de Dios.* Something happened to Joey!"

"No, it's nothing like that," O'Bryan said. "Joe didn't have an accident, and he wasn't shot, if that's what you're worried about."

Mrs. Santos made the sign of the cross.

"My name is Detective O'Bryan," he continued. "This is Officer Scott and this gentleman here is Rick Vaughn. Mr. Vaughn is Zoe Foster's ex-husband. I believe you know Zoe?"

The look she gave Rick was several degrees cooler than the one she gave O'Bryan and the officer. "Yes, of course. Zoe is practically one of the family. But if you want to talk to Joe—"

"Actually, Mrs. Santos, you're the one we want to talk to."

"Me?" Panic flickered in her dark eyes. "Why?"

"May we come in?"

She led them into a small but tidy living room, where the main attraction was a large nativity set on a buffet table.

"What do you want with me?" she asked when they were all seated.

While O'Bryan brought her up to date, Rick watched her expression go from stunned to outraged.

"Are you crazy?" she cried. "You're accusing my son of being a killer?"

"Mrs. Santos—"

She shook both hands. "No, I won't listen. That's crazy talk. My Joey is the best cop on the force. You know that. He would never kill anyone. Who told you he did?"

"We have an eyewitness."

"I know you have an eyewitness, but who is he? How do you know he's not making all that up?"

"Joe will be given every opportunity to defend himself. The problem is, I can't find him anywhere. He doesn't answer his phones."

"Joe always answers his phones. Even when he's not on duty. He's very good about that."

"I know, that's why I'm concerned that he may be in some kind of trouble."

"What kind of trouble?"

"We suspect that he may have kidnapped Zoe," Rick said.

She gave him a frosty look before addressing her next comment to O'Bryan. "That's impossible. He loves Zoe with all his heart. He would never hurt her."

"I hope that's true, Mrs. Santos. In the meantime, with your permission, I'd like to search his room. May I do that?"

A mother is always a mother. "No."

O'Bryan let out an irritated sigh. "Mrs. Santos, I can get a warrant if I have to, but you'll save me and Zoe Foster precious time if you let me take a look at Joe's things now."

"What are you looking for?"

"A clue to where he may have taken Zoe."

She waited a while, pinched her lips, then gave a short nod. "This way," she said, leading the three men down a narrow hallway.

Joe's room was masculine without being too macho and neat as a pin, like the rest of the house. A number of youth sports trophies shared space with more recent accomplishments—a police academy diploma, a marksmanship certificate placing him among the ten best in the entire city, a citation for valor and a New York Yankees pennant autographed by none other than third-baseman great, Alex "A Rod" Rodriguez.

O'Bryan pointed at a file cabinet in one corner. "Vaughn, you take that cabinet. Scott, you check the closet and I'll work on the chest of drawers."

While all three went through the room, Mrs. Santos watched them from the doorway, arms crossed, left shoulder leaning against the jamb. She did not look happy. This was an invasion of her privacy, as well as her son's, and she wasn't going to let anyone forget it.

In the file cabinet's top drawer, Rick found a shoe box filled with photographs of Joe, his family and Zoe, who seemed to have been included in every Santos celebration. He also found several scrapbooks, all containing mementos from the 9/11 tragedy. Judging from the bulging album, Santos hadn't missed a single photo opportunity.

As he closed the last scrapbook, he caught Mrs. Santos looking at him with the same resentment he had noticed when they had first arrived. He couldn't blame her for being upset with him. As the ex-husband who had suddenly reappeared in Zoe's life, she viewed him as the enemy, the one person who stood between Zoe and her son. And the fact that Rick was here, trying to prove that Joe may have harmed Zoe, made him an even greater threat.

Trying to avoid her stare, he opened the lower drawer. That one contained bank statements, all dated and held together with a rubber band, receipts of various items Joe had bought, various warranties and a folder marked Income Tax Returns—1998–2004.

He held up the folder. "Detective? You want to see this?"

"What is it?"

"Tax returns for the last seven years."

"Yeah, let's take a look."

Rick sat on the bed beside O'Bryan, looking over his shoulder as the detective went through each return. The first five showed no changes except for a yearly pay raise and a small increase in Joe's nest egg.

Rick, who was familiar with tax forms, immediately spotted the disparity between the 2003 returns and the 2004. "This is something new." He pointed at two lines on the Itemized Deductions page. One read "Real Estate Taxes" and the other below, "Home Mortgage Interest." A twenty-two-hundred-dollar deduction had been claimed in the first line and another for thirty-one hundred dollars in the second.

O'Bryan turned to Mrs. Santos. "Your son owns property, Mrs. Santos?"

She gave a vigorous shake of her head. "Absolutely not. He's always lived at home, to save money."

"Yet he paid property taxes in 2003." He flipped through the rest of the returns. "And in 2004."

"It must be a mistake."

"It's no mistake. It's on his return."

Looking distraught, Mrs. Santos remained silent. Rick didn't think it was an act. She truly did not know.

"Let's go through that drawer," O'Bryan instructed. "There's got to be a tax bill in there."

Standing by the file cabinet, Officer Scott held up a large printed sheet. "I found it!"

Forty-Eight

After making arrangements to have Mrs. Santos escorted to the Ninth Precinct, where they could keep an eye on her, Detective O'Bryan led the small group outside.

He glanced at the address he had jotted down on a piece of paper. "Either one of you know where New Milford is?" he asked.

Officer Scott shook his head, but Rick went to his car to retrieve a Connecticut map from the pocket behind his seat. He spread it over the hood of the Audi.

"I haven't been up there in a couple of years," he said, tracing the route from Queens with a red pen. "But I used to own a house in Avon, which isn't far from New Milford. In fact, I believe that Lumbock Road, where Santos has his property, is…" He marked the area with an X. "Right about here. No more than five or six miles from the bird sanctuary."

"Is it a densely populated area?"

"It wasn't when I lived there." Rick folded the map. "Why don't I lead the way—"

"Wait a minute." O'Bryan assumed an authoritative stance. "I didn't hear myself say you could tag along. I have no idea what's waiting for us up there, and I don't want to have to worry about the safety of a civilian."

Rick tossed the map in the front seat. "I fought in Desert Storm, Detective. I think I can handle one man, even if he's armed to the teeth."

"I could have you escorted back to the police station with Mrs. Santos."

"Mrs. Santos is being taken into custody because you're worried she'll find a way to warn her son. And may I remind you that you're not the one who thought of that possibility. I was. So you might say that you owe me?"

O'Bryan's only answer was a grunt before he picked up his phone and called his precinct. For a moment, Rick thought he would make good on his threat, but all he did was ask for backup.

"There's been a new development in the Lola Malone case," he told the dispatcher. "Zoe Foster has been kidnapped and is believed to be held in Connecticut by Detective Joseph Santos, who is presumed to be armed and dangerous. I have Officer Scott with me, but I'm going to need backup." He did not mention Rick. "The address is two Lumbock Road in New Milford."

He hung up and turned to Rick. "You said something about leading the way?"

Zoe watched Joe walk across the room to check his laptop. She guessed that he was waiting for Lizzy to answer "Zoe's" e-mail, which would confirm that she had fallen for the deception. So far there had been no response. Either Lizzy hadn't read her mail, or she had realized that something was wrong and had notified the police.

Please, God, let it be the latter.

"How did you do that?" she asked, hoping to distract him. "How did you send Lizzy an e-mail that appeared to come from me?"

Joe shrugged. "Easy. I started a free Internet-based e-mail program under your name, provided a password and a false address, and answered a simple security question. In this instance, they wanted to know what your hobby was."

"What did you say?" As she talked, she glanced around the room, looking for an escape route.

"Sleuthing." He turned the computer around. "You want to see what I said?"

She approached the desk, aware that he still held a .38 revolver he wouldn't hesitate to use if she gave him a reason to. He pushed his stool back as she read

Hi, Lizzy. I know this will sound a little foolhardy, but I just got a lead on Lola's disappearance and I have to follow it through. I'll be out of town for a few days and will contact you as soon as I get a chance. Please relay this message to Rick and Joe so they won't worry. Love, Zoe.

"Relay this message to Rick and Joe so they won't worry," Zoe repeated. "Very clever, Joe, but Lizzy won't buy it. Neither will Rick, especially once they realize that you're gone, too."

"What makes you think that I'm going to remain gone?"

"You intend to commute to work every day? Who will watch me? Or won't that be necessary?"

She gave herself a mental kick for asking that question. Why rush him into a decision? She was in no hurry to die.

His silence spoke volumes. More than ever she was convinced that although he didn't want to kill her, he had no choice.

She was doomed. Unless she thought of a way to get out of here.

Actually, she had come up with a plan, of sorts, but she wasn't sure she could pull it off. At first glance, the scenario seemed simple enough. Maybe too simple. She would wander over to the fireplace, pretending to be cold, which she was, and rub her hands together over the fire. Then, at just the right moment, she would grab the heavy, cast-iron popcorn pan hanging on the wall and hit Joe over the head with it.

She tried not to think of the consequences if she missed. She had to keep a positive attitude. She was a winner, just like Kitty Floyd. And winners always prevailed.

She could feel Joe's gaze on her as she moved toward the fireplace.

"Cold?"

"A little."

"The cabin should start warming up soon. We've only been here about fifteen minutes."

It felt like hours.

Standing in front of the fire, she extended her hands toward the flames. The cast-iron pan hung less than three feet from her right hand, an easy reach. Joe sat at the desk behind her, which meant she would have to make a complete turn before she could strike.

Maybe she should engage him in conversation, something that would distract him, maybe even make him take his eyes off her. A second was all she needed. Well, maybe two seconds.

She looked up at the mantel for inspiration, and found it as her eyes came in contact with yet another photograph of Joe. He was shaking hands with the city's former police commissioner. "Was this photo taken on the same day as the other one?" She pointed at the mantel.

"What other one?"

She nodded toward the opposite wall.

He followed her gaze.

Zoe took a jagged breath. Then, in one swift motion, she unhooked the pan, spun around and—

Joe was out of his chair before she could complete her turn. He grabbed her wrist in midair and twisted it. "What do you think you're doing? You have a death wish or something?"

Tears of frustration ran down her cheeks. "Does it matter? I'm going to die anyway."

He took the heavy pan from her hand and tossed it aside. It fell to the floor with a loud clang. Zoe continued to fight him, kicking and scratching, even though he was far too adept at self-defense for her to inflict any real damage.

"Don't make me hurt you, Zoe."

Her hip hit the desk and something went crashing down. Neither paid attention. "Go ahead, hurt me," she yelled in his face. "Or better yet, kill me. Get it over with."

"I'll choose the time and place, okay?" he yelled back.

A whooshing sound behind them brought the wrestling to an abrupt stop. They turned around simultaneously. Zoe screamed. The Christmas tree was on fire and the flames had already attacked the curtains on the window directly behind it.

"My God, what happened?" Zoe cried.

"You knocked down the oil lamp!"

Joe tucked the gun in his waistband and sprinted toward the kitchen. He reached under the sink, yanked out a fire extinguisher and rushed back. "There's another extinguisher by the stove," he shouted as he aimed his at the Christmas tree. "Go get it. Hurry! This place will go up like a tinderbox."

A second oil lamp exploded, starting a new blaze. Hungry flames found the trail of oil and shot up a log wall.

Zoe pulled at his sleeve. "Joe, don't be crazy. We have to get out of here!"

When he shrugged her off, she ran to the door. As expected, it was locked, and the windows must have been nailed shut because they wouldn't budge.

Behind her, Joe was still trying to put out the fire. One wall and part of the ceiling were ablaze. It wouldn't be long before the entire cabin turned into a raging inferno. "Joe, if we don't get out now, we'll burn to death. Unlock the damn door!"

A spark touched the sofa, igniting a cushion. Joe quickly smothered it with the foamy chemical. "I need that other extinguisher now!"

Zoe's answer was to pick up a chair and raise it above

her head. She was about to hurl it at the nearest window when she heard Joe's warning.

"Zoe! The ceiling! Watch out!"

Zoe looked up in horror as a fifteen-foot section of the ceiling came crashing down.

Forty-Nine

Joe dropped the fire extinguisher and took a giant leap in a desperate attempt to push her out of the way. He was too late. The log knocked her down and fell across her legs, trapping her underneath.

"Joe!"

He was already by her side. His eyebrows were singed and his face was black with smoke. "You're going to be okay. I'm going to get you out of here."

Strangely, she felt the pressure but no pain. "I can't move."

"I know. Fortunately, the larger beam missed you."

"Are you blind? There's a log across my legs."

"A small one. The large one is weighing down on it. I'm going to try to lift it. The moment you feel the weight ease off, you get out. Ready?"

He didn't wait for her answer. He closed his eyes and, groaning with the effort, he tried to lift the heavy log. Nothing happened.

Zoe could feel the heat of the flames behind her, and

the terrifying sound of the fire as it claimed another chunk of the cabin. "Hurry," she said as he stopped to catch his breath.

She heard another grunt, louder this time, then, miraculously, the weight came off. She let out a yelp and wiggled out.

She didn't wait to see if she had sustained any injuries. Knowing that she could move was enough. Gathering every ounce of strength she had left, she picked up the chair she had dropped earlier and heaved it at the window. The glass shattered into a hundred pieces.

Using the chair legs, she knocked down the few jagged pieces that remained and started to climb out. She had one leg over the sill when she heard a spine-chilling scream.

Zoe spun around. Another large ceiling beam had come down and Joe was now trapped under it.

She stood frozen. She could feel the cold wind coming through the window, bringing with it the scent of freedom. All she had to do was climb out and start running.

She looked at Joe. Pain contorted his handsome features and he was having difficulty breathing. "Run, Zoe." She could not hear the words but she read them on his lips. "Run."

She couldn't do it. She couldn't leave him here to die, after he had saved her life. Keeping away from the flames, she ran over to the desk where he had left his cell phone. Fingers shaking, she dialed 911.

"My name is Zoe Foster," she yelled when a dispatcher came on the line. "My friend's house is on fire!"

"What's your location, Miss Foster?"

There was a hiss behind her as the stack of newspapers praising Joe's heroism caught fire. She ran to his side. "Where are we?" she yelled at him. "What's the address?"

She had to press her ear to his mouth to hear his reply.

"Two Lumbock Road, in New Milford," she told the dispatcher. "Five miles north of the bird sanctuary." Joe closed his eyes. "My friend is badly hurt," she added. "He's trapped under a beam."

"Help is on the way, Miss Foster. You just get out of the house now before it collapses. Do you understand?"

Maybe she could lift the log, Zoe thought, just as he had. She didn't have his strength, but she had the will. She remembered the story of a mother who had lifted a car in order to free her child, trapped underneath.

"Miss Foster!"

She let the phone drop and slid her hands under the beam the way she had seen Joe do.

She gave it all she had. Again and again and again. The beam didn't budge. She might as well have been trying to move a mountain.

Rick heard the wail of a siren seconds before he saw the heavy black smoke rise above the treetops. He jammed on his brakes and jumped out of his car at the same time O'Bryan and Officer Scott jumped out of theirs.

"That's Lumbock Road." He pointed up the hill just as a fire truck passed them at high speed, sirens screaming. Two police cruisers followed close behind.

O'Bryan took out his badge, held it up high and stepped in front of the first cruiser's headlights.

The car stopped with a jolt. "Are you nuts?" An angry officer shone his flashlight in O'Bryan's face. "I could throw you in the can for a stunt like that."

O'Bryan remained unruffled. "I'm Detective Jack O'Bryan of NYPD. I'm investigating a possible kidnapping at two Lumbock Road."

"That house is on fire, Detective. I'd advise you to stay—"

Rick jumped back in the Audi, gunned the engine and took off, heading for the house on the hill. He could see the fire now—huge, orange flames shooting through the trees.

His only thought was for Zoe. Had she gotten out in time?

Although dusk had quickly turned into night, the clearing was lit up like a Fourth of July celebration when he arrived. A second truck was already in place, with several firemen hosing down the house, trying to contain the blaze, which so far hadn't spread to the surrounding trees.

The cabin was small, its mossy green roof seeming to rise from the forest floor. The front door gaped open, hanging by the hinges, and thick black smoke poured out of the broken windows.

Rick's heart stopped. Unless Zoe and Joe were already out, it was too late to save them. No one would be getting out of this house alive now.

He grabbed the sleeve of a passing policeman. "Is anyone inside?" he asked.

The policeman shrugged. "Don't know. I just got here."

"Have you seen a woman? A redhead?"

"No, I'm sorry." As Rick started to move toward the house, the policeman put up his hand. "Stand back, please, sir."

Behind him, O'Bryan called out his name, but Rick ignored him. Shoving the cop aside, he raced toward the burning house.

"Hey, you!" someone yelled. "Come back here. What do you think you're doing?"

Two firemen with soot on their faces intercepted him. "You heard the chief, pal. Back off."

"Let me go! My wife is in there!"

"Rick."

He stopped struggling and turned around.

Zoe stood just behind him. She was wrapped in a blanket. Her beautiful red hair was soaked and plastered to her head. Other than that, she looked unharmed.

He shook off the fireman's grip and ran to her, taking her in his arms. "Are you all right?"

He felt her nod her head against his shoulder. He squeezed a little tighter. He could have lost her. He kept repeating those last five words in his head over and over.

"Where's Joe?" he asked when he could talk coherently.

"Still inside. A ceiling beam fell on him. They're trying to get him out." She sounded as if she was about to cry.

"We've got him!" someone shouted. "Coming through."

Rick turned in time to see two firemen lift Joe onto a stretcher. A paramedic slipped an oxygen mask on his mouth.

"Joe!"

Rick didn't hold Zoe back, but followed her to the stretcher. When Joe saw her, he took the oxygen mask off. His lips moved as he lifted his left hand. "Forgive me," he whispered.

Zoe hesitated. Then, with a nod, she took his hand and held it for a moment before she had to let him go.

Fifty

Cape May, New Jersey
December 25—3:50 p.m.

"Have I forgotten anything?" Catherine stood in the Rose Cottage's festive dining room, surveying her dinner table.

"Not a thing, Mom," Zoe replied. "Everything looks beautiful. You've outdone yourself."

The compliment was well deserved. The table shimmered with fine china, sparkling glassware, brass candlesticks and a centerpiece made of fresh holly and red berries. At every setting was a small gold box tied with a gold ribbon, a crisp, white napkin held by a cranberry ring and, just for the fun of it, Christmas crackers in brightly colored foil.

Catherine straightened an ivory candle. "Where did the men go?"

"The beach. I saw Lenny take a football out of the trunk."

Along with Rick, Catherine had invited Lenny and Stretch. Both were single and would have spent the day with Rick at his apartment, eating takeout and watching the Outdoor Life channel. Lou was also part of the festivities. He had flown in from San Diego the moment he heard about Zoe's abduction, and had jumped at the chance of spending Christmas at the Rose Cottage. At the last minute, Lizzy, whose family celebrated Chinese New Year rather than Christmas, had left the restaurant in Jimmy's capable hands and joined them.

Catherine handed Zoe a small stack of place cards in the shape of Christmas trees. "I need to check with Lulu, so why don't you decide where you want everyone to sit." A frown creased her brow. "On second thought, maybe you should come with me. I hate to leave you alone, even for a minute. I know it's silly, but I can't help it. I came so close to losing you—"

"Well, you didn't lose me." Zoe took the cards from her. "So stop fussing and go do whatever you need to do."

"If you're sure."

"I'm sure." As Catherine started to leave, Zoe held her back. "In case I haven't said it yet, thanks for inviting my friends. It was very sweet of you."

"Oh, darling, you know how I love a crowd at holiday time." She walked out, leaving Zoe to her task.

Place cards in hand, Zoe walked around the table. She was trying hard to shake off the awful memories of Joe's burning cabin, and concentrate on the fact that she was here, celebrating this joyous occasion with the people she loved.

Order had finally returned to her life. She had moved

back into the loft, and just yesterday she had turned in Kitty's last strip, in color, for a big Sunday finish. After much internal debate, she had decided that Mona's killer should not be the man the actress was blackmailing, but Alan Ralston, the soap opera actor eager to revive his career. As expected, he had denied any culpability, but the evidence was too damning.

On the reality side of life, Detective O'Bryan hadn't had any difficulty getting Joe to confess. In the hospital, where he was being treated for second-degree burns and a collapsed lung, Joe had made a full confession.

Although the fire had destroyed most of the cabin, the police had recovered the .38 mm revolver that killed Rudy Goldberg and the .30-caliber Remington rifle Joe had used on the rooftop. Tests would determine if the weapons matched the bullets found at the scene of both crimes, but O'Bryan had no doubt they would.

Because Joe's injuries weren't as critical as the doctors had first thought, he was expected to be released from the hospital within a couple of days. A broken rib had pierced his right lung, causing the partial collapse of that organ. Doctors were keeping him under observation with regular X-rays. Murder charges would be filed pending his release.

The Santos family remained in seclusion. Except for daily visits to the hospital, Maria refused to see anyone, even Zoe. With Joe's high-profile trial already in the works and Zoe as the prosecution's star witness, it was doubtful that she and Maria would ever be friends again.

Lola's body, buried in a grave behind the cabin, was exhumed. After an autopsy that confirmed the cause of death as strangulation, Rick had arranged for a quiet burial. She had left everything she owned, including her apartment, to her aunt. Frieda would never need to know about her niece's murder, and the singer would rest in peace knowing that her aunt's excellent care at Sagemore would continue.

In a phone call to Dr. Keefer, Zoe had assured him that she would be coming for regular visits as long as they didn't upset his patient. Buddy Barbarino, present for the reading of the will, had expressed his displeasure at his twenty-five-thousand-dollar inheritance. "After all I did for that woman," he mumbled as he left the attorney's office. "You'd think she would show a little more gratitude."

As for Archie, he was very much the man of the hour. Captain Malfi, of the Ninth Precinct, insisted on thanking him in person, and apologized, in the name of all NYPD officers, for the mistreatment Archie and his friends may have suffered. It was uncertain whether his name was really Archibald Newton III, but no one cared to contest it. To all those who knew him, he was, and would remain, Archie.

Through it all, Rick had remained by Zoe's side, cooking for her, making sure she had enough rest and keeping her spirits up. Once or twice, as they sat together, she caught him looking at her with an odd expression in his eyes. She didn't have to think too hard to figure out what was going on in that handsome head of his. Both were experiencing the same conflicting emotions, afraid to say goodbye and even more afraid to explore the pros and cons of a possible reconciliation. What if they screwed up again? What if those past six years had taught them nothing?

What if they could make it work?

Maybe what they needed was more time. Yes, that had to be it. Time.

"A penny for your thoughts."

At the sound of Lizzy's voice, Zoe turned around. "What happened to you?" she asked. "I was about to send a search party."

"The traffic was insane. I would have made better time on foot." She gazed at the table. "Wow. Your mother has great style."

"Well, she *was* a fashion editor for twenty-five years."

Lizzy looked around. "Where's Rick?"

"At the beach, tossing a football with Lenny, Stretch and his new buddy, Lou. They should be coming in any minute."

"Hmm."

"What?"

Lizzy gave her an innocent look. "What what?"

"That hmm. What did it mean?"

"Nothing. I was just clearing my throat."

"You're so full of it. Something's going on. I can tell. I suspected it when you invited yourself down. You never leave the restaurant on Christmas Day. Only an extraordinary event—"

The front door opened and a gust of cold wind burst in. "The guys are back!" Rick shouted from the entry hall. "And they're hungry."

"In that case, you're in luck," Catherine announced from the doorway. "Because dinner is ready." She walked in carrying her famous beef Wellington while Lulu followed with a cart of mouthwatering side dishes.

After some confusion about who was sitting where, because Zoe had neglected to set the place cards, everyone finally had his or her assigned seat. But as Catherine picked up a carving set, Rick stood up.

"May I say something, Catherine?"

"Why, certainly." She put the carving set down and looked at him expectantly. Zoe caught a little gleam in her eyes.

"First of all," Rick said, looking at the smiling faces that surrounded him, "I would like to thank Catherine for inviting us."

She gave a gracious nod. "You're most welcome."

"I would also like to say, and I'm sure you'll all second this, how happy I am that Zoe is back with us, safe and sound. What happened to her taught us all an important lesson. Waiting to hear the fate of a loved one is nerve-racking. So the next time she wants to investigate a murder, we shoot her."

As Zoe laughed with the rest of the guests, she saw Lizzy whisper something in Lenny's ear. Almost immediately, Lenny glanced at Zoe, saw her looking at him and grinned. Those two were up to something, but she'd be damned if she knew what.

"And because we came so close to losing you, Zoe," Rick continued, now looking directly at her, "I went a little crazy and bought you a present."

As Zoe started to protest, he raised his hand. "I know we agreed not to exchange gifts, but I couldn't resist. This item had your name written all over it and Lizzy agreed, so if you hate it, blame her."

More laughter, but not from Zoe, who pointed an accusing finger at her friend. "I was right. You *were* conspiring behind my back."

"You can thank me later," Lizzy said smugly.

Rick's index finger swept back and forth. "You've all noticed the gold-wrapped boxes on your plates. Inside is a memento of today from Catherine. The one on Zoe's plate is from me. So, Zoe, if you don't mind, would you open yours first?"

Zoe looked at her mother. "You know what's in it, don't you? They all know."

"Actually I don't. Rick wouldn't tell me."

"We don't know, either," the others chimed in, with the exception of Lizzy and Lenny, the two coconspirators, who remained quiet.

"Go ahead, child," Lulu insisted. "Put us out of our misery and open the present."

Zoe picked up the box. Although small, it was too big for a ring, so that blew one assumption right out of the water. She didn't know whether to be disappointed or relieved. With steady fingers, she untied the gold ribbon, ripped the paper off and lifted the lid.

What she saw inside took her breath away.

Nestled into folds of black velvet was a diamond ring. Not just any diamond ring, but the one Rick had put on her finger eight years ago, almost to the day. It had dazzled her then and it dazzled her now. The three-carat, square-cut stone was set in platinum and had an inscription inside the band: From Rick to Zoe, with all my love.

She looked up, eyes misting a little. The table had gone quiet. "It's my engagement ring."

"Well, technically, it's *my* ring. I wanted you to keep it, if you recall, but—"

"I insisted that you take it back."

"You didn't just insist. You threw it at me before you stormed out of the studio."

Soft laughter rippled across the room.

"Didn't you go back for it the following day?" Lizzy asked Zoe.

"Yes. I had second thoughts. I'm not sure why I wanted it back, but I did. He wouldn't give it to me. He said that I'd had my chance and since I was so ungracious about the whole thing, I didn't deserve it."

"Looks to me," Lenny said, "like he's had a change of heart."

Zoe took the ring out of the box. "After six years, you've decided that I should have it after all? Is that it?"

"After six years, I've finally realized that I can't live without you. So, yes, I'd like you to take the ring back. And me. If you should feel so inclined."

Lou leaned toward Stretch. "Is that a marriage proposal?" he asked, loud enough for everyone to hear.

"I think so." Stretch looked at Rick and just waited.

But Rick was watching Zoe. "What do you say, Red? Are you willing to give it another try?"

"In my day," Lou remarked, "a man got down on one knee and put it in proper English. What happened to tradition?"

"That's an excellent question." Rick pushed his chair back, came to stand in front of Zoe, who was holding her breath, and went down on one knee. "I love you, Zoe. I've always loved you. Will you marry me?"

Her heart slammed in her chest. He had taken a huge chance asking her that question in front of her mother and all their friends. But that was Rick, a risk taker all the way.

When she felt as though she could talk without her voice quivering, she looked into his eyes, which were now level with hers. What she saw in them was a reflection of what she felt at this very moment—pure, unadulterated love.

She cleared her throat. "First of all, I keep working."

She heard the gasp of relief around the table. Her mother reached over and squeezed her arm.

"Absolutely," Rick replied.

"Our marriage comes first, not Blue Moon and not Kitty Floyd."

"I wouldn't have it any other way."

"We make decisions together."

"Agreed."

She paused, wondering how far she could push. "You would have to move into the loft."

"I thought you'd never ask."

Loud cheering broke out around the table.

Beaming, Zoe handed Rick the ring. "In that case, darling, why don't you make it official?"